To Jue

Adventures in
the Countryside

best wishes

Giselle
P.

Other Titles by Giselle Rozzell

A Fresh Start in the Countrywide

Adventures in the Countryside

GISELLE ROZZELL

THE CHOIR PRESS

First published in the United Kingdom in 2024 by
The Choir Press

ISBN 978-1-78963-481-5

Dedication

To all my Brightwell friends with love xx

"All dreams can come true if we have the courage to pursue them"

WALT DISNEY

My love of travelling extends to Germany, visiting family from a young age where my late mother was born. I have lived and worked there over the years which I now call my second home country.

Many years later I won the usual goldfish at a fair back in the day, which later extended to hamsters and owning dogs, in particular pointers.

I started writing whilst we were in lockdown and have never looked back.

My motto in life is simply this: believe in yourself, follow your dreams, enjoy the journey and never look back.

God bless
Love Giselle xx

Contents

Chapter One

'Where are my jeans you wore last night?' Issy demanded, after she opened her sister Amy's bedroom door.

'Go away, Sis, not now, chat later,' was her response, as she peered over the duvet with one eye half-open.

Issy closed the door gently behind her so that Amy could catch up on her beauty sleep.

Amy's party went off with a bang, celebrating her 22nd birthday with past and present friends the night before. Their last one before leaving their home in Winchester to move to the new family cottage in the Cotswolds.

Amy's blue elasticated-waist jeans had become a firm favourite of hers, after seeing them on an online shopping site. The sisters were the same size, making it easier to swap fashion items between them, only on the condition that they asked first, which they usually did, unless there was a last-minute hitch; summing up teenagers in one, hearing them squabble upstairs trying to find that perfect outfit for the night. However, Jodie couldn't complain as they were generally good kind-hearted girls, always ready to help others.

They had just turned 22 going on 30. Going out to parties with their mates was becoming the norm, so savour the moment and enjoy it, they thought, as all could change in a blink of an eye.

Life moved swiftly on in the Stevens family now that Jodie and Ralph had finally reunited whilst Amy was still young. Ralph had gone through a tricky period in his life after Amy was born, trying to juggle farm life and adapting to being a first-time parent, which slowly overwhelmed him, leading to a temporary breakdown. Jodie made the decision to move out closer to her mum with baby Amy, whilst Ralph sought counselling sessions helping him to recover.

Jodie returned to her teaching post after navigating him through those difficult days, before he eventually made a career change, becoming a successful carpenter. After a second attempt at saving their relationship and a romantic weekend away, they decided to make a fresh start together, as he moved back in with her.

They bought themselves a lovely cottage in the picturesque village of Stow on the Wold in the heart of the Cotswolds, where they soon settled down with their daughter Amy. All was how it should be.

Seven years later Issy was born; a lovely sister to Amy. They became a family again with their new puppy, Rosie, a cute fawn-coloured cockapoo they rehomed and who now was just five years old, becoming a furry friend to all who entered the house. She was such a friendly bundle of joy as she greeted everyone, lifting her paw for them to shake.

Amy remained in touch with her best friend, Lottie; Sam's girl, growing up together in primary and secondary school. They attended Rainbows and Brownies followed by Girl Guides in the local village of Winchester, before they moved to their new cottage in the Cotswolds.

Sam and Jodie remained best mates, always there for each other, supporting one another through anything that life threw at them. They continued their weekly coffee and cake catch-ups at a new local coffee shop in Stow on the Wold.

Sam found her forever love, marrying Pete, expecting their first child, Grace; a beautiful blonde smiley pretty daughter, now 17 years old, who would no doubt become the apple of men's eyes later on in life.

Then there was James: Jodie's long-lost stepbrother. Dot, her mum, kept a dark secret from her after her dad had died. He had been having an affair, telling nobody, shocking Jodie to the core, leaving her speechless. After Issy was born James was keen to make contact again with her, soon establishing a firm relationship and becoming a valued member of their family.

Daisy the guinea pig sadly joined rainbow heaven of family pets after five years, after contracting arthritis and failing eyesight, one reason Rosie the cockapoo became the latest addition to the family.

All was going swimmingly until one day in September, a day that, no matter how hard they tried, stood out like a very sore memory etched on all their hearts. Issy had shown signs of becoming unwell over the past few weeks. She was checked out by their local doctor, a lovely kind-hearted lady, noting she had a high temperature, thinking it was just a nasty virus going around. She lacked energy, feeling listless and fatigued as she went from bed to sofa trying to get a grip on herself, trying to figure out why she suddenly felt as if a truck had hit her from behind, knocking her off balance in all senses of the word. She was prescribed bed rest and to drink lots of water. Considering Issy was in a weakened state, it didn't prove a chore; she naturally wanted to recover so she could get back on track with her busy life.

After the necessary blood tests, Issy was finally diagnosed with glandular fever, stemming from the Epstein-Barr virus, sadly very common in young women these days. As Issy was an inquisitive soul, she headed over to her search engine to find out more – until she read the three dreaded words "there's no cure", not something you want to read at the tender age of twenty-two, the pinnacle of a young adult's life. A trillion thoughts suddenly flooded her mind, sadly only negative ones, which she tried pushing to the back of her inquisitive mind, despite feeling drained all the time. She had to focus on the positive, disregarding all negative thoughts which could hinder her steady recovery in the long run.

She asked God to help her, claiming the Bible promises He will help in times of trouble, a soothing thought to her mind, body and soul.

Three weeks had passed and finally she was making a slow but steady recovery, yet still not feeling her normal cheery self, this was going to take time. She had to put everything on hold, especially as she was about to embark on a career in caring for the elderly, going into care homes and family homes offering support where possible, a future she was so much looking forward to; the world was her oyster. Remembering this gave her a daily focus, wishing even more for a speedy recovery. After all, nothing had ever fazed her before, and it wasn't about to change this time. *You've got this Issy,* she practised the mantra three times a day.

The days rolled into one another over the next month, as Jodie encouraged Issy to take significant time out for herself, until she felt well enough to face the world again. Too many stops and starts could lead to a relapse, starting all over, which she naturally wanted to avoid. She was getting fed up with taking it easy, she just wanted to get on with her life.

A month passed by, and she gradually started to improve, back to feeling her usual upbeat self. She just needed to slowly ease herself back into a routine again.

A pre-booked holiday to Austria had been arranged by Amy a few months prior to her becoming unwell, a last-minute week's holiday in Austria which they were looking forward to but hoping they didn't have to cancel last minute, due to her fatigue. Fortunately for Issy she made a speedy recovery, enabling them to go. Looking back, it was the best thing she ever did, feeling refreshed on her return. Clearly a sunny week away in beautiful Austria did the trick.

They booked into a beautiful hotel in Seefeld, surrounded by scenic mountains, lakes with cafés selling yummy, mouthwatering Apfelstrudel so with the usual vanilla sauce and a scoop of vanilla ice cream being optional, adding to this traditional luxury dessert; with an iced coffee in a long glass, topped with a scoop of ice cream and freshly whipped cream making it all look very mouth-wateringly scrumptious. This was surely the perfect relaxing treat, sitting outside a café in nature, watching amblers pass by in their shorts and walking boots, often greeted by *Grüß*

Gott, an informal "good day". There were also plenty of benches along the way to sit and relax, breathing in the occasional much-welcome breeze in the heat of the day.

As this was meant to be a time for Issy to recover, they decided to stay in Seefeld, knowing there was plenty to do every day within her capabilities.

They had booked into a lovely hotel in the breathtaking countryside, with balcony views overlooking vineyards where grapes were grown, to be picked later and made into a fruity table wine. All Austrian hotels were wood-timbered chalet houses sitting on hill tops or in quaint villages, adorned by its beautiful scenic landscapes. It was just magical in their wellness areas where life went down a few notches, eliminating all stresses and strains of daily life; mindfulness and yoga and swimming were indeed the heart of Austria, a place to chill and unwind. What was not to like, as they marvelled at the beautiful surroundings.

Austria and Germany were renowned for their wellness places; spa wellness breaks being on offer in every good hotel, loving their saunas and swimming pools and massages to unwind from daily stresses of life, a perfect get-away from it all.

Amy and Issy were very much making the most of their time away together.

On arrival at their 4-star hotel they were handed a flier explaining all about the various spa packages on offer during their stay, with special offers for all guests to be booked in advance at reception.

'Zimmer 101 für Sie, Die erste Etage,' the Austrian receptionist added, pointing to the lift on her left. She spoke with a distinct local accent, handing the key to Amy with its number engraved on a wooden plaque, a beautiful fitting touch, noted by the girls.

'Danke schön,' Issy replied with a smile. Both had taken German at GCSE level, finding it a relatively easy language, until writing with its many grammatical differences soon became more of a struggle thus stopping at A level.

They took the lift with their wheeled suitcases to the first floor to find their room, turning the key in the door to reveal the most beautiful spacious room, with two single beds separated by mahogany bedside tables with one drawer and enough space underneath for all and sundry. A matching mahogany, old-style double-door wardrobe, with wooden hangers for their clothes, added to the old style yet updated bedroom. A well-finished bathroom to the right, housing a double basin set in a wooden vanity unit, made the room fit for king or queen. The girls were living in luxury style for the week.

The usual coffee machine with an oblong woven basket with an assortment of teas, sugar and small packets of biscuits added to the touch of class.

'This is just superb,' Issy remarked, feeling slightly overwhelmed yet loving it all the same. She walked up behind Amy, taking her by surprise, embracing her into a tight hug, placing a slammer of a kiss on her right cheek.

'You're my star, Sis, in a reasonably priced car,' she said, feeling so blessed and thankful to have been given this surprise holiday.

'Oh, get away you, young sibling, wishing you the health and happiness you so deserve. I just pray this will make you feel well again. We can now put this all behind us and start all over once we get back. OK, let's get this holiday started with a splash,' she added, handling some flyers to pre-book their spa treatments later before dinner.

They sat outside on their balcony with the list of spa treatments on the table and a notebook and pen from the room desk, making a list of their favourite treatments ready to book up at reception that evening before dinner.

'I'd say a lovely dip in the pool to start the day tomorrow, followed by coffee and cake in the restaurant. After that, a steady stroll around the lake outside the hotel, taking in the fresh air, listening to the birds and mountain cowbells and the occasional church bell ringers.'

Time was ticking fast, as dinner time approached. A quick change into something smart, before they grabbed their key, not forgetting their important spa treatment list to book at reception. This time they walked down a flight of stairs, giving themselves some much-needed exercise, then repeated after a hearty meal.

'Wonder what's on the menu tonight?' Amy asked, feeling rather peckish.

'Guten Abend, etwas zu trinken?' a pleasant-looking waitress asked, noticing them take a seat by the window.

'Ein Glas weiß Wein halbtrocken bitte für uns.'

'Liebfraumilch oder Hock?' she asked.

'Oh ja, gerne, liebfraumilch,' Amy replied, smiling back at her.

'Ich komme sofort,' she replied, taking away the drinks menus from them.

She promptly tapped their orders into the screen by the till, sending it directly through to the bar opposite. Within minutes she walked over, balancing a tray with their drinks, placing them on beer mats in front of them.

Meanwhile they perused the menu for their mains, ready for her to take their order.

'Zwei panierte Schnitzel mit Bratkartoffeln und Champignons, bitte,' Issy added, practising her German, taking advantage of every opportunity to keep her German going. When in the country speaking the lingo was her motto.

Main meal over, time to check out the desserts. An assortment from apfelstrudel, cheesecake to crème brûlée or a selection of ice creams with chocolate or raspberry sauce. The choices were all mouthwatering. Amy chose crème brûlée as she could never get enough of its yummy texture, with the crunchy sugar crystals on top.

'What do you fancy, Issy?' Amy looked at her with drooling eyes.

'They all look so mouthwateringly scrummy. OK answers please, one two three go.'

'A crème brûlée for me as I'm feeling pretty stuffed right now.'

'Same, I can't pack in anything else either, and two cappuccinos please.'

'Perfect,' agreed Amy.

They relished their desserts and coffees after the young lady brought them over. She added the bill to the room, before they walked back to their room to chill on the balcony.

Once upstairs, Amy opened the balcony doors, to the sound of a band playing from a distance. The evening was still early so they thought they'd check it out. A quick bathroom stop, before grabbing the room key, and they made their way down to reception.

From a distance they heard orchestral music, a band playing in the middle of the square as they played out a variety of Austrian folk songs, the sound of drum kits adding to the rhythm, ladies singing, shaking their maracas and beating tambourines to the beat of the catchy tunes. Onlookers clapped in appreciation as they formed a wide circle in front of the stage, making a delightful evening's entertainment for all in the square.

Seefeld was soon becoming their favourite town with a buzz of melodic excitement, forever etched on their memories.

Eleven o'clock soon came around as the last tune echoed around, which now became a busy centre of attraction. The singers thanked everyone for coming along and joining in the singalong tunes, then bid everyone goodnight as they started to pack up until the following night. They were there for the week, which proved fortunate for the girls.

'Well, that was fun,' Issy raised her voice above the noise of the crowd so Amy could hear.

Feeling tired, they slowly meandered back to their hotel. Day one in Seefeld had certainly gone off with a bang!

Chapter Two

The alarm went off at 8 am. Amy stretched over with her right arm to feel the button to press the off button on the alarm on her bedside table.

'You awake, Sis, time to rise and shine, a quick shower, breakfast in 10 minutes, before they stop serving.'

'OK!' Issy uncurled herself, placing her legs dangling to the floor to stretch out, before easing herself gently upward. She walked over to the balcony window, peering behind the curtain to check out the weather. Blue skies and gradually heating up. T-shirts and shorts today, she concluded.

'Your turn, Sis.' Amy came rushing out with a towel wrapped around her, making a beeline to the wardrobe to pick out her outfit for the day, also choosing the same.

'Guten Morgen,' a friendly lady greeted them as they walked into the breakfast room, which was slowly filling up with other guests.

'Guten Morgen,' they replied as they looked for a suitable table to sit.

A buffet-style breakfast counter was stacked full of the usual different bread rolls, croissants, then a selection of cheeses on a platter with a variety of savoury meats, yogurts and the ultimate German Quark, adding to a colourful, yet healthy, choice of breakfast for those on the go.

A one-touch coffee machine with a selection of juices added to the beverages. A typical continental breakfast to set them up for the day.

'OK, Sis, what's the itinerary for today or what do you fancy doing?' Amy asked with a sense of excitement.

'Well, we have massages booked at 4pm, neck, shoulder and

back massages which should send us into relaxation mode. How about a swim in the pool outside and a sunbathe, something easy, before that all invigorating relaxing massage?'

'Sounds like the perfect day to me,' Issy replied, with a spring in her step.

They finished their health-conscious breakfast, then quickly returned to their room to brush their teeth, before they took a stroll outside, wandering into the town to check it out.

It was beginning to get busy as people meandered around. In the middle of the square were a number of lovely horses and carts waiting for people to ride around the centre which soon became popular throughout the day, a leisurely half-hour walk around the town.

This was special to see as they walked by, children often sitting in the back, finding it all amusing as people waved them by. The downside was the horses left a few smelly parcels along the journey. Luckily a guy used his extra-wide, silver shovel to tidy up the place, leaving the town immaculately clean as the Austrians were renowned for their cleanliness.

'Kaffee und kuchen time!' they announced, high-fiving each other as they descended from their carriage.

'Good idea, Sis!' They walked across the cobblestone square, spotting an outside seating area, grabbing a table before others decided to do the same.

'Grüß Gott.' A friendly lady dressed in a white waist apron came over to their table, dressed in typical Austrian style. Onlookers stared as they served their customers, all adding to the pleasant ambiance. All Austrians loved dressing up in the summer months, giving passing tourists a glimpse at their attire as they went about their day, serving potential customers various drinks and meals.

'Zwei Ice Cafés mit zwei Stück Apfel-Streusel Kuchen bitte.'

'Ja, kommt sofort,' she replied, walking back inside the café.

Another classic cake, apple cake with a crumble topping, loved by millions in Germany and Austria.

She soon came back, balancing a tray with their iced coffees and mouthwatering cakes.

'Gluten Appetit!' She placed them down in front of them.

They devoured their cakes and sipped their coffees, discussing the day ahead, taking everything in their stride.

It was Sunday, a day off from the humdrum of life, time to relax for everything to calm down a notch, to breathe and just enjoy the moment, before a new week started again.

Throughout the town church bells were ringing at different intervals, a peace descending all around, whatever one's belief. Catholicism was rife in Austria with incense swinging in church services, not to everyone's liking, nonetheless a peaceful setting. Many churches were beautiful buildings inside and out, so they decided to go in and take a sneak peek around, taking in the atmosphere. The interior often depicted stained glass windows, telling biblical stories of the Virgin Mary and the crucifixion. A table by the altar adorned with tea lights, waiting for a candle to be lit in memory of a loved one or praying for a loved one in need of the Virgin's help. It was a special place for many who passed through its doors to reflect on life in general. Everyone needed a quiet place to meditate and appreciate what they had, as they walked around with softly spoken voices so as not to disturb the peace.

'I'm going to light a candle, Issy, to say a prayer for our family and friends,' Amy leant in, whispering in her ear.

'Me too, can only be a good thing,' Issy smiled back at her, feeling the love.

They moved swiftly on, pushing the revolving wooden narrow doors into the sunlit streets. They agreed there was only so much time you could spend in churches.

As soon as they got outside they were confronted by a few homeless people sitting on pavements near the church entrance, with their caps laid out in front of them, hoping passers-by would throw in a few cents or Euros to help them along their way, although the girls were not sure what they would spend it on.

Others set themselves up busking in front of crowds, usually with a guitar and amplifier equipment, drawing in passers-by as they watched, clapping in intervals in appreciation. A sight everyone enjoyed seeing on a relaxing Sunday afternoon.

As they walked around they noticed an array of various stalls offering a variety of sweet and savoury dishes. Another all-time favourite was *spätzle;* homemade pasta dough cut into small drops, gently placed into boiling water for a few minutes, before draining them into a sieve, like mini noodles, adding butter to make a tasty side dish to any schnitzel. An alternative was mixing in some grated cheese, lovely but very cheesy, not good for cholesterol and heartburn!

They meandered around Seefeld, window shopping as it was Sunday. Most shops were closed, as they usually are in Austria and Germany, meeting Sunday trading rules and giving staff a well-deserved day off, unlike in the UK. That said, most tourist towns extended shopping hours till early evening, welcoming potential customers as they took their evening strolls along the cobbled streets.

The town gave out a different atmosphere in the evening with shop lights on inside, with streetlamps above, generally making everything look tranquil and beautiful. Lovers walking hand in hand, enjoying their evening stroll, stopping here and there, kissing one another, drawing one another into that all-encompassing embrace, first steps to rekindling their love for each other, a lovely romantic sight watched by many onlookers. One never knows what lurks around the corner as beautiful romances blossom.

A few yards along, kiosks were serving hot chocolate topped with a squirt of whipped cream and marshmallows if desired, making that evening drink extra special. On occasions they held hands, feeling the loved-up atmosphere minus the kissing game, with the occasional peck on the cheek.

Time soon caught up with them as it approached half ten, tiredness started to kick in, so they started ambling back to the hotel; tomorrow was another day.

Monday morning was the start of a busy week for most, loads of business entrepreneurs racing around trying to meet their goals, competing with one another, which was currently far from their minds, knowing that day would eventually come; meanwhile they just enjoyed their mini-break away.

A day trip to nearby Innsbruck was on the cards today, looking at the weather forecast, sunshine all the way. Innsbruck lay in the heart of Austria's Tyrol, where the Winter Olympic Games were hosted in 1964 and 1976. Its lush scenery with mountains and meadows drew millions of visitors every year. There were plenty of galleries and museums to hide away, benches to sit and watch the world go by. They walked into the *Alt Stadt* with its numerous cafés, sipping iced coffee with mouthwatering cakes from the ever-inviting selection of patisseries.

They decided to take a short coach trip, leaving outside their hotel after breakfast, dropping them off in the centre square, picking up the coach later around 5 o'clock, seventeen hundred hours European time. First stop coffee and a small slice of cake to perk them up for the day, then sightseeing till their next refuel stop. They were enjoying being tourists, with no real particular schedule to stick to, bliss being an understatement.

'Selfie time, Amy,' Issy suggested, feeling excited to be there. They stood on the main cobbled square by a statue.

'Come here, Sis.' Amy drew Issy in close, lifting her phone in the air, snapping away as they rotated, capturing the square from different angles.

Off they went on their sightseeing tour. As they walked around, a few buskers stood to the side, setting up their gear for solo singing with guitar in hand, playing catchy hit pop music, pulling in small crowds as they walked past, throwing small change into the laid-out hat, showing their appreciation. Music always attracted lots of attention wherever you went, especially in tourist towns, making it a happy clappy place, lifting people's spirits as they headed to shops or cafés. Little ones dragged their parents by the hand, wanting to see for themselves what was happening, often performing their happy dance regardless of what others thought of them, releasing their endless energy. The square soon sprang into life, everyone going about their day, spirits higher than many probably woke up with, like a magnet, an instant pick-me-up.

However, there was a downside too, seeing sad-looking men, often with their pet dogs lying by their feet on blankets, begging, a very sad sight to see especially where pets were concerned. They often wondered how they got into that position in the first place, their dogs becoming their best friends, as they tended to put their needs before themselves, making sure they had a bit of food and water to drink, which was touching. Paul 0'Grady would be so proud looking down from above.

Onward and upwards. They thought they'd take a cable car from the centre to view the mountains above, a fun ride as the cable car took to the skies from the old town, a half-hour ride with views overlooking the panoramic mountains. A restaurant at the top to sit in or outside. They took the next two-seater cable car that stopped at the bottom, as the operator slowed it down for them to climb aboard. As it left its station, a sudden whoosh hit them, as it swung mid-air off the platform from the pulley above, for some a terrifying moment, sending fluttery, sinking feelings in the stomach which gradually eased off as it levelled out, ascending to the skies above. On windy days all cable cars stopped operating for obvious reasons. However, unknown to them they were about to enter a deep, foggy cloud, causing strange movement underneath the cable car, sending them temporarily into a mild panic. Clunking noises, as if the cogs needed oiling, alerted them that something was adrift mid-air, as it started to sway in a rocking motion until their bubble came to a sudden halt.

'Oh my, what's that noise, what's happening, Amy?' Issy held on tightly to the metal bar along the sides of the window, not wanting to let go lest she should be thrown to the other side of the cable car.

This can't be happening, as a trillion thoughts rushed through her head, wondering if they would ever get to the top, let alone get back to terra firma.

'Don't panic, Miss Mainwaring,' remembering the phrase in Dad's Army, 'we've got each other, at least we're not complete strangers, or have a language barrier.'

'True, we got this, Sis, OK.' Amy placed her arm around Issy's waist, drawing her into a loving hug.

We noticed a tannoy above us which settled our nerves for now, thinking the operators on the ground had to communicate with them somehow. Moments later a voice from above in perfect English settled our theories.

'We have heard of slight turbulence hovering around the mountain area, hence our need to halt all cable cars for your immediate safety. Please do not be alarmed and hold on to the metal bar along the window. We will update you soon.' The German translation followed afterwards.

'That's it then, Sis, we're stuck here for the foreseeable, oh well best get comfy,' Issy said, feeling slightly nervous about how the rest of their pre-planned day would pan out.

'OK, let's see,' Amy said, taking her small rucksack from the floor, unzipping it, to see what treats were lurking inside.

'Where did you get those?' she asked, peering at the various goodies she pulled out, which included a small bag of cashews, a snack pack of milk chocolate biscuits and a banana each. 'Issy, where the heck did you nick these from?'

'Err, who said I *nicked* them, as you so eloquently put it, Amy?' she added, giggling in amusement. 'OK, I might have picked some unnecessary goodies on my travels; all in date, by the way. They will keep us going till we move on. I have a small bottle of Evian for tiny sips, we don't want to be bursting for the loo, do we, Sis,' Issy added feeling slightly amused. 'One thing I haven't brought is a book, as the scenery is pretty enough to distract our minds,' she added, leaving Amy feeling very well catered for, under the current circumstances.

A sudden jerk, which felt like a push from behind, made them both jump, nearly losing their balance, as their clasped fingers had a rush of sweat, causing their hands to nearly let go of the rail.

'Amy, this is getting a bit scary. I can feel the car swaying as I look out of the window,' noticing the other cable cars opposite stopped as they faced the descent to the cable car station from where they had left.

'Our future now hangs in the balance!' Amy chuckled.

'That's not funny ha ha,' Issy remarked with a slight shake in her voice.

'Oh well, you've got to see the funny side of things, or else we would all go insane, and we can't have that, can we Sis?'

'Look at the empty cars going back down swaying in the wind,' Issy added, feeling glad not to be on board.

Instead of the weather improving, it deteriorated into a smog of a misty cloud where visibility was decreasing by the minute. This could turn out to be an interesting day, they thought, although they had enough snacks to sustain them. On the plus side, they were on their jolly holiday, no deadlines to meet or stuck in an office all day long; though they were currently dangling mid-air, much the same thing really.

'Girls, I hope you are OK, we're doing our best to get the cars working as soon as possible,' came another message from above. It was decent of them to enquire about their wellbeing.

'Not much they can do for us, Amy,' Issy responded after it was translated into German. 'Fancy a game of I spy?' looking at Amy, smiling.

'Go on then. Something beginning with C.'

'Err, clouds, of course silly!'

'Yep,' Amy replied, feeling smug. 'Your turn, Issy, this time a little less obvious! F, not being rude, OK,' Amy added.

'Fog! Another obvious one, but a good game nonetheless, as our Brucey would have said in the *Generation Game*.' Issy high-fived her.

'Biscuit anyone?' she swiftly changed the subject.

They lowered themselves gently to the floor, sitting on their cardigans they had tied around their waists that morning.

'Why are we waiting!' they began to sing, waving their arms mid-height, as if in a pop concert.

An hour later and they were finally on the move again, hearing the cogs turning from underneath rumbling away, jerking the car forward, seeing the pulley propel it forward full swing ahead.

'Oh, thank the Lord for that. Gee I need a wee, followed by a cappuccino as soon as we reach the cafeteria!' Issy announced, punching the air with her fist with a big smile on her face.

'Me too, practise those pelvic floor muscle lifts, Amy,' Issy added, trying not to giggle lest she leaked.

'Ha ha,' she replied, trying not to laugh.

The cable car station soon came into sight, as it suddenly slowed down, before it reached the end of the platform. They gathered up their rucksacks then jumped off once it came to a steady halt.

'The cafe is over there,' Amy pointed out, with a sense of urgency to get there, looking for the ladies.

'That's better,' Issy announced once she returned from the café.

'Jetzt zwei Cappuccinos und zwei Stück Apfel kuchen bitte!' she told Amy, who was already standing in the small queue. Clearly not everyone who had got stuck mid-air had had the same idea.

She grabbed a tray from the stack on the counter, pushing it along until they were served by an Austrian lady dressed in her white pinny tied around her waist, eager to keep the queue moving forward. They collected their cake and cappuccinos and paid at the till at the end.

Issy spotted a table for two in the middle as Amy carried their tray over, placing their delights on the table.

'Guten Appetit,' she added, forking a mouthful of cake into her mouth.

'Yummy, just what we deserve in my opinion,' Issy added, taking a sip of her cappuccino.

'It can't get much better than this, Sis, on a mountain top café indulging ourselves with views to,' choosing her words carefully, 'to wow over, we are the luckiest sisters, I reckon.'

'Steady on, though I fully agree,' Amy added, smiling back at her affectionately as she reached out her arm to touch hers.

A buzzing noise and vibration came from her pocket. She pulled out her phone, noticing a call from their mum.

'Mum, good to hear from you, you OK?' Amy asked tentatively, hoping nothing was wrong. She tended to think the worst, not hearing from someone for a while.

'All good, darling, just checking you're having a wonderful time, which I guess you are,' she added, sounding pleased to hear from her.

'We are just sitting in a café up on the mountain top, looking down at Innsbruck. We took a day trip out today.' She thought it best not to explain what had happened earlier. That conversation could wait until they returned in a week's time. Plenty of stories to tell then.

'Great, I'll leave you to enjoy, bye for now, love you loads and stick together,' she ended the call with kissing noises.

'Ah, bless Mum, she sounded all good,' Amy declared with a thumbs-up to the air.

Issy quickly checked her phone for any urgent messages. One stood out as urgent, so she opened it to read:

Dear Issy

Hope this finds you well. I tried to make contact last week, with no success, perhaps you're away, so I thought I'd inform you of a job offer at the local vet practice. We are urgently looking for someone to care for our animals who have had their operations, and we thought you would fit the criteria perfectly, with your love of animals.

Let me know if that sounds like something you'd be interested in, by giving me a call on: 0777 869 2541. Or text me ASAP.

Look forward to hearing from you soon.

Linda
The Rowans vet practice

Amy looked slightly puzzled as she looked at Issy; clearly she looked a bit shocked and excited all in one.

'You OK? You look as if you've seen a ghost, need some water?' she asked, feeling concerned.

'Job offer at the vets!' Issy explained. 'I'd best ring her back, Amy. Heads up, when do we get back?' She wanted to give Linda an honest answer before committing herself to anything or making a hash of things.

'Wow! OK, we'll be home on Monday, so you could potentially have an interview on Wednesday, give yourself a day to recover.'

Issy by this time was about to ring her back whilst Amy told her the details.

'The Rowans, Linda speaking, how can I help you?'

'Linda, it's Issy. I've just read your message. Yes, I am currently in Austria, but will be back on Monday. I'm definitely interested in the post,' she continued to explain.

'Great, could you come for a chat next Thursday morning, say ten o'clock? It's a temporary cover but will become permanent next month.'

"Great, thanks Linda, I look forward to meeting you next Thursday at 10 am,' she added, before hanging up.

'Wow, now that's not to be dismissed.' Issy looked back at Amy, feeling a bit nervous and excited all in one.

'Keep an open mind to see where this could lead to, Sis,' Amy added, feeling excited for her, 'nothing to lose but lots to gain, as the saying goes.'

'Oh, sorry what was yours?' she asked, hoping she had good news too.

'The same, only this one is in the care home, chatting to patients and generally keeping their minds active, etc, sounds perfect, nothing lost. I'll ring her now.'

'Hello, Lucy speaking, how can I help?'

'Oh hello, it's Amy Stevens. You texted me earlier about your post in the care home, can you enlighten me, please?'

'Oh, hello Amy, thank you for ringing me. Yes the offer still stands. We need someone to take a caring role, being a bit creative with our patients, helping them feel upbeat. Does that sound like something of interest to you?'

'Yes, I'd be interested to learn more.'

'Great, could you come for an informal chat next Friday afternoon, about two o'clock?'

'Yes of course, thank you. I'm currently abroad but will be home by then. Thank you.' She ended the call.

'Well, it seems things are looking up, our future jobs await us once home. The only question being, where are we going to call home? We could move in together, buy a flat, perhaps?' Issy added, smiling at Amy.

'Hold that thought for now, we make a great dream team,' Amy chuckled, smiling at her sweetly.

'Most definitely,' high-fiving her.

Time was running away with them as the day just flew by leaving not much else left to see; museums were never big on their agenda anyway, so nothing was lost there.

'Think we'd best start heading back to the bus station to pick up the coach,' Amy suggested, after they had finished their afternoon indulgences.

'Agree, I think we've had enough excitement for today! That said, I've enjoyed it all. Loved the cable car ride,' Issy added, as they walked towards the cobbled square to find the coach stop for Seefeld. Glancing at the digital timetable above, the next one was in ten minutes, which was good. Good old Austria, for their punctuality.

Back on the comfy coach they continued their journey with its twists and turns as it ascended into the forest, becoming quite narrow in places through the mountain passes, a bit hair-raising for the driver to navigate through, that was Austria to a tee. They choose their seats. Amy took the window seat, as she didn't like heights with the twists along the way, feeling a bit queasy at times. Issy preferred the aisle seat, easier to make a quick dash to the on-board loo by the steps at the rear door, not very comfy nonetheless, there in an emergency.

They got chatting, as you do, with two girls across the aisle opposite, also Brits, making communication easier, immediately sparking up a conversation. The usual where do you come from and where are you staying, possibly gaining friends for life, you never know.

'Hi, are you staying in Seefeld or nearby?' one of the girls asked, thinking they did.

'Oh yes, in a Gasthof in the centre, just a few minutes' walk away. A beautiful place isn't it? It's our first time here, we arrived here yesterday, staying a week. We flew into Innsbruck with EasyJet, a lovely airport compared to Heathrow which is now unnecessarily huge in my opinion. I'm Alice, by the way; this is my friend Jess.'

'Lovely to meet you both. I'm Issy, with my sister Amy, we're from the Cotswolds, staying a week here in a hotel. They are so clean in Austria, aren't they, no litter around, putting us Brits to shame, we certainly should learn a lesson there, though we probably won't, being a lazy lot.'

"Is it your first time here in sunny Austria, though it can suddenly all change in a flash, to literally thunder and lightning, *Doner und Blitzen*,' as she shared her experience.

'It is,' Issy replied, feeling amused. 'We come from a quaint village in the Cotswolds too, we were born and bred there in Cirencester.'

'Stow on the Wold,' Amy interjected.

'A beautiful place, we love living in the Cotswolds, such lovely walks and cafés around the area, we don't want to ever move away. Our mum and dad brought us up there many moons ago.'

'Cool, do you fancy meeting up later over a cocktail or something? I'll give you my number,' Alice asked, feeling the excitement in her voice.

'Oh, that would be lovely, thank you. Give me your number. I'll put it in my phone contacts.'

She gave Issy her number and she wrote it in her contacts. 'Send me a message so I can save it.'

'Just got that, great thanks. I'd best add Innsbruck after your name lest I forget.'

'Perfect, we're staying at the Oasis Princess Bergfrieden hotel in the centre.'

'No way! Snap, how coincidental is that, obviously meant to be,' she said. 'OK, room number?' She couldn't help being nosy.

'200, second floor, how about you two?'

'101, first floor, with a balcony overlooking the gardens, love it.'

'Sounds perfect, yeah first impressions of the hotel are magical, we love it here, you can just forget about life for the duration and just chillax – think that's a new word added to the English dictionary. Give us a shout when you feel like meeting up, no pressure, we all need our time to recoup after a day's outing.'

'Will do, here we go, just seen the sign for Seefeld, blue skies all the way, I'm in need of a lie down, though, after our cable car mishaps, we'll explain later.'

Finally their lovely hotel came into view as the coach parked up on the road to drop off all passengers staying in the close vicinity. The front doors opened as those getting off at this stop formed a queue in the aisle to disembark. They were greeted by the humid heat once the doors opened. One by one people thanked their Austrian driver, Johannas, as they stepped off, pleased to return to their hotel.

'Gee whiz, it's baking,' Amy said as she fanned her face like a fan, until she acclimatised. 'OK girls we'll text you in about half an hour to meet up. We've booked dinner at 6.30, how about you?' Amy asked, feeling ravenous.

'Oh, the same, so see you down there, no need to text before.'

On that note they all walked into reception feeling a bit fatigued, a quick brush-up would fix that before dinner.

Chapter Three

After a quick shower and change of clothing, they were all ready to meet up with their new pals, Alice and Jess, in the dining room. They were greeted by a lady at the door taking their room numbers, then they could sit anywhere. They noticed a wave from a nearby table, noting it was one of the girls, though they had forgotten which was which, since they had only just met. A spruced up, looking all glammed up changed anyone's appearance.

'We meet again!' Alice said, as they took their seats by the window.

'Indeed we do, you're looking lovely tonight,' Issy remarked, seeing her in white trousers with a red and white short-sleeved blouse.

'Thanks, so do you,' she returned the compliment.

A young waitress came up to the table, taking their drinks order. She noticed they were all chatting so asked them if they wanted to move to a table for four, so they could continue their conversation. Thinking that would be more sensible, she took them to another table.

'Thank you,' Amy and Issy said in unison, as they sat opposite one another with their friends facing them.

'A bottle of water and a bottle of your house wine, if everyone's happy with that?'

'Absolutely, that's fine. To us girls,' clinking glasses once the wine was delivered to the table.

'To us, and to our health and our future happiness, wherever that may lead. 'Brost', as they say in German.'

They took a menu each to peruse for their mains, before the waitress came over to take their orders.

'So what did everyone do today, the best bits first?' Amy asked first, starting up the conversation.

'We did a bit of window shopping, then sat in a lovely café on the square for coffees and cakes to drool over,' Jess added. 'We then went around a boring museum, just to say we did it, it wasn't that bad to be fair,' she continued, feeling somewhat out of her comfort zone. 'What did *you* get up to today?'

'Oh, we took flight in a cable car, which ended up coming to a halt mid-flight, as we swayed mid-air over the mountain tops.'

'Oh my goodness! Scary or what?' both girls gasped, putting their hands over their mouths.

"Soon after we left the platform at the cable car station, we started entering lots of fog, visibility down to zero, then hearing this clunking noise underneath, we gradually came to a steady halt. The next thing we hear is an Austrian voice from the tannoy above, saying the fog had picked up and visibility became too dangerous to continue for safety reasons. So we just stopped moving, dangling in mid-air. He reassured us there was nothing to be concerned about, a gross understatement in my opinion, but what else could he say, only to keep us informed.'

'Frightening or what, what if you suddenly went into panic mode, having a panic attack with no paper bag to breathe into. I guess you wouldn't go up in the first place, unless you wanted to overcome your fear of heights and enclosed spaces.'

'Are you ready to place your meal orders?' The young waitress stood beside them glancing at them, noticing they were in a deep conversation.

'Oh yes please.' They gave their orders, before she quickly walked over to the till to tap in the order, transferring it to the kitchen staff to prepare the meals.

'Danke,' Amy said on their behalf.

'Bitte schön!'

'Anyway, what was your day like?' she continued, after that all-important interlude.

'Oh, nothing as traumatic as yours, exciting, nonetheless. We decided to check out the zoo, thinking it would be more interesting than going to a museum in this weather. Fortunately, we came out in one piece! The usual bears, elephants, monkeys, you name it, they all gave us a free entertaining performance, enjoyed by the young and old, which was great fun.'

Issy poured some water into their glasses, seeing their meals were carefully brought over on trays by two waiters.

They all had panierte Schnitzel mit Bratkartoffeln und Rotkohl. Suddenly silence descended as they all tucked into their meals.

'This is delicious,' Jess announced after a while, before placing her knife and fork across the plate, indicating she had finished. They waited a while before they perused the dessert menu. 'More wine anyone, they can keep the bottle for another night, so just have another glass perhaps?'

'Thanks, we'll get one another night,' Issy added.

The lady came over to take the plates, then brought over a blackboard listing the desserts on offer, all looking very scrumptious.

'Oh wow, this is going to be tricky,' Amy added, seeing three that took her fancy, knowing she could only choose one. She decided on Panna Cotta, as she thought she often had strudel when they were out and about.

Choices made and ordered the girls delved a bit deeper, finding out about one another's lives.

'Who's going to start this game of finding out about ourselves?' Amy asked after the desserts had arrived. 'I'll start,' she added, as she introduced herself as Issy's older sister. 'This is Issy, my sweet sister, always there for me, a people and an animal lover.'

'My turn, I'm Alice and this is my bestie Jess, we live the next street away in sunny Devon, Barnstaple, no doubt you've heard of it, lovely shopping centre, not much else though.'

'OK, I'm Jess, Alice's partner in crime ... seriously not, I work as a hairdresser in the city centre, after finishing my apprenticeship last year. I'm currently building up my clients and loving it.'

'And lastly, I'm Issy, Amy's double act, working in a care home assessing patients' care needs and supporting their families wherever possible. It's a challenging job, yet very rewarding at the end of the day.'

'Well that all sounded very interesting, thank you, ladies,' Amy concluded with a smile. 'Let's get the bills and continue this conversion in the bar over a cocktail or two, if you fancy that,' she added, feeling a good vibe.

They paid up then headed over to the bar, which was a lovely, comfy modern room adorned with a few breakfast bar-type seating areas, typically Austrian, with long coffee tables with beautifully inset ceramic tiles, all adding to the cosy ambiance of the lounge area. They walked up to the bar, a pretty Austrian lady serving, who took their four Bloody Mary cocktail orders. They spotted a table to the rear with its comfy corner seat, with a long multi-coloured cushion to sit on, and two chequered cube chairs at either end which Alice and Jess bagged. All was well in the cosy group.

'Zum Wohl, as they say over here, meaning to your health!' Amy translated.

'Zum voll,' Alice attempted to say, not sure how to pronounce the "w", "v" being the correct way of saying it, as Amy had learnt in her German studies. They chinked glasses together, raising them high to the sky.

'Any plans for tomorrow or is it a rest day?' Issy asked, trying to get the feel of their agenda. 'We thought we'd take a coach trip out to Salzburg, have a nosy around, take time out to explore while we're here in scenic Austria.'

'Perfect, no we've not decided that yet, we'll have to look at the map to see what's worth visiting. We like the place Mittenwald which is nearby, a picturesque town I believe, yes, we fancy going there, either by train or by coach, the latter probably being the most scenic and popular option.'

'That's sorted then, we can meet up later to discuss our day over kaffee und Kuchen if you fancy?'

They made their way slowly back to reception to enquire about their trips in the morning, feeling like excited kids ready to embark on a fabulous adventure, which to be fair they were. They were given maps of the area and where they could pick up a coach to their preferred destination leaving from the centre, a few minutes' walk from the hotel. They could buy their tickets from the coach driver at a discounted price. The lady stamped a card saying if they stayed at the hotel, they should show it to the driver.

It was an early start, though well worth getting up for.

'Right, we'd best have an early night and pack our bags for tomorrow morning.'

'We offer a breakfast bag to take with you, refreshments will be served on the coach,' she added with a smile, assuming they would be interested, which they were. They would collect their picnic bag from the desk prior to going to the coach stop in the morning.

'OK, good night, I'll probably see you here in the morning,' Issy concluded before they went upstairs to their rooms.

Chapter Four

Mittenwald

Her alarm buzzed at 6 am, giving them plenty of time to get ready. Rucksacks packed, they left their room, picked up their breakfast bag treat from reception, before making their way to the coach, which was already parked up, waiting for customers to board. They checked its destination to Mittenwald on the plaque on the front of the coach.

'Gruß Gott!' the driver greeted them as they climbed on, showing him their stamped card, indicating their hotel.

'Welcome aboard, choose your seats and enjoy today's trip. Mittenwald is a beautiful well-known town in Austria,' he added as they walked past him.

They took their window seats, Issy sitting on the inside. They placed their rucksacks in the overhead lockable compartment which the driver shut after everyone had boarded the coach. Others queued up, waiting to climb aboard, greeting the driver in English and German as they surveyed the coach looking for their seats. Once all were settled they started their hour-long trip to Mittenwald.

'Well, we made it, Sis,' Issy said, patting Amy's knee with a smile across her face.

'Indeed we did, now let's see what's in our goody bag,' Amy continued, peering into it. 'We have a croissant, a pain au chocolat, a cartoon of orange juice, a banana and an apple, a healthy breakfast I'd say.'

Five minutes into the journey, a lovely young Austrian lady was seen pushing a drinks trolley along the narrow galley, sending a coffee aroma as she passed through the aisle.

'Kaffee für Sie?' she asked Amy, who was taken by surprise having not heard her coming down the aisle.

'Ah bitte, zweimal mit Milch ohne Zucker, danke,' Amy replied on behalf of them both.

She started to prepare the coffees while they turned the knob to drop down the table, then passed them their coffees.

They opened up their breakfast bags, taking out the croissant and paper plate which was included, as they enjoyed their drinks and treats.

'Here we go on another adventure, to Mittenwald, known for its violins and craft-making instruments apparently,' Amy said, feeling a bit knowledgeable. 'It's dotted with cobbled streets too, not suitable for high heels,' *a bit of useless information yet very practical*, Amy thought. *Who would want to walk around all day in high heels anyway!*

They arrived at the next pick-up stop. A few more Brits hopped on, as well as some German folk, dressed to impress; typical Germans needing to look their best, standing out from the Brits, comfy casual being their style. One lady brought her dachshund along, so cute in a fawn colour, smooth-coated with a red collar with a little bell. She (assuming she was a girl) strutted down the coach aisle with her owner, wagging her small tail from side to side as everyone looked at her with gawking eyes. A couple of older ladies with walking sticks followed, all glammed up. Lastly a couple of Brits, seemingly, husband and wife, or partners these days, in shorts and T-shirts, with Trilby hats plonked on their heads to shield them from the burning sun.

'All right, love?' the woman asked her husband as he struggled a bit with his leg; probably arthritic, Amy surmised.

He groaned in response as if to say, stop nagging me woman! He probably got his fair share every day. Amy was always fascinated seeing people and their odd responses adding to the comedy of events to the day.

As soon as all newbies were seated, the coach continued its

journey. A couple more stops, and they were well on their way to Mittenwald. The lady came around again with her refreshments trolley, hoping to attract all new customers who'd just joined the jolly trip.

After half an hour the driver pulled up by the central bus station in the city centre. Everyone gathered up their bags from the overhead compartments, before forming an orderly line down the aisle, thanking the driver before disembarking.

'Einen schönen Tag,' he wished everyone as they walked down the steps into the square below.

'OK, first stop a café, as I need the loo, Amy!' Issy announced once they hit the cobbles.

'Absolutely, I'm not keen on coach toilets, such narrow spaces only to be used in desperate situations,' Issy remarked, feeling relieved to get off the coach. As they made their way through the passing crowd, a typically dressed-up Austrian lady, clearly coming out of a café, brought out a round tray with savoury titbits on it; cheese on a stick with a piece of pineapple sticking out from the top. They took one as they walked past her, looking lovely with her white apron with fluted sides as she swished it from side to side, as she strutted her stuff. Her hair in pigtails finishing off the Austrian look to a tee.

After a quick bathroom stop, they spotted a table outside and took out their map to see where they were heading next. There were plenty of attractions to see which took their fancy.

'Grüß Gott,' the waitress announced, seeing them take their seats.

'Zweimal Cappuccinos mit Apfelstrudel mit Vanillesauce bitte,' Issy announced in perfect German.

'Danke,' as she walked off into the restaurant to give them the order.

'I think we earned that, Sis, after all that walking,' Amy said, feeling peckish.

They placed their phones on the table, lest anyone rang them. Lo and behold within five minutes Amy started to play her ringtone, *Any dream will do* by Jason Donovan, her daily kitchen exercise dance routine at home.

'Mum, what a lovely surprise, how are you doing today?' she asked, smiling back at Issy, mouthing, 'It's Mum.'

'Indeed darling, all good here, are you having a lovely time and how is Issy feeling now, back to normal I hope, after that awful spell?'

She passed the phone to Issy, so she could tell her all was tickety-boo.

'Hi Mum, I'm good thanks, no more episodes. Austria seems to have fixed that one, thank God,' Issy explained, much to her mum's relief.

'Fantastic, onwards and upwards, you got this, go my darling and enjoy your holiday,' she said, before Issy handed back the phone to Amy.

'Ok Mum, I'll chat later as we are out and about, love you and Dad,' she added before hanging up.

'Well, she sounded happy, one less thing to worry about.'

The lady brought their coffee and cake over, looking delicious, as they cut into their Apfelstrudel with a fork, dipping it into the vanilla sauce and the scoop of nougat ice cream on the side. *What's not to love around these parts*, she thought.

'Is everything OK?' the woman came over to check all was to their liking.

'Sehr gut Danke,' Amy smiled back at her. 'Die Rechnung bitte auch,' she added before she walked off. *Places to go*, she voiced quietly to herself.

They did some window shopping, noticing a beautiful store selling all things clocks, from grandfather clocks to musical Austrian miniature roof top chalets, with Tyrolean-dressed weather men and women, appearing from their doors, rain or shine. Others were playing Austrian dance music once wound up with a silver key at the back of their chalets, bringing joy and delight to all potential customers passing through the shop. A place where one could hang out for a while to calm anyone's nerves, though it could have the opposite effect after being in the shop all day listening to all the chimes. It felt like Christmas, all of a sudden. All that was needed was *gluhwein* and a waffle or a crepe with Belgian chocolate to tickle the taste buds, and snow outside to add to the picture postcard delight.

'Oh, this is very charming, Amy, isn't it?' Issy glanced at her while smiling.

'Ha Ha, very droll,' Amy nudged her back with her arm. 'Should we take a small musical one home for Mum and Dad, Issy?' she asked as temptation got the better of them.

'Yeah, they'll love that, I could use my Monza card, saving our cash for survival this week.'

They chose a dinky little Austrian house with music playing once she was wound up, perfect with the price being discounted by the lady, making them feel happier before they walked out of the shop. She wrapped it up carefully in white tissue paper, then placed it in a lovely small floral bag. Their musical shopping trip proved to be a winner, leaving them little time to see anything else. They left the shop with spirits as high as a kite!

'How about a walk around some lovely gardens, a walk away from here . . . Heilbrunn Palace seems like a plan,' Issy said as she linked arms in Amy's. 'Another *kaffee und Kuchen* stop!' she added, loving their girly trip already.

Amy, taking the lead, took out her trusty map to find where they were, pointing out the gardens to head for.

After a gentle ten-minute walk they arrived, walking through a big iron gate to the kiosk. The lady said it was free and gave them a map of the area. Naturally their eyes wandered off to the toilet signs and cafeteria area, if they had time before getting their coach home.

The weather was lovely and sunny, no clouds in sight, making the gardens look even more beautiful, with many shrubs and flowers in the borders around the gardens. They took their time to wander around, occasionally sitting on benches admiring the views. They took a few photos and selfies to mark the occasion, adding to their memory box.

A few people came up to them along the way, asking for photos of themselves or group ones, which they kindly reciprocated.

An hour later, they followed the signs to the café for afternoon kaffee und kuchen ... when in Austria! They demolished it within minutes before Amy announced, 'Time check, we need to head back to the coach pick-up point, best get a sprint on lest we miss the last one.'

After a quick walk back to the coach station they saw their coach waiting. They checked the front, noting it was the right one, the driver sitting patiently inside waiting to press the button to open its doors to the sound of whoosh as the turbo doors opened outwardly.

'Grüß Gott,' he announced to them as they boarded the coach, feeling welcomed. As they were the first ones on they had too much choice, eventually taking their seats in the middle. Issy sat by the window, Amy beside her after placing their rucksacks in the overhead compartment. Others were gathering outside to board, the little dachshund making her entrance as she sniffed the floor, led by her owner, who seemed worn out, in need of a rest. Clearly, she had been shopping, carrying a few plastic bags of non-essentials, which she struggled to put in the luggage compartment above her seat.

'Would you like me to help you?' Issy asked her.

'Oh Ja, danke vielen Dank,' pointing to her three bags.

'Kein Problem,' Issy smiled back at her, knowing she was grateful for the help.

All aboard, the driver started the journey back to the hotel.

'Welcome back, I hope you all had a lovely day in Mittenwald. Please take your seats, sit back and enjoy the ride,' the driver said, making them all feel relaxed.

A lady soon brought her trolley round, delighting them all, as they needed a pick-me-up after a long day.

'Kaffee? mit Milch und Zucker?'

'Zwei Mal ohne Zucker Danke,' Issy smiled back at her, feeling thankful. They unclipped their tables whilst she was preparing the drinks.

'I need this after our sprint back here,' Amy added, after taking a sip of her coffee.

'I wonder what Alice and Jess got up to today, no doubt we'll see them later,' Issy remarked.

Forty minutes later they were back at the hotel, ready to flop before dinner later. Walking up to the entrance, two girls came towards them, towels wrapped around them as they handed back a key to the receptionist.

'Oh, hi there,' realising it was Alice, with her pigtails tied in a bun on top of her head.

'Good day to you too,' she replied, focusing on her bright orange towel, indicating they had just been at the pool, basking in the sun. 'We decided a pool day was necessary. After yesterday's trip, a chilled out relaxing day with a good book by the pool, what's not to like?' she added with a nervous giggle.

'Absolutely, good choice, we've just been to Mittenwald, saw some beautiful musical clocks in a shop, I bought one as I couldn't resist,' Issy explained.

'See you later, we're just dumping off our bags, and sprucing up before dinner later,' Amy added.

'OK, first sitting again at 6.30?'

'Perfect, see you later,' they said, waving goodbye as they made their way to the lift.

On opening the door to their room, they were greeted by the lovely fresh scent of room air freshener. The maid had clearly been in earlier and plugged one of those refills into a socket in the entrance hall, which wafted all around the cosy room. Amy placed her rucksack on the floor and walked towards the bed, noticing a chocolate wrapped in a foil wrapper, with a lovely picture on top. She opened it up, popping the chocolate in her mouth, enjoying every second as it melted inside her mouth, then took off her shoes and lay back flat on the bed to unwind.

'Yummy in my tummy,' she added, tapping the bed for Issy to join her, passing her a chocolate.

'I need a shower before tonight, so you go and sit on the balcony and admire the views,' Amy added, walking towards the bathroom.

'Good idea, we've got an hour, which is what we need, Sis.'

Issy opened the sliding door to the balcony, only to notice a long green creature on the floor by the balcony's edge, seemingly enjoying the late afternoon temperature. Usually she would have uttered a short scream seeing a creepy creature but this time she rushed back inside to pick up her phone, to capture the image, adding to her latest fascination with insects.

A light green lizard with four legs poised on the edge of the balcony. Issy snapped a few photos, before bending down to take a closer look. *A bit of wildlife adds to the holiday adventures*, she thought.

Ten minutes later, Amy joined her on the balcony, looking very pretty in her floral pink and cream dress just above the knee.

'Chic or what, Sis!' Issy attempted a whistle with her two fingers in her mouth, which failed, so she gave a twirl instead.

'Thank you,' Amy curtsied back, smiling gleefully. Issy jumped up and headed to the bathroom, entirely forgetting her little green friend, until a screech came from the balcony.

'Er, what's that thing doing?' Amy ran back inside, clasping her hands over her mouth.

'What's up, Sis?' Issy played her at her game, not sure if she thought she had spotted this green lovely reptile.

'Have you not seen that green monster sitting by the balcony's edge, occasionally inching along, *soo* creepy, I can't sit out there, it might jump and attack me, help me before you get in the shower, please!'

'Where, where, show me, I'll grab my phone to snap it!'

'Oh, very funny, I don't think so, it's got legs and sticks its tongue out at me in disgust.'

'Wimp, step aside and I'll take a closer look ... he's lovely isn't he, Amy, I must say.'

'Erm, you're kidding me and how do you know it's a he?' she asked, feeling even more spooked.

'Well, I don't but it's lovely, nonetheless.'

'Okay, I get it, you knew about this, didn't you, Issy? You teased me and played along with it, you know I'm not a fan of all creatures puny and small and freaky-looking!'

'Ha, got ya in one, Sis, you got to have a laugh though, haven't you on our jolly holiday? Look he's harmless, or legless, just take the other seat, time is ticking, I need to shower and glam up before we meet the girls downstairs.'

'Actually, upon closer inspection … he's quite cute in bright green,' Amy admitted out loud, making Issy giggle all the way to the bathroom.

Five minutes later she too appeared in a mini cream-coloured short-sleeved dress, with a flowery short scarf draped around her shoulders, in case they took an evening stroll outside after dinner.

Amy slid the patio door shut, before grabbing their mini shoulder bags to exit downstairs by the staircase to find Alice and Jess waiting at the restaurant entrance to be checked in by their room number.

'Fancy meeting you here,' Amy announced, making Alice jump as she turned to look at them.

'We meet again, all looking very smart, I might add.'

'Ditto,' as they inched forward in the queue, giving the lady their room numbers.

'A table for four is set for you over there, we remembered last night you sat together.' She pointed towards the window seat in the corner.

'Thank you,' Amy added, taking the lead to the table.

The table was decorated with a lovely thin vase holding a red rose in the middle with a glass filled with ocean pebbles and a tea light buried in its middle, ready to be lit by its wick, adding a romantic touch to the display. Four wine glasses with a napkin folded into a fan shape protruding from the top, added to the elegance.

A lady brought them a bottle of Pinot Grigio, something different, as promised by the girls last night.

'Brost,' as the Germans say "zum Wohl" to our health,' they brought their glasses to the middle to toast.

Looking at the night's specials on a printed sheet they chose sea bass and risotto celebrating fish night.

'OK girls, how was your day?' Amy started the conversation off with Jess.

'A day at the pool today for us, with iced coffee and mocktails and a good book.'

'Perfect,' Amy said. 'We took a trip out to beautiful Mittenwald, wandering around the shops, a walk in the palace gardens, a day well spent.'

Their meals were soon brought over by two people as they balanced the plates on their arms, pure skill they thought.

As was their tradition, Amy and Issy took out their phones to take a photo of the meal, sending it to Mum and her best friend, Lottie. Issy took one of the girls as they drew each other into a hug, sending it to their friends, then took themselves, sending it on their family WhatsApp. Within a few minutes Mum sent one back, loving the pic of them both together, wishing them a lovely holiday. Half an hour later they were greeted by four lavish ice creams with a flake and Belgian chocolate sauce poured on them. Just looking at it made their taste buds drool in delight. As always, they headed over to the bar and ordered four cappuccinos, which came with a Biscoff biscuit' it was those little touches in life that make their day. They smiled at one another, feeling the friendship bond between them.

'To our friendship, may it last forever,' Alice added, high-fiving them individually.

'We're going to Salzburg tomorrow if you fancy coming, a coach leaves outside at 8 am; we can get a breakfast bag to go as long as the staff know in advance.'

'Yes please, that sounds like a great plan, we'd best tell

reception now, so they can plan ahead. Drink up, girls, let's head over now.'

They walked to reception and booked their trip and breakfast bag to collect in the morning and made their way back to their rooms to pack, before having an early night.

Chapter Five

Salzburg Trip

The alarm buzzed as usual at 7 am, as Amy slowly turned over to switch it off, no time to hit snooze, as they were off on another jolly to Salzburg.

'Rise and shine, Issy, it's Wednesday which means, not only are we halfway through our week, we're also boarding a coach to Salzburg today to visit Mozart! I'm going to the bathroom now, so sort out your clothes before I'm back.'

'OK boss, don't be long, things to do and all that,' Issy added, teasing Amy all the way.

Moments later, Amy reappeared with her towel wrapped around her to get ready, wearing another flaunty dress as the weather was due to heat up later.

Half an hour later they waited in reception to collect their breakfast bags, then, hearing noises behind them, they turned around to see Alice and Jess waving arms, as if on a runway giving an aircraft the all clear.

'Good morning you two, a lovely day, isn't it,' Amy said.

'It is indeed, and here we are again on our trips,' Jess added, stifling a little yawn.

'Have a lovely trip to Salzburg, the coach is just about to arrive,' the receptionist said, as she walked behind her desk to start her shift.

'Thank you,' they said in unison.

They picked up their breakfast bags from the desk then walked outside to the parked-up red and white coach. With a whoosh, the turbo front doors burst open for them to board.

'Grüß Gott,' the coach driver greeted them as they climbed

the carpeted steps to his cabin. They showed him their pre-booked tickets, and he immediately recognised them from the Mittenwald trip the other day.

'On your travels again, ladies today, enjoy!' he smiled back at them.

They were the first to board, taking their seats in the middle, Amy taking the window seat again.

A few others from nearby hotels boarded, including a couple of pensioners armed with their colourful walking sticks.

Once all aboard they set off on their day trip, collecting other day trippers en route. A whoosh of the turbo doors indicated the next stop. This time a lovely fluffy white westie dog was first to place her two paws on the carpet steps, followed by her owner, a middle-aged casually dressed lady, clearly a dog lover, as the westie wore a red tartan half coat across her middle, as she paraded down the coach isle, causing many stares and smiles.

'Guten Morgen, willkommen auf unseren Bus nach Salzburg, sit back and enjoy the ride,' their driver spoke into his microphone.

'Best get comfy then, we've got two hours!' Issy added with a giggle.

No sooner had they got going than a friendly lady came around pushing her rickety trolley, serving coffees and light refreshments, asking them what they would like.

'Zweimal Cappuccino mit Milch, bitte?' Amy said, smiling back at her.

She passed them their coffees, placing them on their tabletop whilst they opened up their breakfast bags, pleasantly surprised to see a croissant and a brown seeded bread roll with butter and a plastic knife, and a cream paper napkin, adding the perfect touch. The westie lay peacefully opposite, soon raising her head, sniffing the air, smelling out their food, thinking it was irresistibly tasty.

Amy saw her owner turning her back for a brief second, and the little westie took her opportunity to pull herself up, paws on the seat, trying her hardest to pinch the croissant with her opened mouth. Caught in the act just in time, Issy voiced firmly, 'Er no you don't, get down!'

The lady suddenly turned around, pulling firmly on the lead, giving her a firm telling-off.

'Oh my, that was a close call, Amy,' Issy remarked, feeling somewhat amused.

'Oh, I am so sorry, Madame, Bessy can be a bit hasty when she sniffs out food. She is a dog after all. I'm Maria, by the way.'

'No problem, at least I still have my croissant in one piece,' Issy added, smiling back at her. 'I'm Issy and this is my sister Amy,' she replied, feeling friendly.

'Are you from around here?' Amy asked, showing her politeness, despite not really feeling in the mood for conversation; she just wanted some quiet time to savour her coffee and breakfast.

'Oh sorry, you need to eat.' She got the message, making Amy feel even more awkward.

'No problem, I'm just not very awake until I have some food,' she responded, hoping she would back off for now. The owner looked away, feeling a bit embarrassed as she tended to her Bessy.

They returned to eating and drinking and general chit chat, before she bombarded them again with further questions.

'Salzburg is a beautiful city,' Maria announced suddenly out of the blue, causing Amy to nearly spit her mouthful of coffee out!

'I used to live there many years ago, until my husband died. I needed a smaller place to live, and Salzburg is very expensive to live in, being largely a tourist place. Oh sorry, I made you jump!' she gasped as she turned to look at Amy. 'I now live in Augsburg, Bavaria, in Germany where I was born. It's equally beautiful, very near Munich and Stuttgart,' she added.

"We're sisters, our home is in the Cotswolds in England,' Issy continued, giving Amy time to enjoy her breakfast.

'Lovely, I visited Cornwall once, a lovely coastal place with lots of boats and beautiful scenery. Anyway, I'll let you eat, I'm sorry!'

'It's fine, no problem, lovely to chat to you, Maria, have a great day once we arrive.'

'Thank you and you too, no doubt we will probably meet on the bus later,' she ended their chat with a beaming smile.

Half an hour had passed when the driver parked the coach up in a car park a walk away from the town. They thanked him as they got off, wishing him a lovely day.

'I've only just realised, I've not seen Alice or Jess, did they come with us, Amy?' Issy asked, feeling forgetful.

'No, they were going to Mittenwald or somewhere today, or just relaxing at the pool, I'm not sure,' Amy replied.

First stop was the most popular tourist attraction, Mozart's birthplace; he was born in 1756. Germany and Austria loved their classical music, so off they headed to browse round the stately museum. As per usual, on arrival at the entrance hall, they had to place their belongings in a plastic box, to be X-rayed for any harmful weapons. All OK, they continued their tour around the large, yet peaceful building, seeing all the paintings and a few head carvings connected with the famous composer. They took their time to see the important pieces, taking a few pictures, before gradually getting bored after an hour, and making their way back out into the old town. Time for a mooch around the shops, before they found a picture-perfect café for their usual afternoon delights.

'When in Austria coffee and cake all the way,' Amy said, licking her lips.

They soon found a cosy spot in the old town on the cobbles, people watching, their favourite pastime when out and about.

'Etwas zu trinken?' a young lady asked, noticing they'd just taken their seats.

'Zwei Cappuccino und eine Käse Küchen und einen Apfel Streusel Kuchen für meine Schwester bitte,' Amy smiled back at her.

She nodded then walked over to the restaurant to place the order. Within a few moments she came back out with a tray with their delights.

'To us in sunny Salzburg,' Issy lifted her coffee cup to join Amy's.'

Suddenly they heard music. They turned around to see a couple of buskers, one with a guitar, the other a mouth organ, playing some Austrian folk music, putting on a free show, making the atmosphere ... well, atmospheric, putting everyone in a good mood for the day ahead. They finished their delights and paid up, to take a walk over to the Mirabell Palace and Gardens, which was free. A lovely stroll around keeping themselves fit after all the cakes they had consumed so far.

Plenty of tourists from all over the world, to hear with their different languages, trying to guess which country, many from China and Japan, judging by their eyes! Groups gathered to take selfies holding their selfie sticks on poles. They were asked numerous times to take one, so they asked them to return the favour, adding to the memories of the day.

'Did you know that the all-time favourite classic film *The Sound of Music* was filmed here with the Von Trapp family, starring the one and only Julie Andrews? The real Von Trapp family lived here all those decades ago, a piece of very interesting information for us, I didn't know myself.'

'Well I never, just loved watching the movie, it's ageless. Recently re-cast, equally as good, though I prefer the original as we all remembered it ... the hills are alive with the sound of music,' Issy started to raise her voice, throwing her arms out in a V as Julie Andrews did on the hills, singing her heart out.

'OK, time check,' Amy quickly added, feeling the day slipping away from them.

'It's four o'clock now, so yes time is ticking, just an hour left to board the coach back.'

Amy agreed; Issy suggested walking around the new town, to see what was on offer, then a gentle walk back. 'What d'you say, Sis?'

'Perfect, let's go!' They picked up the pace down the cobbles, heading towards the centre.

———

As they walked around, they noticed many chocolate shops selling the most delicious chocolate balls, Belgian dark and white truffles in long milk chocolate bars, featuring post card pictured chocolates individually wrapped in foil, perfect for a present, all very irresistible. After a quick browse inside, they found a few treats for themselves as well as presents for home. Feeling satisfied with their purchases, they started their short walk back to the car park, where they had left the coach that morning. There was five minutes to spare before their driver opened up the front doors. Whoosh and the turbo doors flung open, to reveal their handsome driver, Kurt (from his name tag), welcoming them aboard. His brown hair was tied up in a bun, suggesting he was a casual, yet relaxed caring laid-back man.

Suddenly, as they had just stepped inside the coach, they heard a loud thud, a cry for help, making them turn around to see what the fuss was all about, only to see a lady lying on her side on the floor, with her dog, clearly in distress. Amy immediately disembarked, making way for Kurt to run to her rescue. Her initial instincts kicked in to follow him, as she vaguely remembered seeing the dog ... Maria's dachshund, Bessy, now whimpering at her side, desperately wanting someone to come over and help her. She stood alongside Kurt, trying to assess the situation, clearly seeing no movement from Maria, which was an immediate concern.

'OK, we are here now, are you in any pain?' Kurt immediately asked, despite being an obvious question, a very necessary one. A deep groan in response indicated her answer. Bessy was by her side feeling more distressed not seeing her owner flinch an inch.

'I'm a paramedic, which was my last job,' Kurt continued to explain, hoping she could understand him. 'I'm going to ring the Notfall ambulance, please don't move, we will look after you.'

'Maria, it's me, Amy, from this morning, me and my sister Issy, we will take care of Bessy for you, so don't worry she is in safe hands.'

Within a few minutes a local ambulance, with its sirens sounding, parked up beside her. Maria, unable to get up, due to old age and possibly a broken hip, was gently lifted onto a stretcher by the crew into the ambulance, where she was initially given oxygen via a face mask, to sustain her until they arrived at the local hospital, to be handed over to the staff for further treatment.

Amy didn't have any contact details for Maria, as they had only just met that morning, however, someone had to take her dog, so it was just as well she was a dog lover. Bessy and she had already been introduced, making it less stressful for her. Amy bent down to stroke her, she lifted her head against her face, giving her a thank-you lick in response. Clearly she was comfortable with Amy, making her nearly shed a happy tear down her right cheek. Dogs were a woman's best friend.

The ambulance was on its way to the hospital so Kurt, Amy and Bessy made their way back onto the coach. Once inside, he picked up his microphone to explain what had just happened, telling everyone to keep calm.

"We now have an extra passenger; Bessy the dog. Please give her a stroke as you pass her by, to calm her from her initial distressing situation, thank you. The lady is now in safe hands going to hospital. Amy and Issy will be looking after Bessy,' he added, causing everyone to clap loudly in response, approving of their excellent efforts and dedication.

Amy took Bessy's lead, red with little silver studs around her small collar, with a plastic bag with her bowls and a few treats Maria carried with her, probably everywhere she travelled. Bessy seemed to have forgotten about her stressful incident as she happily walked beside Amy along the coach aisle, all admiring her as she passed by, until Amy took her seat on the outside of the aisle. Bessy lay in the footwell by her feet, ready to fall asleep, Issy taking the window seat this time as Bessy took precedence.

'Oh, look at her now, bless, she's curled up having a much-needed nap,' Issy remarked, feeling all loved-up. The lady soon came over with her trolley, offering them on board drinks which they so needed.

'Two cappuccinos for you, after your kind efforts helping the lady and taking her dog,' she added.

'Oh, that's so kind, we really appreciate this, thank you,' they replied. They put their table down, placing the coffees on a small white lace doily.

Their immediate thoughts were with Maria, hoping she would recover soon, yet aware things could change, overthinking the worst scenario, what would they do with Bessy, could they bring her back to England? They couldn't abandon her now and re-home her here. *Stop this now*, Amy reminded herself, it was too much to bear for now.

They sat and drank their cappuccinos in deep thought, seeing poor Maria lying there had felt very upsetting at the time. Their immediate focus was on Bessy, which wasn't a problem as they loved dogs, and she was no trouble. The hotel was dog friendly anyway and they were sure that, after hearing the story behind her, they would fully understand.

The driver parked directly in front of the hotel, making it easier for them having Bessy on board. Kurt told them he would be in touch with the hotel as soon as he heard from the hospital, to give them next of kin contacts, so they could follow her recovery. It definitely was a day filled with traumatic events at the end, a day they wouldn't forget so easily.

They walked into reception, only to be greeted with further applause from hotel staff standing in reception, making them feel rather overwhelmed, yet a good feeling inside.

'We heard of your traumatic events regarding Maria, we have got to know her quite well over the last weeks, as she regularly sat outside in our garden terrace to the rear, for her kaffee und Kuchen for a hundred hours. She was a lovely, sweet, smart lady, with her gorgeous dachshund. She told us her husband died last year, she felt so alone; we welcomed her here, we sometimes would sit and chat to her, especially on her low days, making sure she was well provided for, often giving her dog meat from the kitchen and other treats. Maria loved the individual attention, showing her gratitude every time,' the receptionist explained, making them well up in emotion, trying to keep it locked in.

'The dog stays here free of charge in your room. We will give you some dog food she likes here, when you come down in the morning,' she added with a smile.

On cue, her mobile rang, which she promptly answered.

After finishing the conversion, she confirmed that it was the hospital, confirming Maria had broken her hip after her sudden fall, meaning it was a long road to recovery. She was due an operation in half an hour due to the level of pain she was in, they would be updated in the morning. At least she was now in the best place, the receptionist added. The girls thanked her for reporting back to them. Amy picked up Bessy's lead to walk upstairs to their room.

Once back in their room Bessy started sniffing her way through the room, exploring all the nooks and crannies, seeking out any morsel of food lurking around the next crevice … sadly none to be found, as the cleaners had got there before her! A few minutes later there was a knock at the door. Wondering who it was, Amy walked over to unlock it, to be greeted by a lady holding a small, brown dog basket in her arms.

'We thought you would like this for Bessy, she loves this cosy bed.'

'Oh, thank you,' and on hearing her name, Bessy came running up, almost slipping on the wooden floor as she came to a sudden halt. Her nose poised to the air, sniffing her familiar hotel bed, she allowed the lady to bring it into the room, placing it near the bed. She soon jumped in, turning herself around in circles, before curling herself up in a ball, making herself comfy for the night. A purrfect sight, with her face lying on top of her two front paws. Issy had to snap this one on her phone, adding to the day's event. The lady bid them good night, shutting the door behind her.

They were shattered after the day, deciding to put their night T-shirts on, taking it in turns to keep watch on Bessy, who by now was away in doggy dream land, faintly snoring.

Their morning wake-up call this time was Bessy as she started to whimper, needing a pee no doubt. Seeing she was wide awake, Amy quickly got out of bed, grabbed her shorts which were slung on the back of the chair, feet in her sandals, walked over to the door, clipped Bessy's lead on her collar, unlocked the door to zoom down the nearest fire exit which led outside into the garden, just in time for her to relieve herself on the lawn.

'Good girl Bessy, I'm sure you feel much better now.' Amy bent down, stroking her silky back, as she wagged her tail in response. They raced back up the fire exit stairs, walking leisurely to her room. She turned the key, noticing Issy was making their morning coffee, taking it to the comfy lounge area. Today was going to be a very different day now Bessy was on board; a gentle peaceful stroll around the area, a pool day sipping mocktails and iced coffees, amusing their four-legged friend.

'Good morning my lovely Sis,' Amy said, taking her by surprise when she walked back in.

'Oh, good morning to you too, my sweet!' Issy teased as she walked past Amy, feeling more relaxed.

'So, what's on the cards today?' Amy asked her, bending down to give Bessy a kiss on her forehead, who was clearly lapping up the attention.

'A day at the pool with Bessy lying on the grass verge, what do you think?'

'Sounds just right ... let's get our swimming gear together and water bowl for Bessy, though I'm sure she'll get spoiled rotten at the pool.'

Half an hour later they took two sun loungers placed under a parasol on the grass verge where Bessy lay down beside them. Amy unpacked her bowl, filling it with water from the tap nearby.

'Guten Morgen,' a handsome young man walked towards them, seeing Bessy chilling on the lawn beside them.

He put up the parasol, making sure they were shielded from the harmful UVA of the sun's rays, then took their orders for two iced coffees, which he made in the kiosk a few metres away. He couldn't resist stroking Bessy before he walked back to prep the drinks.

'She is lovely,' he added before walking off. They smiled back.

'He's dishy, Amy,' Issy looked at her, winking.

'Tall, mid-brown hair, slim physique with his T-shirt and orange shorts ... a cool look,' Amy added, returning the smile.

Within moments he was balancing a tray on his upturned hand, with their iced coffees with a purple umbrella appearing from the centre of the glass.

'Vielen Dank.' They smiled back at him, feeling a connection. He soon came over again with a jug of water to top up Bessy's bowl, which they were grateful for.

'Oh, this is the life isn't it, a lazy day around the pool. I wonder how Maria is feeling now?' Issy asked, hoping they would hear more soon. 'For now, let's just enjoy today, knowing she's in the best place and Bessy is now with us, happy and content.'

'True, let's just kick back and relax, she would want that for us, not worrying about her,' Amy concluded.

'Fancy a dip in the pool, whilst I finish my drink and mind Bessy? I think we should take it in turns until Bessy is settled enough for us to go in together?' said Issy.

'Good idea,' said Amy. 'I'll go first, test the water!'

No sooner had Amy walked over to the pool than Bessy lifted her head, noticing Amy walking off, soon placing her head down again, feeling perfectly safe in her environment, blissfully enjoying sunbathing.

'Ooh it's lovely once you get in,' Amy shouted back, turning towards Issy, hoping she could hear her above the gathering crowd, especially children splashing in the toddler pool. Issy gave her a thumbs up before she took out her book, a holiday romance by Jo Thomas, her latest favourite author.

Bessy got up, walking over to her water bowl, lapping it up with her pink tongue, clearly in need of a refreshing drink, then shaking her little body from side to side as dogs do, plonking herself back down on the grass to cool off from the heat of the day.

———

'My turn next!' as Amy came back looking refreshed, ready to slap on some sunscreen factor 25, before lying back on the blue sun lounger, hoping to gain a tan.

There was a sudden scream from the pool with someone waving arms like a lunatic. Issy soon realised someone was in trouble in the deep end. A young girl was clearly in distress, probably out of her depth. Issy looked around to see if anyone had noticed. Knowing immediate action was needed, Issy couldn't hold out any longer so she ran into the pool, swimming as fast as she could towards the girl, who by now was finding it harder to tread water, clearly swallowing some water causing her to stress more, almost choking. Finally, the handsome man from the kiosk came out to see what the commotion was about. Immediately, he ran into the water, grabbing a life ring hooked on the side of the kiosk, doing the crawl, approaching the girl quickly from behind. Issy was first to place the girl on her back, whilst she turned herself backwards as she pulled the girl back so that she lay on Issy's front. The man was able to put the life ring over her head, making it easier for her to backstroke using her legs. A sudden silence was all around them, as realisation took over what had just happened. Mouths had dropped open, seeing the full scale of the incident, which could have ended very differently indeed.

A few minutes later another man placed a towel on the ground where she was gently placed, after initially being put into a sitting position and patted on the back to spit out any water, before gently being placed on her back to rest.

'Thank goodness you came to her rescue, before I dived in, things could have been very different,' the handsome man added, looking at Issy thankfully.

'Indeed, they could have been, no problem. I did a life-saving course some time ago, and my natural instincts just took over,' she explained to him.

Moments later a lady came trotting over to where they were looking after the girl, who by this point had bounced back after her initial shock, not really understanding why everyone was surrounding her.

'What's happened to my girl, is she OK?' the lady asked frantically, feeling rather helpless amidst some guilt.

'And you are?' the man asked, feeling a bit frazzled and impatient.

'I'm her mother, I only popped over to the toilets. She was with my friend who told her not to go into the pool until I returned. Clearly madam had other ideas.' She looked at her friend sheepishly, wondering what on earth she had been thinking of, taking her eyes off her daughter.

'Don't worry, I've seen this happen many times since I've been working here. All children love to have fun, not always aware of the potential dangers by a pool, despite parents telling them. It's not your fault, we came to her rescue and she won't remember her mistake, so please don't tell her off, she needs your support right now.'

'Yes, you're right, I'm just happy you helped her, I know it's your job. She's only just learning how to swim, having lessons at home in England.'

'Would you like a drink to calm you down?'

'Oh, that's very kind of you, an orange juice please with ice, thank you. I'm so sorry for all this,' she added.

'Well, the main thing is she's safe now, she won't remember much, so the less said about it to her, the better,' the handsome lifeguard waiter reminded her.

'I suggest you go and enjoy the rest of your pool day today.'

Time soon ticked by, all were beginning to pack up their belongings for the day, in time for their evening meals at the hotel or whatever plans they had for the evening. Bessy soon realised things were changing, lifting her head up, noticing they were gathering their stuff up together, packing their gear neatly in their bags. She got up and walked towards them, wagging her tail, feeling happy to be moving on, probably thinking a walk was due, or food.

'Good girl, Bessy, we're going soon, I'm sure you've had enough for today too,' Amy talked to her as she patted her on her silky head.

She picked up her water bowl, clipping her lead to her collar, before they walked around to the entrance of the pool area, heading back to reception. They walked past the reception desk, only to be called back by the lady behind the desk.

'I have a letter for you, I hope you had a good swim,' she called out calmly, smiling back at them.

'Oh, thank you, yes it was a lovely afternoon and this one,' pointing to Bessy, 'enjoyed sunning herself on the grass,' she added with a chuckle.

They carried on to the lift taking them to their room. On opening the door, they noticed the usual chocolate on both beds, indicating the maids had been in to refresh the room. Amy was always fascinated with the little wicker basket in the bathroom, with little shampoo and conditioner bottles amongst the mini soaps wrapped up and a bottle of hand and body lotion, emanating a lush aroma once the bottle was opened. All being part of a jolly hotel experience.

'Who's having a shower before we take Bessy out before dinner at 6.30?'

'I'll go first,' Amy said, 'then we can look at the letter afterwards, knowing we are ready to eat. I wonder who it's from?' she added, feeling intrigued.

Ten minutes later they sat out on the balcony, dressed up in a different dress for tonight's meal.

'I'll open the letter to see who it's from, if you like, Amy, I'm intrigued to know. OK, here goes,' Issy added, placing her thumb underneath the sealed envelope.

To whom this may concern

That sounds formal and rather serious,' Amy added, feeling slightly on edge as she sat up straight in a more formal position.

It is with deep regret that Maria has taken a turn for the worse in the last 24 hours and remains in hospital suffering from a stroke. Therefore, she can no longer look after Bessy. She was able to tell us that she would like you both to look after Bessy, as she seemed to enjoy your company. Maria has no other person to hand over Bessy to, so Bessy is now officially yours.

I hope you will both enjoy giving her the new forever home she rightly deserves.

Kind regards
Dr Muller
on behalf of Maria's instruction.

'Well, I was kind of expecting this, as Maria didn't look at all well and is in her twilight years, no doubt. She never mentioned siblings, so I just assumed she was on her own, possibly the last surviving one in her family,' Amy added, feeling slightly bereft yet happy to take on Bessy, as they both were beginning to love her, unable to give her back or rehome her. 'Well, that changes everything for now, depending on what we do next. Fortunately, we haven't booked a return flight, so we now need to take a train or coach back home. For now, let's concentrate on our meal tonight, and think about the rest tomorrow. After all, Bessy is now ours. Poor Maria, I hope she continues to recover a bit,' Amy added, smiling down at Bessy, who looked up into her eyes, as if to say thank you for having me.

'Well, you're very welcome, my beautiful furry friend Bessy, you're now part of our family.' She knelt down to tickle her belly, which she loved, rolling over enjoying the love, wagging her little tail from side to side as it knocked on the floor. All was well in her world and theirs too.

'It's nearly time for dinner, Issy, let's go. We can chat about seeing Maria, though not sure it's wise to take Bessy,' Amy added.

After a quick walk outside for Bessy to do her business before they went into the restaurant, they were greeted by a friendly Austrian lady who escorted them to a table by the window, with a window bench for extra comfort. Bessy lay down under the table, feeling she finally belonged, a happy contented dog.

'OK, on the menu tonight is sea bass with cabbage and baby carrots and classic kartoffeln, if that's your thing?' Amy read out, making Issy jump. 'I'm definitely having that, I love fish, a healthy option too. How about you, Sis?'

'The same, fish night it is then!' feeling accomplished.

'Ready to order?' The young waitress came over with her iPad ready to tap away.

'Drink first; 2 orange juices with ice and 2 sea bass please,' Issy replied, looking her in the eye.

'Danke schön!' she replied, tapping in their order.

Within minutes she brought their drinks over which they lifted up, clinking them, celebrating the news of adopting Bessy, though obviously aware that Maria was unwell. She would want them to give Bessy the best life, for which they were eternally grateful. A quick check on her, suddenly lifting her head in response, they felt all loved up having her.

The lush-looking square plates with a well-presented sea bass dish set before them, they were ready to tuck in with gusto.

'Guten Appetit! as they say here, Amy, and to us three!'

'Indeed, to us!' Amy lifted her glass in response, staring into Issy's eyes. 'Wait one, haven't you forgotten something, Issy?'

'Oops, a photo for the family WhatsApp, good thinking, Sis!'

An ice cream with Belgian chocolate sauce finished the meal off nicely. They skipped coffees as Bessy needed a walk, before they returned to the lounge, ordering coffees later on.

They finished off their juices, taking Bessy by her lead and walking out through the front entrance, along the street, where she soon performed. Having a plastic bag with them, they kept the place tidy by depositing it in the nearest dog litter bin. They decided to wander around the town until they found a quaint café and took their seats, Bessy lying by Issy's feet, to order two cappuccinos. A lovely stroll around the town breathing the fresh air, people-watching, was the better choice having Bessy too. A buzzing noise; noting it was her phone ringing in her bag, Issy quickly pulled it out before it stopped ringing. 'It's Mum, best take this, Amy, before she worries herself more,' she swiftly added, knowing she'd want a full update.

'Hi Mum, are you OK, how's life?'

'Fine, what's your latest news?' she replied, sensing the excitement in Amy's voice.

'Well, a lot has happened in the last 24 hours. We've adopted a gorgeous dog, whose owner took a bad health turn on our way back from Salzburg, the other day. She sadly had a fall by our coach, was taken to hospital, then suffered a stroke the following day, not good I know. We received a letter from her doctor, saying she wanted us to take her dog, whom we had fallen for, as she has no immediate family to pass her over to. We felt honoured to give this wee dog a forever home. Obviously, we feel for the lady. Maria is in her late 70s so, sadly she may not survive much longer,' Amy recalled the story in full.

'Oh, that's so sad, yet lovely you are now the new dog owner. What's going to happen now, will you bring her home soon?'

'Yes, once we are finished with our holiday here, which is on Saturday. We will probably book a train home, as we can't take her on a plane. It will be much nicer taking the scenic route.'

'Sounds like a great idea, a perfect end to a jolly holiday. We can all work out the rest once you're back.' Mum sounded excited to meet this fur baby.

'Her name is Bessy, by the way and she is so adorable, you will love her, Mum. OK I'd best go as we're out having a coffee in

---

town. We'll be in touch soon with the details. Bye for now, Mum, love you and Dad,' she concluded before ending the call.

Fortunately, their cappuccinos had only just arrived or else they would have been cold.

'Well, Mum seemed happy with that, one less thing to concern ourselves with. See, everyone loves dogs, don't they?' Issy added, giggling. 'Cheers,' Issy continued, as the cappuccinos had just arrived with a lovely amaretto shortbread on the saucer with 2 brown sugar sachets, of which they only used one as the coffee was a bit on the strong side.

'To our new life with Bessy!'

'Wherever that takes us,' Amy added, feeling excited.

Chapter Six

They were now nearly at the end of their jolly holidays; what an adventure it had been thus far. They had visited many beautiful Austrian towns with their folklore, consumed lots of coffee and cake along the way, met up with interesting people, a satisfying expedition, filled with lasting memories to be cherished forever. Soon, however, they had to face reality once back home, new beginnings and pastures new. They were ready for a new vibrant challenge.

Mum and Dad had also moved on and bought themselves a spacious bungalow in Stow on the Wold, where they could stay temporarily until they found a place to rent, once they started their new jobs. They loved dogs, so Bessy would definitely be a welcome new member to their extended family. Life was indeed looking good, lots to look forward to as long as everyone stayed in good health, which sadly no one could predict the future.

They decided on a flight back home, after extensive enquiries about taking Bessy on board, thinking it would be the quicker and less stress busting option for her; the airline finally agreed as Bessy was a small dog. A check up with a local vet 24 hours before with a necessary rabies injection and they were all good to go. Bessy was the perfect patient, once lifted onto the vets table and suitably distracted with doggy biscuits, the injection into her fur around her neck. Bessy was wagging her tail again banging down on the table, eager to be lifted down onto the floor, her ordeal swiftly forgotten. The vet praised her all the way, making her feel special. She was ready to quickly exit his room, into the reception area to be rewarded with yet more treats, whilst they paid for the damages, before they were handed her own blue passport with her name on it, listing her latest checkups and vaccinations.

Saturday morning finally arrived, the day of their departure from beautiful Austria as they travelled on the coach to Innsbruck airport. They had had a lovely time with an extra special memory, adopting Bessy from Maria. She was so lovely, yet sadly could no longer look after Bessy, due to ill health and no other family to care for her. She entrusted her to them, which they were not expecting, yet for which they were overwhelmingly grateful. Bessy had taken a shine to them prior to Maria's fall, – so sad, yet had felt certain her beloved dachshund was in the best of hands – now looking forward to her new forever future. Bessy certainly grabbed everyone's attention once they boarded the Boeing 747 to London Heathrow. As they walked down the aisle, children stared at her, as she walked to heel through the narrow corridor, whilst Amy and Issy perused the seat numbers above, looking for theirs; aisle C4 and 5. They took their seats, Amy by the window and Issy by the aisle, in case she needed to take Bessy out. The air hostess brought over a special, small halter, to clip onto her seatbelt, to keep her safe during take-off and landing. Bessy was all for the amazing attention she was receiving on board, lapping up the gentle pats and strokes along her silky-smooth back. What's not to like, she thought, no doubt!

After a few pre-landing jerks and bumps, they were soon back on terra firma, slowly cruising into the parking bay stop, engines off and seat belt signs overhead turned off, ready to disembark. Naturally all the passengers released their seat belts, standing up, turning round facing the overhead compartments, claiming their hand luggage, some distinctly heavier than others. Bessy, despite sniffing everyone who passed her, showed definite signs of frustration, as she eagerly tried to pull herself off Issy's lap, clearly wanting to have her freedom back, after the hour's flight.

After a quick check over by ground staff in the lounge, they were all ready to go and collect their red wheeled suitcases from the carousel to the exit, to the express coach homeward bound. Looking at the LED timetable above, they had half an hour to spare, enough time for a toilet stop for all of them, much to Bessy's relief. They bought two cappuccinos from a nearby kiosk, selling yummy cranberry flapjacks and carrot cake slices. They bought one of each, ready for the final trek home to Stow on the Wold. Mum would then pick them up from Tesco car park, as she was more comfortable making this short car journey; age was slowly creeping up on Mum and Dad, meaning long-distance car journeys were no longer doable.

The coach finally parked up in the car park, they collected their luggage from the coach storage underneath, after the driver disembarked to open it up, placing all luggage in the car park to be collected. They soon stood up, wheeling their cases over, seeing Mum waving her arms about to gain their attention, calling from afar. Bessy desperately tried to speed them along, wagging her tail frantically, knowing the end was in sight.

'Oh, hello you lovely doggy,' Mum bent over to greet Bessy, who by this time, was so excited to see her, making Mum nearly lose her balance, as Bessy weaved in and out around her ankles.

'Mum, this is Bessy, our new member of the family, Bessy, meet my mum, Jodie.'

'She's a beauty, Amy, oh and hello, my lovely girl, Issy,' bringing them both into a tight hug, nearly making them feel breathless.

'Let's walk over to the car,' a new VW Golf in a light metallic blue. 'We swapped it last week, thinking this will be our last car, something smaller and automatic.'

'Very fancy, Mum', Issy said, liking their choice.

Within a few minutes, Mum parked up outside the bungalow. They were all eager to get out, ending their long travelling day. They walked up towards the front door, greeted by Dad, who no doubt heard them all trundle up the lovely newly paved drive.

'And who do we have here?' He bent down to Bessy's level, patting her on her side, as she swished her tail from side to side, catching his brown corduroy trousers, slapping them rhythmically.

'Dad, meet Bessy, the latest addition to our family,' Amy added, loving the all-round excitement.

'Come on in, all of you and welcome to our new bungalow.' He opened the door wide enough for them to wheel the suitcases in, trying not to scratch anything in the process.

'I'll play mum to you, by making us a brew, as neither of you are familiar with the layout yet,' Dad added, feeling chuffed to be in charge for once. 'Just leave your cases and rucksacks in the hall and hang your jackets on the coat stand, please, or else Mum will start nagging, we don't want that, do we, girls?'

'Who said I was going to nag, mister, thank you!' Mum clearly eavesdropped on his comments.

'Oops, I've been told off, sorry girls', he added, giggling into his hand clasped over his mouth.

'You're all right, Dad, we love you . . . now where's that cuppa and cake, we're thirsty?' Amy added, placing an arm on his shoulder.

As they walked further into the kitchen an aroma of food steadily drifted from the Aga, making them feel rather ravenous.

'I've made a lasagna for later for dinner, thinking you'd be hungry,' Mum added, then wondered what Bessy could eat, until she had a light bulb moment . . . some of Rosie's food, till they bought some more in the morning. 'We've got spare bowls too, so we're all good tonight,' she added to confirm.

'Thanks Mum, you've covered every possible aspect,' Amy added, smiling sweetly back at her.

Bessy was now sniffing around, familiarising herself gradually to her new surroundings. They all could soon settle down around the long, oak kitchen table, whilst Mum finished laying it for dinner.

'Talking about Rosie, where is she, Mum?' Issy asked, suddenly realising she hadn't come up to greet them.

'No worries, she's with Sam and Pete, since earlier, Lottie

drove over to us. She's very keen to meet up with you guys tomorrow, or whenever.'

'Oh great, we haven't seen one another for weeks now, be lovely to catch up over a coffee perhaps. I'll text her now, so she can plan her weekend,' Issy added, feeling excited to see her. They had become best friends over the years. A few minutes later, she messaged her back.

Oh my gosh, you're back, yay. Yes we must meet up, I'm free tomorrow, I'll pick you both up at 10, and take you to the new coffee house in town, it's lush. Xx

Great, looking forward to seeing you in the morning. Oh and we have a new doggy too xxx

Interesting, exciting times ahead, Lottie concluded.

Mum gave them the grand tour of their new bungalow, which was beautiful in itself; the best being no stairs to climb, helping them later in life as they faced possible mobility problems. The idea was to make their lives more comfortable and enjoyable, which was key once reaching those twilight years!

Five bedrooms with two en suites, as well as a main bathroom when guests came to stay. All individually decorated with pastel colours, with a large canvas photo depicting an autumnal scene, a central feature in one of the en suite bedrooms. Double beds in all rooms with mahogany bedside tables either side, with touch sensitive lamps, for easy reading. All rooms had oak floors throughout, eliminating any nasty moths which might snuggle into the depths of carpets, being the modern updated layout in today's world.

'Wow, Mum, this is all very plush and impressive, we love it, good choice and congratulations on your new abode. This will give you many years of joy and happiness.' Amy beamed at her, placing a hand on her left shoulder for good measure.

'Ah, thank you darling, we are more than happy. We had Rob the painter to touch up the bedrooms, then the lounge, money well spent, he's a lovely friendly chap, just gets on with the job, no fuss, he's no trouble at all, remembering one of Ronnie Barker's sweet shop sketches quotes,' Mum added with a giggle, trying to keep a straight face! 'Your rooms are at the far end, giving you the space you both need, until you find yourselves a place of your own . . . no worries, we're not giving marching orders . . . yet!'

'Ha ha, I should hope not. You need to get to know Bessy first, once she's introduced to Rosie, which will be fun. Good job they are both girls!' Issy added, giggling.

'We'd best be around once Rosie returns, as they sniff each other out and get to know each other.'

'Thanks, Mum, you're our star mum in . . . you know what comes next!' Issy feeling very comical, seeing her mum's reaction in her face!

'Well on that note, I'll bid you goodnight and don't let any bed bugs bite!'

'Night Mum,' they said together, 'see you in the morning.'

They walked back into the hall to wheel their cases into their rooms, not forgetting Bessy's bits and pieces; her bed and lead in case she needed a wee in the early hours.

'I'll take her tonight, we can swap tomorrow night, pending how she adjusts. Bessy will also meet Rosie tomorrow, so big day for our baby girl. Indeed, OK, you're with me tonight, Bessy," Issy told her, patting her head gently as she bent down, licking her cheek in response, assuring her all was well in her world.

Their first night went without any hitches, as Issy let Bessy outside before bed. She pulled up the blind by its white cord to reveal the lovely garden with patio sleepers and a quaint summer garden house, ready for the warmer months. She assumed some pretty garden furniture was housed within, or yet to be bought, a sneak peek was a must before they eventually moved out one day.

'Good morning girls,' as Mum passed them by walking towards the kitchen. Issy put the kettle on for tea or coffee.

'I remember you are meeting up with Lottie today in that new coffee house up the road, which just opened a few months ago and they are looking for staff to cover busy periods, if you're interested, something to tide you over until you get sorted perhaps. Every little helps these days, I say,' she added, having her girls' interests at heart.

'Two teas to keep us going with a piece of toast if that's OK Mum, as we'll probably have a full English later with Lottie,' Issy replied with an air of excitement in her voice; they couldn't wait to see Lottie and hopefully Rosie too.

'Teas and toast coming up as you like it, girls,' Mum replied with a happy smile plastered on her pale face. 'While you're out, bring your washing in to load up, get it all done and out of the way,' she added.

'Thanks Mum, we appreciate that, lots to catch up on now with interviews, etc. I'll fill you in later on, OK, don't worry for now, we got this Mum,' Amy added, putting her finger on her lip.

Bessy's ears suddenly pricked up at the sound of a horn outside in the front, no doubt Lottie, as she parked up on the drive. Amy dashed to the front door, ready to fling her arms around her bestie, whom she hadn't seen for what seemed like a decade!

'Amy,' she screeched with excitement. 'It's so good to see you after all this time, how are you, pal, and where is Bessy? I'm dying to meet her. We just love our dogs in our families, don't we, darling!' Lottie pulled her into the tightest hug, nearly deflating her!

On call Bessy came running into the hall, nearly sending her flying as she screeched to a halt in front of Lottie, who by now was head over heels in love with this bundle of fun. Lottie bent down to stroke her and pat her, before Bessy rolled onto her back for a belly rub, which she loved every second of, getting up immediately to shake her body from side to side like all excitable dogs do after being given lots of attention.

'Amy, are you coming?'

'See you later, Mum,' she shouted back up the hallway to hurry her up, their chariot awaiting them.

Within minutes they were ready to walk up to her car, a Fiat Uno, a quirky little red Italian car, despite not having much room for more than two people and a boot to fit the size of a small suitcase.

'Bessy can sit with one of you in the footwell in the front, if that's OK, it's only up the High Street, so she'll be safe, I promise,' Lottie added with assurance.

They pulled up into Tesco car park and got out, making sure Bessy's lead was hooked to her red collar, before she pulled on Amy to the nearest grass verge to empty her small bladder from excitement or nerves being confined in a small space. Arm in arm, Lottie and Amy led the way to the café, noting dogs allowed from the sticker in the window, on best behaviour only . . . owners included!

'Good morning, ladies,' the lady behind the counter greeted them on hearing the *ping* above the café door.

They walked over, returning the morning greeting.

'A lovely one too,' she continued. 'Anyway, what can I offer you today? I have a Victoria sponge, lemon or coffee, and walnut, carrot cake or chocolate brownies, all freshly baked this morning. An assortment of coffees too, of course.'

'Oh wow, OK, a latte and two cappuccinos, please, with a lemon Victoria sponge and two slices of carrot cake,' Amy said, taking out her card to pay. The lady handed over a loyalty card to stamp every time they went in, then handed her the card reader to pay.

'Take a seat and I'll bring your order over,' she raised her head with a smile.

They took their seats at a table by the wall, not wanting to create much attention. Bessy lay by Amy's side in total obedience, as if she sensed she had to be on her best behaviour! Within minutes the coffees and cakes arrived on a large tray, Issy playing mum, placing them by each one. 'Well, to us girls reunited from our school days, Lottie!' They picked their coffees up, clinking them together.

'Hold that thought, we need a selfie.' Lottie withdrew her phone from her body bag.

The lady behind the counter, noticing their intention, went over to them, suggesting she take a few photos of them, making it easier all round.

'Oh, that's very kind of you,' Lottie smiled up at her, as they all huddled together, arms around one another, as they glared into the camera.

'Thank you,' Amy added, before she returned behind the counter to serve customers.

Bessy clearly wanted to be in on the act, raised her head, nose to the air, sniffing the aroma of cakes, licking her lips occasionally.

'OK, I've got some gravy bones in my jacket pocket, Bessy.' Amy took a couple out, handing her one as she said, 'Gently,' as she met her mouth with the edge of the bone, very gently removing it from her lip.

'Good girl.' She patted her smooth head, praising her. 'That's the way to train a dog,' she said, 'to respect you, which they actually enjoy. They have a brain which has to be nurtured and effectively used, or else boredom kicks in,' she added, feeling proud of herself.

Bessy soon settled down again, taking her rightful place by Amy's feet, placing her smooth fur head on her outstretched paws, looking so cosy and cute, adored by onlookers passing by, noticing the odd twitch from under the table as they walked past.

'So, what's the next plan of action, now that you're both back from your holiday adventures?' Lottie asked inquisitively. 'I'm all ears, no, seriously, if you need a doggy sitter, then look no further, pending on my diary, of course.'

'Aww, thanks, we might take you up on that.'

'Well, we've both got interviews coming up next week; mine at a care home, Amy's at the vets. Whilst away, we both got emails inviting us for interviews early next week, so we'll see how they go, before deciding our next move. Obviously, staying with Mum and Dad is only temporary.'

'We thought we'd share a flat or something, a place of our

own. Mum and Dad are getting older now, the reason they moved to a beautiful bungalow, no stairs, making life much easier as they hit their twilight years,' Amy added, forking a slice of carrot cake into her mouth. 'Oh, this is yummy,' licking her lips after she swallowed it down.

'Sounds like you've thought it all through,' Lottie replied, feeling very optimistic for them. 'I really hope everything works out for you both, I'm always here if you need me, forever friends.'

'Aww, I know, and we are both here for you too.' Issy reached out her hand, giving Lottie a firm squeeze of affection.

'Thank you, Issy, this could be our new big break in the world of work . . . for the next few years at least!' Amy high-fived Lottie, feeling optimistic. 'Onward and upwards.'

On that high note, they left the café, hearing the *ping* above the door as they walked out.

Chapter Seven

Monday morning soon came around after a lovely catch-up with the girls over the weekend, a great start to a new interesting week, potentially life-changing, following our interviews. Austria soon became a distant memory, yet never forgotten, a pure much-needed adventurous experience, certainly kicking glandular fever's butt being the aim, sunny days and adopting a beautiful dog at the end. They heard with sadness of Maria's passing a few days later; heartbreaking as it was following a heart attack, she was now at peace, which settled their aching hearts. Due to the forthcoming interviews, they sent flowers online to cover their condolences, which they knew she would have fully appreciated and understood as they'd only just returned. Most importantly she had been grateful they had adopted Bessy, saving her from having to be rehomed to complete strangers.

'I've got a text!' Issy announced, like being in the *Big Brother* house, not that they really followed it, an overrated lovers' retreat in their opinion.

'About the interview?' Amy asked, feeling excited for her. 'Cool, spill all, do I need to sit down?' she asked, feeling nervous.

'Very droll! Monday at ten o'clock, with Trudy, a care assistant.'

'Perfect, Sis, pleased for you, fingers crossed and all that. Oh hello, I've just got one too now!'

'Clearly our day, Amy!'

'OK, yeah, Thursday morning at 10.30 with Jenny, at the Rowan Vets, up the road.'

'Excellent, we're both winning!'

'Indeed we are, dress code trousers and a jumper I reckon, suitable for our future jobs.'

They high-fived one another triumphantly, knowing their future was waiting just around the corner!

'Best let Mum know about our potential life-changing news, she'll be really chuffed for us,' Issy added with a chuckle.

They walked into the fabulous new kitchen, all kitted out with the necessary tech; an Aga oven heating up the kitchen toasty warm, taking a few attempts to perfect the cooking, but worth every penny. Then the twin air fryer, being far cheaper to run than an ordinary oven, the main difference being that you didn't have to wait until it reached temperature.

'Mum,' Issy called out, entering the kitchen, knowing she would be sitting around the long table in the middle, sipping a cup of coffee. She called out again, still no reply.

'Perhaps she's hiding, or upstairs,' Amy added, sneaking in from behind, nearly scaring her.

Suddenly, we heard footsteps, plonking sounds, big man's feet as they stomped onto the rustic tiled floor.

Oh Dad,' Amy turned around to see where the noise was coming from.

'Oh, sorry to disturb the peace, thought it was just me in here.'

'Where's Mum?' she asked.

'Oh, she's having a lie down, wasn't feeling her best this morning. I took her up a lemon green tea, to soothe her weariness. She'll be down in a sec, she's been there a while now.'

'Who said I was unwell? I was just feeling tired in my old age,' Mum stormed in, wondering what all the fuss was about.

'That's good to know, as we wondered where you were when we came in this morning,' Amy added, feeling relieved to see her mum, although looking a bit pale, probably in need of a coffee.

"We've got some promising news this morning, both of us got texts, re interviews for jobs this week.'

'Excellent, girls, we're really happy for you, crossing everything.'

'Thanks Mum, Issy added, blowing her a kiss. 'I'll switch the coffee machine on, I think we all could do with a coffee, considering it's nearly eleven.'

'What do you fancy, girls?' Mum asked, once the machine was ready to start up.

'Two cappuccinos for us and whatever you and Dad want,' Amy said, before Dad interrupted.

'Did someone mention coffee?' pretending to sniff the air like Bessy. 'A latte for me, if there's enough milk.'

'Of course, dear, silly,' Mum added, smiling, looking all perky hearing their good news, as he walked in, taking a seat at the table.

Amy helped her mum bring over the coffees followed by some mini brownies, placing the coffees on silver coasters by each one and a plate of brownies in the middle, for all to help themselves.

'Thanks, Mum, the brownies look yummy, very moist and moreish!' they all commented together.

'They're from the new café up the road, a new secret recipe apparently! Moving on, your interviews, when are they?' Mum asked inquisitively, so she could prepare for the week ahead.

'Well, mine is on Monday and Issy's is Thursday this week.' Amy filled her in with the details, knowing she'd probably forget tomorrow, at least she had told her now.

"We've got a few things to look up beforehand, to make sure we don't say the wrong things, nothing too difficult, should go well I think,' Issy added, looking at her mum.

"Great, any plans today? We have a GP check-up in an hour, the usual MOT for us oldies, making sure we're not dying yet!' she giggled, finishing off her cappuccino before putting her mug in the dishwasher.

At that moment Bessy wandered in, nudging Amy, reminding her she needed a walk, swiftly followed by Rosie, hearing Bessy's paws patter all over the tiled kitchen floor.

'OK, I get it, you both need a walk like me and Issy, a bit of fresh air will do wonders for our stuffy heads,' bending down to pat both in turn.

On that note, everyone left the room to do their own thing, keeping themselves busy to pass the time of day.

_____

69

'Good luck with your MOTs,' Amy shouted back at her parents before they disappeared out into the hallway.

All togged up, they grabbed the dogs' collars for a quick walk to a hidden local nature reserve, where most dog owners met with their fur babies, where they could run freely around in search of their furry regulars, depending on the time of day. A great catch-up for dog owners as they passed one another along the way. Some lasting friendships were made, leading to coffee mornings or other social gatherings, young and old, there was something for everyone, a happy-go-lucky community.

There had been a bit of a downpour in the night, leaving the odd puddle here and there ... perfect for muddy paws to dash through, never a good look on white Westies though, their owners' biggest nightmare when they came home, heading upstairs for a bath or a hose down in the garden, depending on the weather.

They carried on walking around the path, avoiding any remaining puddles as well as they could, until, with no warning, a dog came hurtling up from behind. Skidding to a halt, unaware of the dangers, he crashed into Amy's legs, causing her to briefly lose her footing, nearly sending her flying. Thankfully just a muddy wet splash over her trousers was all that remained. A few rude words left her mouth, raising a few heads from passers-by.

'Oh, I'm so sorry!'

Amy turned around to see the horror on a middle-aged lady's face, as she briskly walked towards her.

'My pooch is still very much a youngster, full of life, unaware of the dire consequences of her actions. That's dogs for us, I'm afraid,' she spluttered out, trying to convince Amy of the innocence of her pooch's actions; she did have a valid point, as they were all playful mates together, having the time of their lives.

'Oh, don't worry, it will all come out in the wash, no broken bones, that's the main thing. As a new dog owner, I'm aware, we all have dog-walking clothes, especially coats, as you just don't know what's lurking around the next corner on our dog walks.'

'Thank you for being so good about it, not everyone is, I can assure you. People bite back and become angry. These are the sad times we live in. Revenge gets you nowhere, in my opinion.'

'Come on, you two,' Issy turned around, smiling, encouraging them to walk beside them. It was a lovely feeling, one's own dog was behaving well, putting other owners to shame.

They returned home after their breath of fresh air with the dogs, intending to help Mum after getting a few essentials from Tesco, considering they were her new lodgers for now.

Mum had already put a list together on their return, adding a few non-essential yummy items; everyone needs a treat or two!

'Oh, you're back,' Mum announced as the dogs came running in, wagging their tails frantically, as if they'd been away for weeks … that's dogs for you, always bringing joy to their owners, brightening up their dullest of days, not that this was one of them.

'Indeed, Mum, they loved every minute and have become the best of furry mates. They couldn't be separated now, joined at the hip forever!' Issy added, stroking the dogs in turn, which they lapped up, raising their heads, licking her face, feeling loved.

'OK, I'll take over, you go with the list, here's my card,' Mum added.

'Back soon, we'll get something easy for dinner,' I winked at her, grabbing the shopping bags before leaving.

'OK, surprise us!' Mum waved back enthusiastically. The family all loved surprises.

An hour later a wholesome leek and chicken pie was cooking in the Aga, wafting mouth-watering aromas around the kitchen and beyond, as everyone walked through. Even the dogs turned up their noses like Samantha in *Bewitched*, as their nostrils twitched in the air, wondering where the sweet scent was coming from.

'Cup of tea, anyone?' Amy asked as she waltzed into the kitchen, feeling all shook up! 'The kettle on the Aga is about to boil,' she said, grabbing mugs from the cupboard above.

'Did someone say tea?' Dad chuckled, as he sneaked in from nowhere, causing them to turn around briskly, as he crept in from behind.

'Oh Dad, you made us jump, ordinary or Earl Grey?' Amy asked, feeling amused.

'Earl Grey for me, love, thanks.'

He took his usual spot at the table whilst she added a tea bag to a ceramic blue teapot, enough for two, placing it in the middle to stand, before she poured two mugs of tea for herself and her dad.

'Er, excuse me, what about me Sis? Sorry I'm a bit late, I was just sorting out clean washing, got bored, so here I am, in need of a brew!' Issy gave Amy a cheeky grin as she too crept up from behind, placing her arms around Amy's waist, drawing her into a lovely embrace.

'OK, OK, another tea bag in the pot,' as she refilled the kettle, placing it back on the Aga.

'Where is Mum, is she napping again?' Issy asked, noting this was becoming a habit at this time of day.

'I'm here now, just attending to the dogs, giving them a bit of TLC.'

'A quick cuppa, before dinner later?' Amy asked her mum. 'Dinner at 6.30 prompt, just gotta make some cheesy mash and peas, then it'll be ready.' Amy smiled back at her mum.

'Sounds like a perfect combo.'

'I'll set the table once we've all had our cuppas,' Amy replied feeling organised. 'We can catch up then.'

Mum and Dad went back into the lounge to join the dogs, who by then were all curled up in their individual beds by the patio doors, where they could always lift their tired heads to peek outside. They took out the Scrabble from under the long coffee table, feeling in the mood for a relaxing game, before the girls announced that dinner was ready. On grabbing the box, she noticed a small, red box next to it, with a lid you could just lift off. Wondering what it was, she picked it up, feeling very inquisitive, then sat back down next to Dad, who by then was eager to start playing. He opened the Scrabble, placing the board in the middle, removing two tile holders from their slots, placing them either side of the board. Next, the small green drawstring bag with the letter tiles, a quick shake to mix them up, before he removed seven tiles, placing them in alphabetical order on his tile-holder.

'Right, that's me sorted, now it's your turn. You can see what's in the box after, we probably only have 45 minutes until they call us in for dinner.'

Mum did as she was told and sat next to Dad, despite wanting to open the mystery box. Definitely not a jack in the box, a bit small for that, she mused.

After Mum had picked her seven tiles they were off. Mum picked one from the bag. Whoever had the highest letter could start, which was Dad.

They soon got into the swing of things, until Issy interrupted the flow by announcing dinner was about to be served.

'Oh well, we can resume later,' Mum added thoughtfully.

'Absolutely, done deal,' Dad added, giving her a friendly squeeze on her knee, sending quivers around her body, like when they had first set eyes on one another all those years ago.

'Oh, this looks fabulous,' they said, seeing the table laid out for a banquet.

'Well, take your places and we'll serve up,' Amy added, smiling at them.

Issy placed the veg in several bowls; broccoli, carrots and green beans in the centre of the table, with serving spoons by each one to help themselves. Amy placed a large bowl of cheesy mash on the other end, which looked so yummy, as the mash stood up in peeks.

'Wow, you've worked hard, girls, we must have done something right bringing you up,' Dad chuckled, catching their eye whilst they walked by, placing hot dinner plates with the pie on each place mat. The place mats depicted local country scenes, which were quite fitting seeing where their parents lived.

'It's a pleasure, and thank you for all your hard work, navigating us through life whilst you two carried on with your jobs, can't have been easy with the farm as well,' Issy remarked.

'We were younger then, so we had more energy, we couldn't do it now,' they concluded as they dished out the vegetables, passing the bowls around in turn. 'Now it's your turn to take over, as we enter our old age!' Mum said, smiling.

'Enough of that, tuck into your meals before they get cold,' Amy announced, feeling amused.

As it was a Sunday, dessert followed, everyone's favourite, profiteroles with Belgian chocolate drizzled over the top ... what was not to like, unless cream was a diet issue, which in their family it wasn't! Issy gathered up the plates to be stacked in the dishwasher later, as Amy brought out the profiteroles, followed by clear glass bowls, placing them on everyone's mat with dessert spoons.

'Well chosen, girls, our favourite,' Dad added with gleaming eyes.

'Help yourselves, four each, nothing more!' Amy added, smiling at her dad. 'Coffee will be served in the lounge after, followed by a board game of our choice, as long as we have it,' she giggled.

'There's nothing like a bit of competitiveness, in my opinion,' Mum elbowed Dad, feeling ready to challenge everyone. 'I think Monopoly is high up on the list, unless you don't feel like being a banker!' Things could easily become very competitive.

They all agreed on Monopoly, bringing out the competitive side in the family, ideal for a Sunday afternoon's entertainment. Mum removed the bits from the box, opening the board up and placing it in the centre of the table. They all chose their favourite counters, from the famous iron to the horse and boat. The money was dished out equally, with Amy acting as the banker. They took it in turns to throw the two dice, hoping a '6' would soon land to start the game off. Issy's turn first, followed by Mum, Dad and Amy.

'Let the competitiveness start in earnest,' Amy announced, feeling plush.

'This could potentially go on for hours, let's set our watches for an hour, lest we get too tired or lose interest,' Issy concluded.

The game was all going so well, everyone in full swing until Rosie appeared from her bed nestled in the corner, nudging Mum to let her out as nature called. She made her move, before getting up and walking into the kitchen with Rosie trotting on behind, eager for the back door to be opened, to relieve herself by the nearest bush.

'Good girl,' Mum patted her head, after she came running back in.

She followed Mum back into the lounge, finding her happy place in her comfy bed. Monopoly continued for a further hour, before everyone called it a day. On a final count, Dad took the trophy, owning numerous houses scattered around the board and one lonely red brick hotel.

The board was soon back in its box, with the money neatly arranged in order of the coloured pounds for next time alongside the counters. A final drink before bed, then letting the dogs out before they finally curled up in their comfy beds.

'Good game, let's play again soon,' Dad said, feeling rather pleased with himself being the winner.

'Next week could be a winner, as Issy and I have our interviews, potentially changing our lives for the better, so watch this space, Dad, hence an early night is needed.'

'Oh yes, I forgot about that, best of luck to you both, good night my lovelies.' He turned around, high-fiving us whilst he walked out into the hallway.

Chapter Eight

Monday morning and the alarm went off at seven, giving them plenty of time to surface followed by a leisurely breakfast, then taking the dogs out for their brisk morning walk before thinking about Issy's interview, scheduled at ten at the care home. The usual chaos, everyone milling around the bungalow, trying to organise themselves, rushing about like madmen, going back in time when they were younger before the school run.

'Good morning, girls.' Mum walked in, feeling upbeat, ready for the day. 'It's the day of reckoning, your interview, Issy, feeling nervous?' she announced, placing her hand on her shoulder.

'You know what, Mum, I've got a good vibe about this one, so I'm excited for once. I want this job and everything else will just fall into place. Amy and I are going to get our flat or a two-bed semi perhaps, then all will be well in our world.'

'A good positive start to the week does wonders for the soul, love your enthusiasm.' Mum smiled back at them whilst gathering up essentials for her breakfast.

'Onward and upwards, as they say, and bring it on, being another lol!' Amy added with a chuckle.

'Tea everyone?' Issy interrupted, mindful of the time.

'Two greens and an Earl Grey for Mum, if that's right, Mum?' Issy announced, as the kettle had just boiled.

'Perfect thanks, I'll get the mugs out.'

Half an hour later, the race was on, looking in the mirror, making sure she was suitably dressed for the interview, by now Issy was feeling slightly nervous. A ping on her phone, seeing a reminder of the interview, soon put her mind at ease, knowing she hadn't got the days mixed up.

The only change was the name, Liz; most likely the

coordinator, not Trudy. She was satisfied with her look, grabbing her keys from the table in the hall, bending down to pat Rosie and saying, 'Wish me luck,' before unlocking the front door and dashing to her car, parked next to Mum's, making a beeline up the road towards the care home.

The care home had recently been opened by the mayor of the town, drawing a big crowd on opening day. It was named after a large oak tree in the arboretum, after a name was randomly picked out of a hat: Oak Residential Care House.

The building itself was very plush with its black exterior cladding, with bedroom balconies above overlooking the front with well-maintained gardens to the car park. The entrance was easily accessible with steps and a ramp for wheelchairs and visitors with pushchairs and buggies, catering for everyone's needs, a must in any new building, complying with the latest disability guidelines; Equality Act regulations 2010.

Issy drove into a suitable space, gathered up her coat, bag and key fob and, locking up, walked towards the grand front entrance.

A lady behind the reception announced, 'Lovely day today, welcome to Oak house.' She greeted Issy with a smile, beaming from ear to ear.

'Indeed it is, my name is Issy, I'm here for an interview with … Trudy; the care assistant position,' she continued, feeling a little more nervous, though not sure why. Probably reality kicking in, as she very much hoped that she would secure this post, her new future in the making.

The receptionist looked at the open double page in front of her, noting the name, placing a red tick by it, acknowledging her arrival.

'Lovely, Issy, please take a seat, and I'll let Trudy know you're here.' She pointed to the blue chairs to her left. By this point Issy felt more at ease, welcomed by a friendly face with good vibes, she thought. She noticed a few brochures about the place amongst other interesting leaflets fanned out on the table.

'Trudy will come and get you shortly, meanwhile can I get you a coffee? They come highly recommended!' she announced, making Issy feel more at ease

'Oh, yes please, I'll have a flat white if possible,' Issy smiled back at her, feeling very relaxed.

'Good choice, coming right up.' Within minutes a flat white was carried out on a small circular tray, with a Biscoff biscuit on the saucer. Twenty minutes later, a young lady with large, light-brown glasses stood by her side, taking her by surprise. She quickly drained the last of her coffee, before she reached out her hand, saying 'Issy, lovely to meet you,' shaking her hand a few times.

'I'm Trudy, very pleased to finally meet you, thank you for your patience. I see Susi gave you one of her yummy coffees. Love those pods you just put in the coffee machine, bringing out a lovely froth! Come on through to my office,' she continued, leading the way down the corridor. Her name on a plaque on the door made it look more official. Typically, the room was neatly decorated, with a large desk where she sat down, in her black swivel office chair.

As Issy sat on the other side, ready to be interviewed, nerves began to kick in, yet she was made to feel instantly at ease by the interviewer.

'Lovely, so what brings you here today? What could you offer to this new position?' Trudy asked, taking her by complete surprise, causing her to think quickly on her feet, hoping she could give the best response possible.

'Well, I loved reading about the diversity in the job description. I've worked in old people's homes before, as a teenager, loved serving the elderly refreshments, then having a good natter about their day, or anything really. I found it all so satisfying and rewarding, I don't think that ever left me, if I'm honest.' Issy managed to navigate a true answer, easing herself into the interview after a few minutes.

'That's what I like to hear, your enthusiasm means everything in this place. Many of our residents don't have local family or friends, so they truly rely on us to offer that extra special support, especially on difficult days, if their health has deteriorated and they feel they are a burden to society. We are a very dedicated team here, our patients' well-being is our highest priority,' she added, smiling at me.

'Perfect. Well, you would be very much part of this beautiful home. The hours are usually 9 to 5, with a half hour lunch break, though we are all flexible, sometimes you may need to step in during busy times. Does that sound like anything you could give us?'

'Oh yes, definitely, I'd love all that, there's nothing like giving back in society these days.'

'That's very true. There would be an initial trial period, to see how you adjust,' she continued, before asking, 'How soon could you start? We need cover ASAP, as our last assistant sadly had to leave under difficult circumstances.'

'Oh, I could start next week or sooner, I've just had an extended holiday abroad, so no holidays are planned,' Issy added, feeling good vibes already.

'Great, thank you, Issy. I will be in touch by the end of today. I just have one more to see today, but so far, I'm very impressed.'

Trudy stood up to shake her hand again, before opening the door and leading her back to reception.

'Thank you again for coming, bye for now,' Susi the receptionist added, as Issy walked through the automatic front doors.

Within minutes she was back in the car park, trying to remember where she had left her car, still in a daze from the interview as it all churned around in her head. She hoped she'd receive that all important phone call later, offering her the position as care assistant, one she'd been dreaming about since she finished college.

'Issy, wait, fancy a catch-up?' She turned around, seeing legs scampering towards her, causing her to suddenly turn around, before unlocking the car with her key fob.

'Amy, what brings you here? I thought we'd meet back at Mum and Dad's, unless they've sent you out on an errand, of course?'

'No, I just needed some fresh air, they need their space, as much as we need ours, so here I am, now let's have a coffee. You can tell me how you got on. I promise I won't spill to anyone.'

"Ha ha, there's not much to say at this stage, she's still got one more to interview before the winner is announced!' Issy chuckled back cautiously, not wanting to raise her own hopes.

'Lock her up and we'll head over to the new café, my treat,' Amy insisted, placing a friendly hand on her left shoulder.

'Oh, we could get used to this, after just returning from Austria, coffee and cake every morning, what's not to like?' Issy smiled at her with a cheeky glint in her eye.

'Oh, you're back again,' the lady behind the counter spoke out, clearly remembering Issy from her last visit, hearing the *ping* above the shop door.

'Yes, can't resist that carrot cake you had on the counter earlier in the week,' Issy smiled at her, feeling rather peckish.

'Well, you're in luck, I've got two slices left. Two cappuccinos?' she asked, reading their minds. Amy smiled back, feeling excited.

'Take your seats and I'll bring them over in a sec,' Pippa replied, as they noted the white name tag on the blue apron tied around her waist.

They pulled their chairs out on either side of a table by the window; their favourite spot for people-watching as they walked on by, a story behind each one. Moments later, Pippa carried over a tray with their coffees and cakes, waiting to be demolished within a few minutes.

'Enjoy,' she added, before returning to her workstation.

'So, how did it go, Sis?' Amy asked, wanting to know everything.

'Like I said, all went swimmingly well from the moment I walked in. I felt welcomed with open arms, a few initial nerves soon settled within minutes.'

'Sounds promising, I think you've nailed it, your lucky day for sure,' Amy confirmed, feeling upbeat. 'Just have to wait for that all-important phone call, I guess, how exciting, Sis,' extending her arm towards Issy, placing her hand on hers, giving it a firm squeeze.

'My time soon won't be my own anymore, as the reality of life kicks in. I can't complain as I'm ready for my next adventure to start in earnest.'

They finished their coffee and cakes, enjoying every last mouthful. Amy got up to pay at the counter as Issy gathered up the bags to head back up to the car park.

Whilst she was walking along, she heard a buzzing vibration coming from within her bag, stopping her in her tracks, thinking this may be *the* call she was waiting for. She located her phone under a pile of non-essentials, quickly swiping it to answer.

'Hello, is that Issy? It's Trudy from the care home,' the voice continued, sounding smiley down the line.

'Oh, hi Trudy, thank you for ringing me back so quickly,' but thinking about the worst scenario at the same time, having a glimmer of hope and taking a deep breath.

She continued, 'Well, I have some news, and it's good news. We would like to offer you the job, pending a two-week trial, which is just routine procedure as I know you have the enthusiasm and skill to offer and our patients will love you from the start, so please don't concern yourself with this,' Trudy concluded, waiting eagerly for a positive response.

'Oh my goodness, err, really, you want me? Oh my, I'm bowled over, that's just ... fantastic, thank you so much. I promise you you won't regret it, I won't let you down.' Issy tried to keep her emotions together, though she could tell Trudy sensed she was overjoyed and on the verge of shedding happy tears.

'You're very welcome. I was very taken by your responses this morning, knowing you would fit the criteria above and beyond expectations, Issy, so congratulations again. Would you be able to start next Monday morning? I'll email you the details and we can take it from there.'

_____

'Perfect, thank you, and yes, Monday is fine.'

'Great and on that note, we'll see you Monday week, have a great week. Bye for now.' She hung up.

'Wow!' She looked at Amy with a huge smile plastered from one end of her mouth to the other. 'I've got the job, you were right, it's my lucky day, Amy.' She jumped up, nearly losing her balance, falling into Amy's already open arms ready to catch her, planting a big kiss on her forehead for good measure.

'Told you you'd get it Issy, you're the winner of the day, Miss Stevens.'

'Thanks Amy, I clearly am. Onwards and upwards, here's to my next adventure in the glorious Cotswolds!' They high-fived one another.

'That just leaves me to be successful, on Thursday,' Amy concluded, feeling slightly jealous.

'No pressure then, Sis,' Issy added, feeling her willingness to succeed, despite hating that new phrase.

'OK, enough of that, let's head back to Mum's, see what they've been up to.'

Moments later they parked up alongside their mum and dad's car on the drive by their new bungalow. She beeped the horn on the steering wheel and moments later, Dad appeared in his worn-out old, brown cord trousers.

'Hello girls, had a good morning? Where did you go again?'

Dad's memory wasn't quite what it used to be a few years ago, she remembered.

'I had my interview, Dad, at the new care home up the road, the posh one with black cladding all around, with balconies facing the front and rear.'

'Oh yes, I remember now, you told us at breakfast. So how did it go, what's the verdict, did you win? I'm guessing you did, cos you're smiling, being a clever girl.'

'It's not about being clever, Dad, although that does help. It's how you sell yourself and what you can bring to the job. The short answer is . . . drum roll . . . I nailed it! She rang me back and offered me the position as care assistant, which I'm naturally over the moon about, and have clearly accepted the job. I start next Monday.'

'Brilliant, I knew you would, congratulations from me and Mum,' he added, feeling very proud of his girl.

'Where's Mum, by the way?' wondering why she hadn't joined him on the doorstep.

'Oh, she's just having her usual nap, she gets very tired these days, docs are testing her for CFS or an underactive thyroid gland.'

'Oh, she never said, probably not wanting us to worry unnecessarily,' Amy assumed, hoping she was OK, and realising that age was creeping in. These things happened at her time of life, oestrogen levels constantly dropping over the years.

'What's going on here?' Mum crept in, shocking us all standing by the kitchen door.

'Oh nothing, love, we were just congratulating our Issy on her new position as care assistant, at the new plush residential care home up the road.' Dad filled her in on the intricate details.

'Oh, that's excellent news, darling, we'll come to you when the time comes, needing extra care in our old age. I can see you being a lovely caring person to the elderly, lifting their spirits on bad days.'

'Thanks Mum, my new adventure starts next week, and I'm ready for it.'

'Let's celebrate at the weekend after Amy's interview. We've got a good feeling this will be the year of new beginnings for you both,' Mum affirmed, feeling positive.

'What if I'm not successful?' Amy hesitated.

'You will be, even if it's not this time, what's right will be,' Dad interrupted. 'We're going out anyway, a family affair. That's settled end of.'

It felt like a family meeting had just drawn to a close, Mum and Dad heading into the kitchen, initially to check on the dogs, who by this time were feeling restless, in need of a good walk.

Amy's phone suddenly sprang into life. Seeing it was Lottie, she swiped to answer. 'Good morning stranger, how are you doing?' Pleased to have the distraction.

'All good, fancy a walk in the park? Our new puppy needs some exercise.'

'What, you've got a new fur baby? How sweet. Come over, I want to see this one.'

'OK, I'll be around in ten mins. Don't worry, Floss is a girl, so no worries there, all girls together, hopefully they'll all get on swimmingly. We chose her from the local dog shelter, one less for them to re-home,' Lottie explained, before quickly hanging up.

Amy walked back into the kitchen, which by now was smelling rather doggy, Rosie and Bessy getting all excited, eager to hear the word 'walk'. Mum was becoming a little flustered and frustrated with them.

'Don't worry, Mum, I'm the bearer of excellent news. Lottie just rang me, they've only just rehomed a new puppy, and she's popping around in a moment, so we can take these two rascals for, well, you know what. Can't say the word lest they go mad circling the place with excitement.'

'Is it a girl? We don't want any love birds here, thank you!' she exclaimed, feeling even more flustered.'

'Don't panic, Mum, it's a girl, Floss. You'll soon meet her. We're going to take them to the park, we'll soon find out if they are a friendly bunch,' Amy tried to reassure her.

A loud rat a tat tat at the door alerted the dogs as they scampered through to the hall, moaning and whimpering, pressing their noses against the door, eager for it to be opened up.

'OK, move away so I can open the door,' Amy gently pushed their bodies back, whilst she grabbed the key from the table to unlock it.

'Woof, woof,' from the other side, as if to say, 'Let me in.'

Mum called them to her as she grabbed their collars, before giving Amy the thumbs up to open the door.

'Hey you,' Lottie stumbled in, leading Floss in tow, engulfing

Amy into the biggest embrace, as if they hadn't seen one another in months.

'Well, introducing you to our latest addition, Floss the spaniel, with light brown, furry ears. We picked her up last week, about three years old, fully house trained and jabbed up. Poor little mite was itching to be released from her kennel. Seeing us as we walked past she pawed the kennel, hoping that we were the ones to give her her forever home. ... we couldn't resist her, so here she is. Her last owner abandoned her, the RSPCA were called out to rescue her. She was left to starve, they came just in good time, before the real deterioration set in. The lady was subsequently charged by the police with neglect, issued with a six-month warning warrant, not allowing her to own any further animals. Sadly, a common case these days, especially after Christmas and with the current inability to afford pet food, obviously that was often out of their control. Still the motto remains: think before you buy a pet.'

'Absolutely, come in and meet Bessy and Rosie, all girls together, let them sniff each other, before we take them out to the park, they're itching to be let loose.'

'Jodie, you're looking well, hope you're adjusting to your girls and the two dogs living with you again now in your lovely bungalow,' Lottie smiled back at her.

'It's only temporary, we've been told, until they find their own place. They are most welcome here, plenty of space to escape to for everyone's sanity,' Mum added, putting leads on the dogs, before they went wild.

"Great, we're off to the park now to catch up, see you later. Don't worry about dinner later, see where the day takes us, we will return the dogs though!'

Off they went as Amy took their two, Lottie taking Floss. They all walked to heel, then saw a huge, black St Bernard galloping towards them with no signs of stopping, seeing Floss, who became increasingly anxious as he/she approached us. It seemed clear that this huge dog was a 'he', as he was only interested in one thing, sniffing Floss's rear end, leaving poor Floss to shake her body more, whimpering, eager to be lifted up, away from this nutter of a dog.

'No, go away,' Amy raised her voice, the second time more seriously. 'Where's your owner, you're frightening little dogs out of their wits, shoo, off you go.'

He wasn't having any of that, he lingered until his human stood alongside him, trying to grab hold of his collar, placing his choke chain over his head, yanking him frantically away from them, their dogs yelping, frightened to death by this 'horse'.

'Take your dog away, please, he's way too big for these three little ones.' Issy insisted as she ran towards them, seeing trouble brewing. 'Can't you tell they are so scared?'

'I'm trying, I'm so sorry, he's not usually like this, his testosterone levels are clearly through the roof today,' the lady answered, feeling guilty.

'You shouldn't let him off the lead if he's like that. He's creating havoc with other dogs, especially the smaller ones who only came out to have some fun, dashing about, letting off steam, making it easier for their owners later once home. That's how unwanted pregnancies happen, they get all excited, start romping the ladies, then, hey presto, three months later a litter of puppies is born. It only takes one sexual act then your life for the next 56 days is shared with puppies. Then the hard work starts, as lots of fur babies need constant attention day and night, leaving you with little or no respite. How does that sound?' Amy spoke out feeling so annoyed.

She got the picture, dragging her beloved hound from the crime scene. She left in a hurry, feeling very put out and leaving them to pick up the broken, anxious dogs.

'Thank goodness you turned up, before everything kicked off, that dog was full on to say the least and she seemed unaware of the consequences,' Lottie added, feeling all hot and bothered.

'OK, let's not ruin our day anymore, leave the dogs on a long lead to have some space, before we turn around to head home. Come on girls,' Issy added, 'you're safe now.'

They meandered around the path, glad to be out of sight of Mr St. Bernard, the frisky dog, full of testosterone, putting all little dogs off sex for life. They chatted about everything, especially young Floss, Lottie's latest family addition. The sun finally appeared from behind the clouds, giving them some much-needed warmth.

'So, any news regarding jobs after returning from your travels?' Lottie asked, wanting to be in the know.

'Oh yes, I forgot to say, I had an interview this morning at the new all plush care home up the road ... and was offered the position as care assistant, starting next Monday. How cool is that? I was well chuffed after the lady rang me back, giving me the good news,' Issy continued.

'Oh wow, that's just brilliant news, Issy, you must be thrilled, as it's right up your street, excuse the pun, none intended.'

'Oh, I am, Lottie, I can't wait to start my new career. We now just need to find a place to live, to buy or rent, depending what funds are available and what's on the property market. Amy and I agreed on living together for now, ha, until one of us meets Mr Right, though not planning that anytime soon,' she added, knowing anything could happen.

'Sounds like a perfect plan to me, your future is out there, just grab it with both hands, eyes wide open, and you'll be going full steam ahead. Oops, another pun not intended.'

Once home Amy unlocked the front door of the bungalow announcing she was back, followed by both dogs and Issy. She unhooked the dogs' leads, who were eager to go straight into the kitchen, desperate for a drink from their water bowls.

'Oh, hello you two, good walk and clearly very thirsty too?' Mum patted them as they walked past.

'Yes, they enjoyed their walk, until this huge St Bernard bully of a hound decided to hurtle towards us, nearly pushing us over, clearly only interested in sniffing the girls out, which they took a distinct disliking to. They were so scared, they froze with fright, shaking their little bodies. His owner came running towards us apologising, only saying he was full of testosterone, hence his persistence. Issy told her to be more careful and not to bring a dog out who is so frisky. I mean anything could happen, a quick rump behind the bushes, and hey presto, three months later, a handful of puppies could be born, and believe me, your work is definitely cut out then, day in day out, no respite for the wicked, so I've heard.'

'That sounded awful for them, their first encounter with a frisky dog twice their size. Well at least they survived it, no damage done,' Mum added, feeling a bit disturbed hearing the experience. 'I'll put the kettle on for a nice cuppa, sounds like you could do with one.'

'Thanks, Mum, what have you been up to?' Amy asked.

'Oh, nothing strenuous, we thought we'd have a game of Scrabble, your dad used to love that when we first met all those years ago. Love's young bloom brought us closer to each other, before we got back together again after his minor setback, the rest is history, and here we are, celebrating thirty years of marriage, and here's to many more!'

'How sweet, you're going down memory lane, clearly relishing every special moment, love that, Mum. The secret to a long relationship,' Amy said, with a hint of emotion.

'Remind me when your doctor's appointment is, it looks like a week of appointments!' Amy smiled at her mum, feeling slightly concerned.

'Oh gosh, thanks for reminding me, love, it's tomorrow morning. Ten o'clock with the nurse, taking blood to send off to the hospital for analysis.'

'Is Dad taking you or do you want me or Issy to?'

'Dad can't, as he's meeting up with his mate Jack, who he met in the pub last week over a pint. They got chatting, found a common fishing interest, so they're going out on their first fishing trip together by a lake nearby. I forget the name, but it sounds like fun. I'm really proud of your dad, finding an outdoor hobby, breathing quality fresh air and listening to the birds twittering away. So relaxing at his stage of life,' Mum continued with a chuckle.

'Well, I'll drive you tomorrow morning, Mum,' Amy confirmed, 'we can do a food shop after if you need to, or coffee or both, your choice.'

'Thanks, Amy, let's do that. I'll go and make a list of essentials, one less thing to do in the morning,' she concluded.

Chapter Nine

Tuesday morning came around, with everyone rushing around the bungalow, sorting themselves out, before gathering for breakfast. Amy was already up early, getting everything ready in the kitchen. The dogs were milling around, getting under her feet, trying to get her attention, they needed feeding too. She let them out first whilst Issy spooned their meals out into their bowls and filled up their water bowls.

'Good morning, Mum's just getting dressed, she's not a morning person, gets a bit moody too, as we all have those tendencies occasionally,' Dad added as he walked into the kitchen.

'Take your seats, a fresh pot of tea is ready to be poured. Help yourselves. I'll make a round of toast for anyone who wants one,' Amy added.

'Morning all!' Mum appeared from nowhere, still looking a bit tired. 'Thanks, girls, for doing this.'

'No problem, sit down, here's a mug of tea, Dad just poured it out. Time is ticking,' Amy reminded her, 'doctor's in an hour, Mum.' Amy gently hurried her along.

Issy placed the toast in one of those old-fashioned metal toast racks, for all to help themselves, like you see in hotels. *No slumming it here*, Issy thought.

Breakfast finished and dishes neatly stacked in the dishwasher, a quick bathroom stop before Issy grabbed her car fob, bag and coat, heading out into the cold air to her car.

'I'll stay here, as I've got a few last-minute things to swot up before my interview on Thursday,' Amy added, seeing her mum and Issy walk out the door all togged up. 'Enjoy your coffee after, see you later.'

'OK Sis, text me if you need anything from Tesco.'

They parked up at the doctor's surgery, walked in and filled out the initial online registration on the screen before taking their seats in the main waiting area. These days everything was automated, a TV screen above, with names appearing, giving them the room number for the appointment, along with a voice request.

'Mrs Jodie Stevens to Nurse Watkins, Room 15.' Mum jumped up hearing her name best arm giving a good blood flow,' she explained to her, trying to make her feel more at ease.

'Oh yes, I won't look, while you do the necessary.'

'A short scratch and it will be over in seconds I promise,' she reassured her. 'Perfect. They will go off today, I'll ring you once I get the results back, she added before showing them to the door.

'Coffee, Mum? You did well, so my treat.'

'Oh, yes please and a slice of cake will do for me.' Mum felt lifted up after her ordeal.

'Good morning, ladies, a bit of a chilly one so far, a warm drink will sort that one for you. What can I get you both?' Pippa asked, feeling perky this morning.

'Indeed it is, we'll have two cappuccinos and whatever cake my mum wants.'

Issy looked at her mum for an answer, then back at Pippa, who turned to start making the cappuccinos.

'OK, I'll have a slice of carrot cake and a slice of walnut sponge for my daughter, please.' Mum turned to Issy, hoping she had chosen the right one for her. She nodded in agreement.

'Perfect, ladies, choose your table and I'll bring it in a jiffy,' Pippa added, smiling at them.

'Oh, this is lovely Issy, you're so good to your old mum.'

'Less of the old, Mum, you're most welcome. Thank you for sharing your home with us. We won't outstay our welcome, we promise.'

On cue, her phone buzzed into life, an unknown contact, which she still swiped it to answer.

'Is this Miss Stevens?' a young-sounding voice asked.

'And you are?' not wanting to divulge anything.

'Oh sorry, my name is Jess from the estate agent. Miss Amy Stevens informed me you're looking to buy or rent a flat. We've got a few for you to view, if you're interested.'

'Oh, err yes, I wasn't aware that she had rung you, that would be lovely, though we can't do this Thursday.'

'No worries, can I send you details via email, you can look over at your leisure,' she added before hanging up.

'Gosh, Mum, that was an estate agent saying they have a few properties for us to look at. What's Amy been up to? She's obviously rung them. We're on the hunt for our first property together,' Issy gasped, feeling rather excited.

'That's great.' Her mum smiled at her as if she knew something was going on.

Pippa brought their coffees and cake on a tray, placing them down in front of them to devour.

'Oh by the way, how do you know the lady's name here, Issy?' her mum asked, wanting to be in the know.

'We came in the other day with Lottie, who read the name tag on her apron. She's really friendly, isn't she, Mum?'

'Absolutely, she is lovely, a real bonus these days, spreading a little kindness everywhere.'

Issy took her phone out to quickly send Amy a text, wondering if she knew anything about it. She fired one back, saying she had randomly messaged them one day, whilst she was bored, clearly it had paid off.

I'm just waiting for details of the properties, then we can start looking in earnest, Amy replied, sending quivers up her spine.

Issy replied, *See you at home,* placing the phone on the table.

'Well, it seems our day is mapped out, Mum, places to see, people to meet, ooh how exciting.'

'Oh yes, I'm nearly finished, we can go back.'

'No hurry, Mum, it's not a race.'

Her phone lit up, a new email which she clicked to open. The estate agent had sent through the relevant details of two different properties. The first was a two-bed flat in the same town of Stow (its nickname). The other was a small semi-detached house, with a lovely small garden with room for two cars on the paved driveway.

'Oh, look at these, Mum, which one do you prefer? I think the house would be better long-term, saves us moving again,' passing her her phone to look at the pictures which had been sent through.

'They both look a great starter. I prefer the house though, like you say, saving you another move at a later date. We would give towards it, which was our initial plan anyway. Let's go home and see what your dad thinks, I'm sure he'll agree!' Mum added, spooning the last of the froth from her cappuccino into her mouth. 'That was yummy, let's go home and tell your dad the news.'

Ten minutes later they were all back inside the warm kitchen, dogs racing around like no tomorrow. Mum called out for Dad, before he appeared from the back door.

'Oh, you're back, did you all have a good catch up? Your brother rang a few minutes ago, fancies a catch up with his sister. I told James you were out with our Issy, and you'd ring him later,' Dad announced, placing a smile on Mum's face.

'Well, it's all happening today, isn't it?' she voiced out to anyone who was listening.

'It certainly is, now we've got some news to share with you, Dad. So take a pew and listen up!' Issy insisted.

'Yes, miss, I'm all ears. This had better be good,' pulling out his chair from underneath the kitchen table.

'Big breath, here goes!' Issy continued. 'Whilst we were at the café, I received a message from the estate agents. They have two properties for me and Amy to view, a potential solution to our property dilemma.'

She pulled out her phone from her pocket and opened the email with the two attached photos. She placed it in front of her dad, who immediately wowed each one.

'Oh, these look good. I love the house, with its low maintenance garden with shrub tubs along the side of the garden, making it look very attractive to any buyer. I think this is a winner, what do you think, girls?'

'Well, we thought the same, save us from moving again. I think we should arrange a viewing as soon as possible. If you're OK with this, I'll give the lady a ring, nothing like the present, is there, Dad?'

'Good thinking, give them a buzz now, while we're all in the flow of things,' he confirmed, already feeling excited. 'I'm prepared to make you an offer, to help you get started,' he added, willing us on.

'Sounds like one of the Dragons, though not quite the same, obviously,' Amy chuckled, feeling amused by it all, yet very excited.

'Shh, here goes,' Issy said calmly as she clicked on the last caller.

'Oh Issy', Jess answered, 'thanks for ringing me back. I take it you liked the two pictures I sent over and assume you would like to view one or both?'

'Definitely, they both are lovely. We are particularly interested in the house. Any chance we could see it later or tomorrow morning?'

'You're clearly very keen. I'll ring the owner now and see if I can arrange a viewing. I'll ring you back shortly,' the lady added, before ending the call. 'My name is Jess, just ask for me when you next call.'

'Thank you, Jess, chat in a moment,' Issy concluded, feeling more positive.

"All we can do now is to be patient, Dad, we've set the wheels in motion,' Amy added, placing her hand gently on his.

A few minutes passed and Issy's phone buzzed into life.

'It's Jess from the estate agent again. I've just spoken to Mrs Roberts, the lady of the house. She's free this afternoon in an hour, four o'clock, if that suits you,' she added, expecting an immediate answer.

'I'll just ask my sister,' mouthing her the answer.

'Four o'clock is perfect for us, thank you,' Issy told her, feeling excited.

'Great, I'll confirm that with her and she'll be happy to show you around. She's a lovely lady,' she added, before hanging up.

'Well, that's sorted then, best get a move on, excuse the pun, as time is of the essence,' Amy added, pushing her chair back to get up. A quick bathroom stop, and a look in the mirror to check she was ready to go. She grabbed her keys, hurrying Issy along before they walked out to her car. Amy punched the postcode into the built-in satnav, noting a short journey, a mere twenty-minute drive to the other side of Stow.

They pulled up outside, parking on the pavement in front of the house. Their first glance at the garden, with various terracotta tubs with sprouting daffodils, left a good impression.

The house was a quaint-looking, cottage-style house with a path leading up to a red wood-like front door.

'This looks interesting, let's go and meet Mrs Roberts,' Issy said, loving the house already.

They locked the car and walked slowly up the garden path, hoping she wouldn't be peering out of the window in the lounge. Two knocks and footsteps were soon heard as she unlocked the front door. After a slight tug, she appeared from within. She was a smartly dressed, short female with shoulder-length blonde hair tied up in a bun, looking like she'd just changed to impress.

'Hello, are you the ladies who wanted to view my house?' she asked tentatively.

'Yes, we are, I'm Amy and this is my sister, Issy. Jess the estate agent sent us,' Amy explained.

She opened the door fully to let us in.

'Thank you, your house looks beautiful, 'Issy added as they walked on through.

A narrow yet adequate hallway with a small round table to place essentials on, such as house and car keys to the left, and a coat stand next to it. Further along, walking into the lounge, a bottle-green settee with two matching armchairs with nesting tables either side, leaving the room looking cosy and charming. It wasn't over-furnished as some places are, which was an immediate appeal factor.

'Follow me into the kitchen. It has just been updated with cream gloss finished cupboards and drawers with ample storage for pots and pans for all cooking equipment. A lovely space with the usual whites: a washing machine and tumble dryer next to one another, a double oven and a microwave on one of the work tops. Three good sized workstations suitably placed around the kitchen, adequate for chopping and prepping meals,' she continued.

A small, yet light conservatory to the rear, leading out into a small garden, with a patio for the summer months, was more than they had expected.

'This is lovely,' they said in unison, causing her to smile. They followed her back inside.

'Follow me up the stairs to the bed and bathrooms. I hope you like them.'

A light oak, straight staircase took them to the first floor, housing two good-sized bedrooms with one en suite; a walk-in shower, a loo and vanity basin with a heated chrome towel rail on the wall. A window looking out into the back garden.

'Lovely,' Amy added as they walked through to the other bedroom. Another double bed and a double built-in wardrobe, with bedside tables either side, with a comfy cube chair in one corner to throw your clothes on, making the room very pretty and impressive.

A small, but equally adequate bathroom, with a roll-top bath, set the relaxing scene for someone who needed a luxury bath after a busy day at work.

'So that's the house, I hope you like it. All recently upgraded and decorated by my late husband; I sadly lost him a few months ago, the reason I need to sell up and start afresh elsewhere. The house has too many memories. I need to have closure to enable me to move forward. If you have any questions please ask, I won't bite, feel free to wander around by yourselves if you wish.'

'Thank you, we're happy with everything,' Amy added, seeing her smile broaden on her face.

'Great, well thank you for coming, all the best to you in your search.' She stretched out her hand to shake theirs in turn, before opening the front door, sending a slight breeze throughout the house.

'Well, she seemed pleasant enough,' Amy said once she had closed the door behind them. 'Yet, a sad story, losing your husband, that must be so tough. I can understand she needs to sell up. Unless you bring closure, it's very hard to move forward in life,' she concluded.

'I propose a coffee, and a good chat about the house. I saw a lovely coffee house on the High Street as we drove past.'

Amy unlocked the car and drove off to find a car park. They parked up at a Morrisons car park up the road, just a few minutes' walk to the café. They marched in, setting off the bell above the door, and walked straight up to the counter, which displayed an array of mouth-watering cakes. A black board above with various coffees and other drinks listed, made their decision slightly easier.

'Ladies, what can I get you?' the young girl asked, ready to tap in their order onto the screen.

'Two cappuccinos, please and a slice of carrot cake and a walnut cake for my sister,' Amy replied.

'Coming right up, take your seats and I'll bring them over,' she added whilst Amy swiped her card on the card reader to pay.

They took the usual window seat so they could people-watch, that being their favourite pastime when in a café. After ten minutes, Issy's phone began to buzz. Thinking it would be Jess from the estate agent, she was right, so quickly swiped it to answer.

'Hi there, it's Jess from the estate agents, just checking how your viewing went this afternoon. She's a lovely lady, isn't she?' she added.

'Oh yes, we decided to chat in a café up the road. So here we are. Yes, the house is beautiful and just what we're looking for. I think this could well be a contender. Can I get back to you later after my sister and I have had a good chat about it?' she asked, sending her a good vibe down the phone.

'Yes of course, I thought you'd like it. It's a great starter property for you girls. At the moment you're the first to view it, no others yet. Mrs Roberts is after a quick sale and is open to offers nearest to the asking price. The house won't stay long on our books, so the sooner you decide, the better.'

'Thank you, Jess, we'll need to make up our minds soon I guess.' Issy ended the call, eager to drink the coffees the girl had brought over, drooling over the cakes.

'Well, what's your verdict on the house, least favourites and the best?'

'Overall, 10 out of 10, really nothing to fault. Two good-sized bedrooms and a lovely pathway leading up to the front with those terracotta tubs, very pretty, what's not to like. I could see us living there. We are close to the shops and to our work, depending on whether I get mine,' Amy added hopefully.

'Best of all we could just move in, as it's all just been freshly decorated.'

'I feel the same way, Issy, I think we should now discuss it with Dad to see if he's willing to help us out, which I'm sure he will,' Amy concluded by draining the last of her coffee and forking the last crumbs off her plate.

Turning the key in the door, they heard the dogs scampering to the door with wagging tails, waiting to be greeted.

'Anyone home?' Amy shouted down the corridor, holding out for some response.

'In here, just having our afternoon nap, before life starts again,' Mum shouted back before they entered the lounge, seeing her lying back on the sofa. Issy placed a kiss on her forehead.

'Have the dogs been out recently? They seem a bit scatty. I'll let them out of the kitchen, and put the kettle on, we've got some news.'

'Sounds promising, I guess it's about the house this morning. Your dad's just popped out, he'll be back soon.'

'Earl Grey or ordinary, Mum?' she asked, feeling slightly impatient.

'Earl Grey for me, love, thank you.'

Issy and Amy walked back into the kitchen, letting the dogs back in, making sure their water was topped up.

'Hello, you two, did you miss us?' Issy bent over, patting the dogs in turn on their bellies.

Dad suddenly appeared from nowhere, looking rather pleased with himself.

'I've been fishing with Jack, the guy I met at the pub last week. We caught a pike, before releasing it back into the lake. A lovely specimen too, beautiful scales,' he told us his story, feeling very chuffed with himself.

'Wow, clearly a successful morning's catch then, Dad, cuppa?'

'Oh yes please, how was your morning at the house, did you like it?'

'Loved it, Dad, it ticked all the essential boxes, it's a winner in our opinion.'

'Grand, well, if the price is right, and as I said I would give a lump sum towards it, go for it, if your gut feeling tells you. Always trust your own instincts, they are usually right.'

'We need to phone the agency back today, if we want to be in with a chance, as she said it won't be on their books for long, before it gets snapped up by some enthusiastic buyer, like us!' Amy hinted, looking at her dad with an air of hope in her eyes.

'OK, let's talk about finances, girls. We'll offer half the money, if you are able to cover the rest.'

'Really, that's very generous of you and much appreciated. If you're really sure, I'll ring Jess back now and take it from there, Dad,' they agreed, as she took out her phone, hovering her thumb over the last caller ... Jess. She made the call, explaining they would like to make an offer on the house. Jess would get back to them after she had spoken to Mrs Roberts.

Dad then reminded them of the story about Mum finding her lost brother James.

'Mum was left a lump sum after her dad passed away, which I've placed in a high-rate savings account, to be used later for such occasions. She had a solicitor's letter land on the doormat one day after work, whilst living in Winchester, when you, Amy, were still very young. She subsequently opened it, seeing it was a solicitor's letter, initially wondering why she had received it. Reading further she noted that a dormant account was still in her Dad's name, a year after his death, which clearly had gone unnoticed. They were obviously wanting to close the account, hence the letter, asking for her permission to transfer any monies over to Mum.

'Initially it was a shock, as she thought everything had been sorted out after his death, which was clearly not the case. That's how Mum also found out more about your uncle James. Her mum, Dot, secretly had an affair without Mum knowing about it, which understandably upset and annoyed your mother. Still, that's history now and we've since met up with James and got to know one other more. He is now your mother's long-lost stepbrother.

'He has since moved away and was living in Cambridge the last time we messaged one another. He did come and see you, Issy, after you were born, which was good. That reminds me, I must get in contact again with him soon and give him the latest update on our family. He may even drive over and come and spend time with us, if he's willing to make the effort for us. Sorry, that sounds a bit mean, but Mum can't forget what happened. However she has since forgiven him, which is the main thing.'

Dad put us in the picture, for us to digest and draw our own conclusions.

'Oh my, Mum, that sounded like a complicated time in your life, far from easy,' Issy added as Mum listened to every word.

"We're glad it's all sorted now, despite him not being very good at communicating, definitely a man thing I'm afraid!' Amy added, feeling upset for her mum.

'Onward and upwards girls, it's a new year and a fresh start,' Jodie concluded, before getting up to fill the kettle up for another pot of tea.

Issy finally made that all-important call to Jess, who explained that she would inform Mrs Roberts and ring Issy back later. Dad told her to make her an offer and see if she would accept it. It was now a waiting game, crossing everything and praying for a good outcome. The excitement and the nervous wait were becoming too much yet would be over in no time.

Mum placed a fresh pot of tea in her blue ceramic teapot in the centre of the table, with fresh mugs, ready to pour out once the tea had stood for a while, with a jug of milk and four teaspoons.

They all sat in silence as Mum poured out the tea, on tenterhooks, waiting for Jess to ring back before the day was out.

A few minutes later, Issy's phone vibrated on the table, leaving them all at sixes and sevens, itching to know the answer.

'Jess, thank you for ringing back,' Issy replied, feeling slightly on edge.

'I've spoken to Mrs Roberts, who has agreed to your offer, subject to all the usual surveys. There is no link in the chain, so all should go according to plan. She's very keen to sell as soon as possible, so we could be looking at a few months before moving in. I hope that sounds satisfactory. I'll be in touch shortly when I hear any further updates.'

'Yeah,' they shouted, clapping their hands together after she had hung up. Things were definitely looking more positive than they had that morning. Issy and Amy high-fived one another despite it still being early days.

'Here's to our next chapter, Issy, yippee.'

Chapter Ten

Thursday finally arrived when Amy's alarm went off at 7am. She pressed the snooze button just once before her day started in earnest. Her interview at the vets was at 10.30, so no lie-in today.

A quick shower to kick start her into action then, pulling on a pair of smart jeans and a jumper, she dashed into the kitchen. Greeted by the dogs, she let them out, whilst preparing their breakfast.

'Morning,' Issy's voice echoed down the corridor on entering the kitchen. 'It's the day of reckoning for you, how are you feeling?' she asked nervously.

'Oh, you know, what will be will be. Actually I feel optimistic.'

'That's the spirit, Amy, we've got lots to look forward to, with our new house, and our jobs. It's going to be a good year, I can feel it in my bones!'

'Let's hope so, I really need this new start,' she added, feeling positive vibes about everything.

Issy let the dogs back in and noticed their breakfast already served up in their bowls, whilst Amy laid the table and placed a pot of tea with four mugs in the centre for all to help themselves.

'Good morning, girls,' Mum graced them with her presence a bit earlier than normal.

'Morning Mum, you're up early today. Had a bad night or just couldn't sleep?' Amy asked out of curiosity.

'I remembered it was your interview today, so I thought I'd get up to wish you all the best.'

'Oh, thank you, Mum, there's a pot of tea ready on the table.'

'I'll pour it, Mum, just sit yourself down and relax,' Issy added, knowing she was a bit slower in the mornings.

Just then her phone sprang into life. Seeing it was the doctors' surgery, she thought it best to take the call.

'Is this Issy Stevens? It's the surgery regarding your mother Jodie,' the lady explained.

'Oh hi, yes, I'm Issy, one of her daughters. How can I help?'

'Well, she needs to come into the surgery sometime this week to see the doctor to discuss the results of the blood test she had the other day. It's not urgent but she needs to be seen this week, please.'

'Thank you, I'll relay that message to her, and we'll get something booked in as soon as possible,' Issy confirmed, before she hung up.

'That was the surgery, Mum, they wanted to discuss your recent blood tests. We'll chat about it later on once Amy gets back from her interview . You could of course ring the surgery and book an appointment yourself, sooner rather than later as they suggested. Don't worry about it for now, Mum, OK?' she added, knowing her mum would feel slightly concerned about the results.

On arrival at Rowans, the vet practice, Amy was greeted by a few barking dogs, scratching and sliding along the grey, vinyl floor, clearly excited to see one another, knowing they probably would get a dog biscuit from the counter after they'd been seen by a vet, their reward for being good. The owner's reward was a bill!

'Good morning, how may I help?' the girl asked, noticing I was pet-less.

'Good morning, I'm Amy Stevens for an interview for the vet assistant position.'

'Brilliant, please take a seat and Lucy will be out shortly.'

Amy took a seat along with the waiting pet owners. A cat's kennel was beside her with a tabby face poking out, making her feel right at home.

A few minutes later, a young lady appeared, dressed in blue nurse's attire, with dark brown hair tied back in a ponytail. She walked out to shake Amy's hand, before they wandered back into her room.

It was clearly an interview room, with a small black desk with a swivel chair. Amy sat on the other side, on an ordinary chair that had a slight wobble to it as she brought it closer towards the table.

'Thank you for coming this morning,' looking up from her sheet of paper in front of her, summarising her details, giving her a quick overview.

'Have you worked with animals before?' She started the interview with what seemed like an obvious question to Amy.

'I have two dogs, one I recently adopted from my last holiday abroad. The short story being, the owner suffered a heart attack on a coach we were about to board in Austria, but sadly died 48 hours later. We had already met prior to this unforeseen incident, and become friends, seeing that I showed my affection towards her dog. Sadly there was no one else to take the dog. I became smitten and just couldn't bear to rehome her elsewhere, so I adopted her. I took her to a local vet to check her over and to be given a rabies injection, before bringing her back into this country. My best friend here has also just bought a lovely spaniel from a rescue centre,' she added, hoping that would suffice.

'Wow, that sounded full on, lovely that you adopted her beloved dog. Well, we are looking for someone to assist in caring for our day care animals, after they have had surgery or who have been brought in, lost or looking to be rehomed. Does that sound like something you could give? You clearly are a very caring person and a keen dog lover.'

'Yes, that sounds like something I'd like to do. Would there be any reception work too, giving a variety of duties?' she added, hoping she could muck in when required.

'Oh yes, I was leading on to that, you would become a valued member of our team, stepping into other roles when required. Variety is indeed the spice of life. The hours are flexible, generally 8.30 to 5 o'clock, with an hour for lunch, any good?'

'Brilliant, I'd definitely prefer a variety of different things during the day. Gives a great insight into a day in a busy vet practice.' She felt more satisfied.

'Lovely, well, I'll leave you to ponder on that, oh and I assume you could start next week?' she added.

'This would be my first job since returning from my travels,' Amy concluded as she drew the interview to a close.

'Thank you, Amy, I'll be in touch later today.' She stood up, walking over to the door to show her out. 'Have a lovely day,' she added with a smile.

Amy walked briskly out of reception with her head held high, unsure how she felt about the job. Then again, it was a starter which could lead to other possibilities, or she could just review it as time ticked on by. She took her phone out to ring Issy, who might shed more light on the situation.

'Amy, how did it go at the interview? I'm just around the next corner, fancy a coffee to chat it out? Meet you in five in our usual place.' She hung up, before Amy could say anything.

Next thing Amy felt a touch on her shoulder and turned around to see Issy, with Bessy walking alongside her.

'Oh hello you.' Amy bent down to make a fuss of Bessy, who loved every second, wanting to lick her face.

'Escape again from the oldens as they have a nap or a game of Scrabble?'

'Something like that. Bessy needed a walk so I thought I'd leave Rosie, who didn't show much interest in going out, she'd rather be curled up in her cosy bed with them, making it easier all round. Honestly, I can't wait for our new home, our space, as they clearly need theirs,' she added, wanting it to happen sooner than later.

'Ditto, Sis,' they agreed as they approached the café, pushing the door open, seeing it was already filling up quickly.

'Good morning, ladies, you're becoming regulars, what can I get you both?' the woman asked, peering down at Bessy, then quickly grabbing a small treat from nowhere. She must have a few stashed away for customers bringing in their furry friends.

'Two cappuccinos and two slices of cheesecake, please.'

'Coming right up, choose your table and I'll bring them over.'

'Thank you.' They turned around, noticing the last window seat, their preferred spot for people-watching.

'Here you go, enjoy, ladies.' She promptly brought our treats over on a tray.

'OK, spill, would you fancy working there with canine friends and the odd cat?' Issy asked, knowing full well she preferred dogs to cats. Cats have a tendency to hiss like a snake when disturbed, and they scratch like no tomorrow.

Amy hissed back at her with claw like-fingers, reminding Issy what it feels like. 'OK, yes, it's a great opportunity into the animal kingdom. I would be a fool to turn it down, if offered to me.'

'Good, that's settled then, now get your claws around that mug, and teeth into your cake, as these times could be rare, once we start working, though I'm sure we could sneak in lunch on odd occasions.'

'Absolutely, we can't give this up so easily!' Amy added with a cheeky wink.

They finished their morning treats. Amy walked up to pay, not forgetting to stamp the loyalty card. They headed back to the car, Bessy lying in the footwell by Amy, to return to the bungalow.

No sooner had they stepped inside than Amy's phone vibrated in her pocket. Seeing it was the vets, she took a deep breath before answering.

'Amy, it's Tracy from Rowans. I'm sure you want to know about this morning, so I can confirm we would like to offer you the job, if you are still interested. I clearly saw you are a dog lover, meeting all the criteria for this position. We would gladly welcome you on our team. If you could start next Monday, that would be even better,' she continued.

'Oh, thank you, and yes, I will gladly accept your offer to start on Monday morning,' Amy replied, raising a thumb and letting Issy know the news.

'I'll send you an email confirming our offer, if you could reply as soon as possible, please. I'll see you on Monday,' she concluded before ending the call.

'Ace, you've done it, Sis, now we're both in the world of work. Onwards and upwards,' giving her a tight hug.

'Just one more hurdle, a big one at that … the house, which could take a while after all the necessary surveys are completed. That said, I've got a good feeling about it, let's claim it. We'd better tell Mum and Dad.'

'Anyone home?' Amy shouted as they continued through into the kitchen, switching the kettle on to make another brew for anyone who wanted one.

'Oh, I was just about to do the same,' Mum said, walking in looking sprightly. 'Well, how did it go?' she asked, eager to be in the know.

'Another one in the bag. I've got the job; she just rang me, telling me the good news, Mum.'

'Oh, that's brilliant, definitely worth a cuppa and that meal we were going to have this weekend. A double celebration with both of our clever girls and the potential house too, epic.'

'Steady on, we don't want to tempt fate.'

'It will be fine, what could possibly go wrong, unless the surveyors find major problems, which I doubt will happen.'

'Right, who's for that cuppa and a digestive you can dunk in!'

'Yuck, they get soggy bottoms, not very ladylike!' Mum added pulling a face.

'That's the idea though, in and out, straight into your mouth,' moving on, Amy added, amused.

'Where are the dogs?' they asked together.

'Oh, Dad's just out with them, they all needed to stretch their legs, including Dad.'

A knock on the kitchen back door; seeing it was Dad bringing the dogs back in one piece, Mum got up to let them in. No muddy paws to wipe as it was cold and dry outside. They soon scampered in all excited, before that all-important shake, making their tails wag then wanting attention, as they nudged Amy, nearly causing her legs to buckle.

'Steady on you two,' she said, whilst they made a beeline for their water bowls, clearly thirsty work trotting around outside. 'Now go in your beds, while we have our tea.'

'Will someone keep me up to date with the latest job news? Seems like our lucky week,' Dad asked, hearing voices.

'Oh yes, I've got the job at the vet's, Dad, starting on Monday.'

'That's my girl, one thing left now ... the house and you're quids in,' Dad gestured with a big smile.

'Absolutely, any news about Mum's tests?' quickly changing the subject.

'Oh, that yes, she heard yesterday, we didn't want to say. Mum has a thyroid problem, hence the fatigue. They have prescribed some tablets, one a day, to see if they help. Nothing to concern ourselves about for now,' he added.

'OK, that's good, at least they've found the root cause, a common problem as we age,' Amy added, feeling relieved to hear.

'We can now plan our meal out tomorrow or Saturday. There's a lovely Italian restaurant just opened in Stow which I noticed this morning, fancy going there? I could book a table later.'

'Our favourite, yes please, our favourite food,' Mum and Dad agreed.

'Great, say tomorrow evening at 7pm. I picked up their menu with their contact info, so I'll give them a buzz.'

Amy picked up her phone from the table, about to punch in the number, when it rang. Seeing it was Jess from the estate agents, she thought she'd better take the call.

'Oh, hi there, Jess, how are you? I take it you have news regarding the house?' she asked tentatively, secretly hoping everything was going according to plan.

'Oh yes Amy, no problem this end. Just giving you options of possible moving in dates, as Mrs Roberts is very keen to move things along as quickly as possible. The building surveyor is going over tomorrow to file his report, which I think will go well, unless he detects something major. So, how about Friday in two weeks, unless that's too much of a rush?' she concluded.

'Wow, that is quite soon, can I discuss it all with my family over the weekend and get back to you on Monday morning? My sister and I start new jobs then, so it will be a busy start to the week.'

'Absolutely, there's no real hurry. I assume you need to buy some beds to start you off, so please don't stress yourselves for now.'

'Indeed we do, and the rest we can do in slow time. The main thing being, we can move in. Meanwhile we can carry on living with our parents, which will help them out. Feeling excited already.'

'Perfect, I'll get back to you as soon as I have any further updates. Have a great weekend.' She hung up.

'That all sounds very exciting, possibly going at more of a pace than we thought, but that's OK,' Amy added, feeling slightly nervous, but in a good way.

They had discussed earlier about visiting some second-hand furniture shops and antique shops, for inspiration, adding a different style to their new home. They liked the idea of upcycling furniture as seen on TV, where once-precious items, having been discarded in a waste tip, are carefully selected by an interior designer to create something unique from them, selling them on to someone else, who appreciates such transformations. The idea being that you can upcycle any old piece of furniture, making it into something really special.

They started to make a list of the most essential pieces they would need; the list soon became endless, yet they could build it up over time. Secretly they hoped that their mum and dad would offer them some of the unwanted items they had accumulated over the years, and which were stashed up in their loft. They had had a massive clear out before they moved, though their style of furniture was way different from the girls', being from a different era.

Their weekends were soon going to be busy, as they drifted from one furniture shop to another. This became their new hobby for now, until their new home was fully furnished to their liking. Happy days, they high-fived one another, feeling accomplished.

The Italian restaurant was booked for 7pm, giving them plenty of time to get ready and dressed up. The dogs had been walked, fed and watered, one thing less to worry about.

'How's everyone doing?' Issy asked, as she walked through the bungalow. 'An hour left before we need to go,' she warned them, hoping someone was listening.

'We heard you loud and clear, girls,' Dad tutted back, feeling amused.

Mum appeared shortly from their bedroom in a cream blouse and red jumper with black trousers, not wanting to get cold later on. Dad followed, dressed in his light brown chinos with a bottle-green jumper, looking very dapper for two oldens!

Issy and Amy also dressed in smart casual trousers, loving the comfy cosy clothes feeling.

'Are we all ready to hit the Italian in style?' Amy asked for the last time, seeing her parents all coated up, making their way out into the cold early evening air.

They arrived all excited for their family night out, taking an already set table over by the window, with a lovely bench seat for extra comfort. Mum and Dad took their places, whilst the girls took the chairs on the other side.

"Good evening.' A handsome Italian waiter stood by their table smiling at them. 'What drinks can I get you tonight?'

'No alcohol for us; four orange juices with ice, please,' Amy replied, smiling back.

'Gracie!' he added as he punched in the order on his screen.

A few minutes later he walked over with their drinks, balancing a tray on his upheld hand.

Amy and Issy perused the menu, remembering their childhood days, going out for family meals with Mum and Dad as they looked back, remembering those good old days, as they gathered around the table once again. It was so lovely to repeat the experience now that they were older, all living together under the same roof.

'To us, happy days, may it continue!' They lifted their glasses together after he had brought the drinks over and placed them on the table.

'Have you chosen your mains?' he politely asked, fingers ready to tap away.

'Two carbonara for us girls, and two spaghetti bolognaise for our parents, please,' Amy confirmed as he tapped away merrily.

'Gracie!' he said, collecting the menus and walking back to the till, sending the order directly to the kitchen staff.

They chatted a while about all and sundry, before two people walked over with their mains, which all looked scrumptious.

'Thank you, gracie,' Issy replied, practising her much-limited Italian.

'Prego!' he smiled back at her, as she noticed his lovely blue eyes.

'Buon appetito! As they say in Italian,' Issy added. 'This all looks so delicious, tuck in and enjoy.'

They tucked into the mains with gusto, in silence, with the odd remark in between.

'Is everything alright with your food?' Mr Blue-eyed Boy walked back over, as they all looked up, smiling back at him.

'Buon appetito,' he winked back, feeling the love amongst them.

'He's a lovely cheerful chap,' Mum added, 'and a good-looking one too,' she chuckled.

'Steady on my love,' Dad stared back at her, nudging her gently on the arm.

Issy and Amy looked at one another, about to burst into laughter. After half an hour, he collected the empty plates, returning with dessert menus. It didn't take long before they had decided on desserts; when in an Italian restaurant, tiramisu times four followed by coffees after, finishing the evening off on a high. The bill being bitter-sweet, yet a good night was had by all. They made their exit, bidding their goodbyes as they passed the staff on their way out.

Walking into the kitchen back at the bungalow, the dogs were desperate to go into the garden, not wanting to leave a puddle in the kitchen.

'Good girls,' Issy said, acknowledging their good behaviour once they swiftly came back into the kitchen. They went straight back into their beds by the Aga, keeping toasty and warm. It had just turned half nine. Mum and Dad were ready to turn in for the night, seeing them walk into the kitchen looking tired.

'Anything I can get you two before bed?' Issy asked Mum as she bent down to kiss the dogs goodnight.

'No, we'll just head off for bed. Thanks, girls, for a fabulous evening, it was lovely, goodnight,' smiling back at us before disappearing down the corridor.

'Night you two, see you in the morning.'

Amy and Issy decided on having a final drink to wind down, before they too turned in for the night. A camomile tea would do the trick. They were still so excited about the new future about to unfold. They thought they'd make a start looking around second-hand furniture shops, to see what they could pick up. Dad said they could temporarily store some in his garage, as long as they didn't fill it up to the rafters. After half an hour, Amy placed their mugs in the dishwasher whilst Issy let the dogs out one last time. Amy checked everything was locked up, before closing the kitchen door once the dogs settled in their beds, then turned off the lights before they walked down the corridor to their room.

'Goodnight, girls.'

Chapter Eleven

The weekend was finally here with lots to accomplish before starting their jobs on Monday. They planned on visiting a few local furniture shops, selling new and old items, to assess what they needed for the new house. Clearly they had a limited budget, focusing only on essentials, until they had saved up, putting money away in a savings account whilst working their socks off. Busy times ahead, so they had to keep focused.

First things first, that all-important morning coffee comparing our lists of items to buy.

'Good morning, girls,' Dad walked into the kitchen, all dressed up for another fishing day ahead.

'Morning Dad, you're looking very smart in your fishing trousers this morning! I assume you're meeting up with your mate Jack from the other day?' Issy asked, noting he was up earlier than usual on a Saturday morning.

'Thank you, yes, we planned another fishing trip, hoping to catch something unusual, then off to the pub later for brunch. Mum's off to the hairdresser and meeting her new friend Elaine after, to check out that new cafe you went to in old Stow. She misses a good natter during the week, does your mum. I've told her she needs to join something, take up a new hobby or interest. She likes reading, so she could join a book club. She needs to visit the local library, they could advise, I'm sure.'

'Good for you, Dad for encouraging her, it's not easy deciding what to do once you get older and after everyone flies the nest. Loneliness sets in quickly, leading into other health issues, so prevention is always the best answer. So, Jack is picking you up? As I need my car today, Dad, will Mum be alright?'

'Yes, we take it in turns and it's his turn, so that works out well.

Mum has her phone, if she needs me. I can message you too, so all will be OK girls, please don't worry,' he reassured them.

'I'm making a coffee if you want one, before we all leave.'

'Thanks, but we're going soon, Jack is due any time soon.'

On cue there was a loud knock at the front door, alerting the dogs as they jumped out of their beds, scampering down the corridor, barking as they went. Dad beat them to it, opening the door, grabbing their collars, lest they dash outside.

'Jack, come on in and meet these two rascals, and my two girls, they aren't rascals! Steady on girls, calm down and let Jack in before you jump all over him, not that you should be doing that anyway,' Dad warned the dogs, as they quickly turned around, as if they understood every word he was telling them.

'Right, are we ready to hit the lake for another day's fishing? I've got all the gear in the car, including two folding chairs, blankets to sit on, for our morning coffee and snacks. Wiggly worms in a plastic box for bait, not forgetting the most important fishing rods.'

'Great, I'll grab my parka coat and rucksack with mugs and spoons and we'll be off. See you later everyone, enjoy your day, love, with Elaine,' he called back as they walked out of the door, locking it behind them.

Secretly they were pleased to have the kitchen to themselves, to go through their lists together whilst sipping their coffee before Mum appeared. It was their space, the reason they couldn't wait for their own place.

Mum appeared half an hour later, all dressed up ready to go out with Elaine. The hairdresser was five minutes' walk up the High Street where Elaine would meet her to walk to the café afterwards.

'Morning, Mum, you're looking lovely this morning, ready for the hairdresser and meeting up with your friend after?' Issy remarked as she walked through.

'Yes, busy morning for us girls, love having my hair done. Have a cup of tea, I've just made a pot if you want one.'

'Sit down and I'll get a mug out. What time is your appointment?' Issy asked, to keep a check on the time.

'In an hour, that's enough time for a cuppa. I thought it's best I leave the dogs here. They keep one another company as long as I let them out beforehand.'

'OK, Mum, we're going to start our shopping trip for furniture, so have a lovely day of pampering and see you later,' giving her a kiss on the cheek as they walked past.

They all left the house heading in different directions. Mum walked to the hairdresser in town, where she would meet up with Elaine afterwards and have a coffee at the café on the High Street.

Issy and Amy parked in Morrisons car park and took a stroll down the High Street, noticing an array of antique shops along the way. This was the perfect place to start their bargain hunt for furniture for their new abode.

Stow is renowned for its many antique and craft shops and art galleries. A beautiful place to amble along then have a coffee stop at the café on the High Street with a lovely variety of cakes to choose from.

'This is a beautiful place, Amy, a picturesque town with lots of antique furniture shops. I'm in the zone already. Let's go bargain hunting, Sis, coffee and cake after . . . our perfect day, I say!'

'Onward and upwards, Issy!'

The bell pinged above the first antique shop, alerting new customers, which was jammed full of knicknacks littering the place. Plenty of display cabinets aligned the walls as they ambled through, careful not to knock any larger pieces of furniture en route. It was a place where one could escape for hours, lost in your own world, enjoying everything you saw. They spotted a few items such as a lovely coffee table with a few mosaic ceramic tiles neatly inset in the coffee table-top. Further to the rear of the shop, a couple of two-seater sofas and armchairs. Table lamps, coat stands, ideal for the hall. A small round mahogany table for placing all and sundry, including keys when you enter the house.

Lots to explore. They decided on buying new beds from the bed shop a few shops along, knowing it was best buying new with a firm mattress, it was hardly going to break the bank these days. On their initial walk around they mentally noted the items they needed the most. The rest they could build up in slow time.

'Good morning, ladies, have you seen anything you like? I have a van, so we can also deliver within a 10-mile radius, if that helps. Just ask and I'll see what we can do to help.' A handsome chap with a small brown beard whittled on, well-meaning and eager to help them. Amy took an instant liking to him. He seemed friendly enough.

'Thank you, we are looking for furniture for our new small house, there's plenty to choose from here. The house is in Stow and we would be interested if you could deliver.'

'That's lovely, we can definitely deliver to you free of charge as it's just up the road. I suggest you amble around and make a list of the items you're interested in and we can take it from there. There's no hurry either, if you fancy a coffee in the café, I'll reserve the items for you.'

'That sounds great, thank you. I think a coffee break will be well needed. We'll let you know in a few minutes.'

'OK, let's look at the essential items. I like the coffee table and the small round table for the hall. The coat stands and that lovely burgundy sofa with the two matching armchairs, perfect for the lounge. That's my choice so far,' Issy suggested.

'Great minds, let's reserve them, then get a coffee, what do you say? We can negotiate on the price after.'

Amy spotted the chap wandering around, so she asked him to see what they had chosen. He placed a red reserved sticker on all of their chosen items, whilst they happily walked out of the shop, up the High Street to the café for their long-awaited visit, to mull it all over.

'Good morning, ladies, back again! What can I tempt you with today? Lemon cheesecake or a Nutella sandwich cake, freshly made this morning?'

'Oh yummy, two lattes and a lemon cheesecake for both of us, please.'

'Good choice, I'll bring it over shortly.'

They took a table by the window, as this time they needed to get their heads together about the furniture with their set budget. So exciting yet a bit scary. That it was progressing as planned was the main thing.

'Here you go, enjoy!' She brought the delights on a tray, placing them on the table. Issy played mum, handing out the coffee and cakes before they relished their treats.

'To us.' Raising their cups, smiling at each other, feeling happy.

An hour passed and they were back in the shop to negotiate their items with the owner.

'You're back, so what's the verdict? I can do everything for a good price. We can deliver too, just give me an address, and we can arrange a date and time that suits you. I can only hold the items for a few days though,' he explained.

'Perfect, we have storage in our parents' garage until we can move into our new house. I'll write down the address for you, if you have a pen and paper,' Issy explained as he peered over his black-framed glasses.

'We deliver on a Friday afternoon if that's OK, this Friday if you prefer?'

Just then his mobile rang, giving them a window to decide on the time and a delivery date. After a quick chat about it, they opted for this Friday, freeing up the space for anything new coming into the shop.

'Sorry, back with you. What have you decided? I'm flexible.'

'This Friday would be perfect if that's OK, thank you.'

'Certainly, say three o'clock?'

'Great, thank you,' Amy added, feeling excited, smiling up at him.

'Here's your invoice.' He handed her the card machine to pay and then the receipt.

'Have a lovely afternoon and see you on Friday at 3pm.'

He walked towards the shop door, opening it like a gentleman.

On opening the front door, they were greeted by the dogs, plus one other face yet to be introduced to them.

'Hello, you two and who do we have here in our midst?' Issy asked as she bent down to stroke her dogs as they circled around her feet. 'Let's go and find Mum, I'm sure she's in the kitchen or lounge.'

They took off their coats, hanging them on the coat stand, left their bags on the table and wandered into the kitchen, the girls following closely behind.

'Hello, you two, meet Elaine, my friend, and her cockapoo, Sadie. She rescued her a week ago from the vets, after seeing a poster on the notice board by the post office, explaining she had been handed in after no one had come forward to claim her. She was found wandering the streets one afternoon and was handed in to the Rowans vet practice. Elaine lives alone now, so needs a companion and here she is, isn't she adorable!' Mum recounted the story.

'Oh, lovely to meet you both, yes, she's a cutie, you'll definitely have fun with this one, and she's definitely taken with our two pooches,' Issy said, seeing the happy doggies all bonding together.

'One happy family, you will also see me soon at Rowans, I'm starting a new job there on Monday. It's all happening in our family,' Amy added with a chuckle.

'I'll put the kettle on, and you can tell me how you got on this morning.' Mum changed the subject before anyone could say anything.

'Just one more cuppa, as this one needs a walk,' Elaine replied.

'Oh, we can arrange that one, come on girls, you pop in the garden and have a play,' Mum added, opening the back door before Elaine could change her mind.

Mum took mugs from the cupboard and put milk in a jug, placing them on the table. Issy filled the teapot, placing two tea bags in, to stand for Mum to be ... well, Mum!

She started to recount the morning's events, bringing Mum up to date, especially about the handsome chap in the antique shop with his brown beard, giving her something to amuse herself with.

'He's delivering the furniture on Friday, to store in your garage as dad said we could, until we get the keys for our new home.'

'Bravo girls, a good fruitful morning, it all sounds very exciting,' she concluded before pouring the tea out and handing round a plate of digestives.

There was a loud knock at the front door, causing Mum to jump up and walk quickly over to see who it was. Opening the door, she saw Dad with his rucksack over his shoulder, looking totally wiped out. No doubt his fishing trip with Jack had been an equally successful day, judging by his smiling happy face.

'Oh love, you look worn out. I've just made a pot of tea, come in, out of the cold and join us for a brew.' Mum noticed Jack's rickety old Mark 2 Land Rover struggling to engage into reverse, with a clunking noise, before disappearing down the road, leaving behind a puff of smoke, adding to the non-clean air zone.

'I'm guessing Jack, your fishing mate, is heading back home.' Mum was not impressed with his old Land Rover, leave alone the clunking noises it produced.

'It was a long day, catching good-sized fish, weighing them, then releasing them back into the water. I took a few photos, holding a trout and a pike.' He showed Mum the pictures he had taken, once he had taken off his outer layers of clothing to join them for a mug of tea.

'Wow, they look huge and colourful,' she remarked, noting the scales on their skin.

'The bigger, the better. Some weigh 30 pounds and more, amazing. We've watched that *Gone Fishing* programme on TV. It's brilliant. They go on a day's fishing, on the River Wye for example, then turn up at a stunning overnight location, where they have loads of fun and great food. Those two men are hilariously funny. Such a fun, relaxing hobby for men in their old age,' Dad told us.

'You didn't bring our tea then, a fresh salmon would have been lovely, though I don't fancy cutting its head off, poor mite, still it's food on the table,' Issy said, feeling a bit squeamish.

'Perhaps next time.'

'I bought one of those lovely leek and chicken pies on our way home for later. I'll put it in the Aga later, broccoli and carrots, meal sorted,' Issy smiled, feeling accomplished.

Moments later everyone gathered around the table chatting about their day and drinking tea, until they exhausted themselves. Elaine went home with Sadie, to feed her. As it was their turn to cook, Issy served the veg whilst Amy placed the pie on a baking tray ready for the Aga. Rice pudding was for afters, shop-bought as it had been a busy day. They set the table ready to eat in an hour.

Amy's phone lit up with an unknown number, which she was always wary of, dismissing it this time. They'd ring again if it was that urgent, she told Issy.

Ten minutes later, the same number appeared on the screen, to her amazement. She thought she'd be bold and answer it. She was so glad she did, as it was her friend Lottie.

'Did you just call earlier? I didn't recognise your number. Have you changed it, Lottie?' Amy asked, feeling relieved it was somebody she knew.

'Oh, it's Mum's old phone, mine is kaput, getting an upgrade next week,' she added. 'So, how's life with you, how's that lovely pooch of yours, gorgeous and cuddly? Just wondering if you fancy going to the pub later, there's a quiz night on, nothing too daunting, just a laugh, what do you say?'

'OK, lovely, just having a pie here with Mum and Dad, we could come after that, what time is it?'

'Starts at half seven, you're both invited, it will be a laugh, meet a few people, men even?'

'Oh, not ready for dating yet, too much going on with our jobs and potential house, girls only for now!'

'Perfect, pick you up at 7ish,' Lottie confirmed before hanging up.

'Issy and I are going out after Lottie picks us up for a quiz night at The Lion Pub, so I'll leave you to lock up and we'll take a key. Make sure the dogs go out before you hit the pillow,' Amy instructed them in case they forgot.

'Yes boss, have a great night. I'm sure you will,' Dad smiled at them.

When seven o'clock arrived, they were ready, standing in the hall, seeing a car pull up on the drive with its lights beaming their way. Their cue to exit, an escape to join a bunch of quizzers at the pub.

'We're off now, see you later,' Amy announced, grabbing a key and locking the door behind them.

'You've escaped, lovely to see you both again. Let's hit the pub!' Amy leant in for a quick peck on the cheek. Issy jumped in the back.

The Lion was an old quirky-looking pub, probably dating back to the 18th century, judging by its wonky wooden beams inside. A few stag heads around the walls made it very gamey-looking, yet cosy. Clearly the owner loved the outdoors, a deerstalker perhaps.

They pulled up in the rear car park and walked to the front entrance. A warm welcome with the bar in front, many mingling around waiting to be served. It was a busy night.

'Half an hour before the quiz starts,' a tall chap wearing a red checked shirt announced into a handheld microphone, 'so order your drinks now, before kick-off.'

Issy grabbed a table further in where a fire was already in full swing, whilst Amy ordered two orange juices with ice, and a packet of peanuts, a classic pub snack.

'Last orders please, before we start,' a bell rang from the bar.

A lady made her way around the tables with the quiz sheets and biros to jot down the answers. Two other ladies joined them at their table. Once Amy had brought over the drinks, they introduced themselves to their team. They had to choose a team name, after a wild animal. They chose Wild Boar.

'Good evening, ladies and gentlemen, welcome to our quiz night. You should all have been given a list of questions with a biro to write your answers. So, without further ado, let's get this quiz started. Pens to the ready, no cheating and enjoy the game,' the chap announced over his microphone.

'Here we go, girls. I'll write the answers down, if you're OK with that. Let's confer and give me your best answer,' Amy said, liking the idea of being team leader.

'First question,' he began talking into the mic. 'One. Name as many wild animals as possible. Two. What animal is this?' A picture was shown of a face on the sheet. 'Three. What sort of food do they hunt on the ground?'

The questions continued until the end, when the same lady came around to collect their sheet, swapping with the next table. They had to check each other's answers, before the quiz master read the answers out loud then totted up their sheet, before passing it back to the original table. The winning table could choose a prize from the bar. A box of Cadbury chocolates, a bottle of white wine or a meal voucher for two.

'And the winner is … drum roll!' Everyone thumped their tables as they eagerly awaited the answer. 'Table number 4!' which was theirs!

'Yeah, that's us!' they shouted out so the guy could hear them at the front. Amy jumped up to attention, making her way to the bar to choose from the prizes. She chose the voucher for two, thinking they could have a celebratory meal, once they had moved into their new home. The other girls chose the chocolates instead of the wine, a good night was had by all.

They ordered more drinks to celebrate their victory, before heading back home. The other two made their exit after the end of the quiz, probably thinking the girls wanted to chat on their own, which was true.

Issy swiped her phone for any missed messages, Mum just

saying they'd had a game of Scrabble before they turned in for the night. Issy quickly sent one back, telling her they had won the quiz, wishing her goodnight and saying they'd be home shortly.

We got chatting about this and that, sipping our cappuccinos, until the door swung open, to show a scraggly looking dark-haired unkempt man, seemingly drunk, in a poor state of health as he stumbled towards the bar, nearly missing one of the bar stools as he approached the front. He clearly smelled of booze as he leant over the bar, holding his hand to steady himself. Everyone soon became aware of his behaviour, as he gazed up at the barman, asking for a drink. The barman clearly saw he was in no fit state to drink anything alcoholic, so he offered him some orange juice instead. The barman seemed to know this man, coming out from behind the bar to chat to him, leading him to a table around the corner for some privacy, carrying his orange juice in one hand, as he supported him, putting his arm through his. leading him to the table.

From hearing others chat around us, he was clearly a regular visitor to the pub, explaining he slept rough along the High Street, one of many homeless rough sleepers around the area, despite the area being an upmarket, tourist place.

The pub owner often offered him a hearty meal with at least two veg, before he headed out for the night, armed with his sleeping bag and a blanket he'd been given by the owner of the pub. A sad story all round these days, with no real long-term solution. It made Issy and Amy think how very privileged they all were, taking everything in life for granted. Just having a place to sleep isn't available to all.

We finally got home after eleven o'clock. All the lights were out, everyone was tucked up in bed. After a quick check on the dogs, who were curled up in their beds not wishing to be disturbed, they turned in themselves.

Sunday morning soon arrived. Hearing the dogs whimper and bark, Issy quickly got up, walking into the kitchen, seeing noses pushed up against the back door, eager to be let out.

'Good girls for telling me you need to go out, I couldn't sleep much longer either,' talking to the dogs as she usually did. She put the kettle on the toasty warm Aga, getting a mug from the cupboard for an early brew. She loved this special time alone with the dogs, a peaceful sanctuary before the others invaded her space.

She rushed back to her bedroom, grabbed her phone now fully charged, put her joggers on and placed her feet in her sea-blue Crocs, before letting the dogs back inside. She changed her mind about tea, choosing a frothy coffee pod, putting it in the coffee machine to kick start her day.

The weather had a sharp chill to it as the lawn had a smattering of frost, turning it into a pretty picture. She gave the dogs their breakfast and refilled their water bowls, so they were sorted. She took a breakfast bowl for herself, added a few bran flakes and berries and mixed it up with some yoghurt for a healthy start to her day along with some walnuts and pecan nuts.

She checked her phone for any new messages, not expecting anything at eight o'clock in the morning. Thinking Lottie might be up she asked her if she fancied taking the dogs out for their morning walk.

Still in bed, sorry, enjoy the fresh air, me time, love you xx

Issy had secretly hoped that it would be just herself and the dogs, giving her some head space.

She put the leads on Bessy and Rosie before grabbing her coat, hat and scarf, quickly exiting the bungalow before the others disturbed her space.

They enjoyed a gentle stroll to the nature reserve, before she unhooked their leads to sniff and explore the place to their hearts' content. It wasn't long before she noticed that bully of a dog, Mr St Bernard, trotting briskly towards them. Her immediate instinct was to put their leads back on, lest he become frisky again.

'Oh, not you again,' Issy tutted under her breath, hoping his owner wasn't anywhere close by. She soon came stomping up, pleading with him to behave, clearly remembering their last encounter.

'Good morning, sorry, he's at it again,' she remarked with a sharp tone to her voice.

'Not to worry, my two are back on their leads, so no harm done this time,' Issy added, hoping she would pull him away by his collar.

Her phone buzzed. Seeing it was Amy, she thought it best to answer.

'Where are you and the dogs?' Amy bellowed down the phone, clearly panicking as to where they were.

'Good morning to you too, Sis, we're out on an early Sunday morning walk by the nature reserve. Tell Mum not to panic.'

'Phew, she told me to ring you, seeing they weren't in the kitchen and nowhere to be seen.'

'I'll be back soon.'

'No probs, I'll let her know. They suggested a meal at the pub later, to save anyone cooking today.'

'Sounds good to me, before our working week starts in earnest next week.'

'Absolutely, a lazy Sunday sounds like the perfect day. I'll ring the pub and book a table.'

Twenty minutes later Issy opened the door and saw Mum looking all dolled up, ready for Sunday roast at The Lion.

'You're looking lovely, Mum, off anywhere nice?' Issy pretended not to know about going to the pub.

'Amy told me we were going out for lunch, so I thought I'd make an effort, add a bit of lippy.'

'She did indeed and yes, I knew, Mum. A table has been booked for one o'clock.'

'Oh, you got me there, anyway I'm ready to go when your Dad is,' Mum added, smiling.

On arrival at the pub, seeing how it was jam-packed full, they weaved in and out, pushing and shoving, till they reached the bar.

'Hi, I've booked a table for four at one o'clock.' Issy raised her voice so he could hear her above the crowd. After a glance at his booking sheet, he confirmed the name.

'Can I get you any drinks before you eat? I do suggest you grab a table beforehand, as it's a bit busy at the moment,' he added.

'Four orange juices with ice please. I'll pop back with the table number in a while,' she replied.

'No need, I've found table number 10 in the middle by the fire,' Dad reported back after his search.

They followed him to the table, soon followed by a young woman with their drinks, who placed them down on the beer mats.

'Cheers to new beginnings,' Dad raised his glass as they met him in the middle.

They all wanted a roast dinner, so one by one they made their way to the carvery, where a choice of chicken, beef or lamb with seasonal vegetables was on offer. On another table was a selection of sauces, in little dishes with serving spoons; they helped themselves, then returned to the table, tucking in before it all went cold.

'Tomorrow is the big day, then, girls,' Dad added, feeling delighted for them.

'Definitely is, life will never be the same again, our next new chapter begins in the heart of the Cotswolds.'

'Who's for dessert?' Mum interrupted.

Looking at the menu, bread and butter pudding seemed a firm favourite and chocolate brownies with ice cream for the girls. A waitress noticed we had finished, coming over to collect our plates, taking our dessert orders.

They tucked into our desserts, all wanting coffees after, making the most of family mealtimes.

Once home, they took the dogs out, as they were itching to go for their walk, before settling down in the lounge for a game of Scrabble, their Sunday afternoon family pastime. This time they succeeded in beating Dad.

Chapter Twelve

Monday morning arrived, with the realisation that their lives were about to change for the better. Issy pulled the white cord on the rose-coloured blind, only to reveal a blanket of sharp frost covering the small lawn in the back garden. A chilly frosty morning was enough to send shivers down her spine. Why can't it be a bright spring morning instead, she thought, not being keen on winter mornings.

She had sorted out her clothes the night before, placing them neatly on her chair. She wanted to leave a lasting impression on everyone she met on her first day, staff and patients included. A quick glance in the mirror; she was happy with her outfit.

'Good morning, love,' Mum appeared in her burgundy dressing gown and slippers.

'The kettle is sitting on the Aga ready to make that all important first drink of the day. You're looking very smart, I must say, for your first day!' she added, giving Issy the once-over approval.

'Aww, thanks Mum, I thought I'd go for the casual look being more appropriate.'

'Now where's your sister? she asked. 'It's her first day at the vets, all very exciting.'

'I'm here, behind you, Mum, ready to face my first day at Rowans,' Amy announced as she walked into the kitchen.

'Tea everyone, or coffee?' Issy asked, as she took four mugs from the cupboard with the teapot, placing them on the table.

She made herself and Amy coffee, being their preferred beverage in the morning. Mum and Dad were having a leisurely breakfast later, after they had left. The dogs nudged her for theirs as she walked around.

'A quick reminder to walk the dogs later is all we ask,' Amy reminded her mum, before she bid her farewell, grabbing her coat and bag and key, walking out into the cold air to her car as Issy followed behind, being given a lift to the care home first.

'Have a lovely day, girls,' Mum added before getting on with her day.

'Good morning,' a young lady greeted Issy as she walked up to reception.

"Good morning. I'm Issy, on my first day as a care assistant,' she said, feeling a bit nervous, yet excited at the same time.

'Issy, welcome to Oak House, I hope you enjoy your stay with us. I'll buzz Trudy now. She'll show you around to meet everyone,' she explained, punching an extension number into her phone.

Within minutes Trudy appeared, equally casually dressed, stretching out her hand to greet Issy.

'It's a bit chilly this morning, come on in and meet all of us. I'll take you to the staff room first, show you your locker, and you can hang the key on a lanyard. I'll take a photo of you later for your ID card, identifying you as one of us.'

She showed Issy the essential tea and coffee making facilities and drawers and cupboards housing the crockery. There was a fridge for sandwiches and drinks for a quick snack and a pick-me-up during break times.

Issy removed her phone, placing her coat and bag in the designated red locker, as Trudy handed her a blue lanyard with the key on it. She then followed Trudy through to meet her new colleagues. Most were out on duty in the various areas, so they continued their tour into a lovely spacious lounge area, where most of the residents gathered during the day for meals and socialising.

Colleagues were only just wheeling patients in for breakfast, perfectly timed, so she would be able to get a good idea of their daily routines. Some were more mobile than others, able to walk over to their designated table to sit on one of the chairs.

Wheelchair users remained in their chairs for a meal. Some had a carer beside them if they needed help, which was now part of her job description, one she was truly looking forward to; something very rewarding by which she could give back to helping others in society.

Issy was paired up with an older lady, Freda, probably in her late seventies, with no real immediately obvious mobility issues; perhaps she had previously lived alone, her husband having died, no longer able to look after herself, so had she opted to make this her new home. She was a talkative soul, loving the company of others, making the day more bearable and special.

'Freda, this is Issy, your new helper for today. It's her first day here, she will become part of us, so please welcome her and be on your best behaviour!'

'Oh lovely,' she turned her head towards me.

'Welcome, Issy, to our crazy home, well not really, we're all very friendly here, Issy, you'll see,' Freda added with a chuckle, winking back at her, placing a hand on hers.

'Oh, I'm sure you all are, I'm really pleased to be here. You can tell me if I'm doing anything wrong, just let me know what you like or don't, we can then learn from each other, 'Issy replied, feeling more at ease, smiling back at her.

All was going according to plan, until Issy heard a lady shouting. She turned her head around, noticing a lady waving her arms about saying, 'Leave me alone,' giving Issy the impression she had dementia or something. She turned back to concentrate on Freda, not wishing to be alarmed by her actions.

'Oh, that sounds like Muriel, poor thing, she's got dementia, one of the older residents here. She's been here several years now, sadly has no local family I don't think, bless her,' Freda explained to her, helping her get to know everyone.

The breakfast staff came around, asking those who could understand what they wanted, a choice of cereal and toast and a lightly cooked breakfast, scrambled eggs with salmon or bacon or just a yoghurt for those who fancied it. A coffee machine offered a variety of coffees and hot water for tea. Everything seemed to run smoothly as they all tucked into their morning treats. Once breakfast was finished, those who needed to return to their rooms were escorted by a helper. Freda stayed with Issy, telling her about the next event of the day.

Today was craft day, a popular, lovely therapeutic day where everyone was shown simple tasks, such as colouring or creating a collage on paper, using different textured materials. There was something for everyone. A member of staff came round snapping pictures of their individual creations, later posting them on their social media pages. Advertising the care home helped outsiders choose the correct care home for their loved ones as they got older.

The day progressed well. Issy took an early lunch before helping patients with theirs, which was always a busy time. Today they were one staff member short, so it was all hands to the pump.

Issy took the opportunity to text Amy to see how her day was going.

All good here, plenty of dogs this morning, gets a bit noisy at times, just how I like it. See you back at the ranch. Amy fired one back in minutes, as she was probably on her break, too.

Five o'clock finally arrived, Issy was ready to go home, feeling exhausted, but in a good way. She definitely loved her new vocation in life, caring for others, giving something back to the world.

She decided to walk home, for some much-needed exercise and fresh air after being cooped up indoors all day. The fitter she became the better she would be with looking after the patients, was her initial thinking. She texted Amy, letting her know she was walking home.

Issy turned the key in the front door of the bungalow, to be greeted by two lively dogs, circling around her as if they hadn't seen her for hours, which was obviously the case.

'Anyone home?' she raised her voice, hoping someone had

heard her. The dogs followed her into the kitchen. She filled the kettle up for a cuppa, hoping Mum or Dad would soon walk in. She assumed they must have gone out so she made herself a lemon green tea. She let the dogs out; judging by their waggy tails, they were desperate to go out, making her think they hadn't been for a walk in hours. She sat down with her cuppa and pulled out her phone to give her mum a ring, hopefully she had her phone turned on. After a few rings, it went to voicemail, which started to concern her, hoping she was OK. No doubt she was with her friend Elaine, the widow, so she left it at that, not wanting to spoil her afternoon. Ten minutes later, Amy appeared behind her, sneaking in without her knowing, placing her hand on Issy's shoulder, making her jump.

'The nurse returns,' Issy teased, as she got up to grab another mug to make her a cuppa. 'Sit down and tell me all about your day, all the details, nothing left out,' she teased as Amy smiled back at her.

'Well, apart from it being very busy for a Monday, lots of dogs and a few cats meowing in their cages, all went swimmingly well.'

'Perfect, what about the staff, any dishy men I should know about, Sis?'

'Sadly no, they were all women, we'll see at the end of the week!' Amy added, feeling amused. 'Thanks for the tea, now if you're sitting comfortably, I will recall my day as it unfolded.'

'I was greeted by waggy tails when I opened the practice door. I walked up to the reception and announced my arrival. I was then taken to the back where I could dump my coat and bag in a locker in the staff room. I had an initial tour around the sick bay, where all dogs and cats were either recovering from their operations or were about to have one. Others had been brought in overnight, either having had an RTA or had been abandoned on the streets. All sorts came through those doors, so never a dull moment. That in a nutshell, sums up my day at the vets ... I loved it.'

'That makes us two happy girls.' They high-fived each other.

Amy's phone soon buzzed into life; seeing it was Dad, she answered it. 'Hi Dad, are you OK? Where are you? Issy and I are home now, we wondered where Mum was,' she questioned him.

'Mum is with her friend, Elaine, they went for lunch and a walk. I'll pick her up after my fishing trip with Jack on the lake. We caught a few lovely specimens. We won't need tea tonight, so suit yourselves, just you and the dogs.'

'Thanks for letting me know, we'll see you later. We will probably meet up with Lottie, take the dogs out.'

Amy rang Lottie on the off chance she was free. She soon messaged back, she could do with some company and would be over soon, with Floss.

Fancy a takeaway later, Mum and Dad have already eaten.

Perfect, see you in a mo. She fired one back.

Ten minutes having passed, Lottie was standing out in the front, with Floss wagging her tail in excitement.

'Hello, you two, let me grab the dogs and tell Amy you're here, then we can head out to the park,' Issy said, whilst putting the dogs' leads on as they raced through to greet her. 'Are you coming, Amy? The dogs and Lottie are waiting patiently.'

We soon walked out with all the dogs in tow. We leisurely walked off to the park, chatting about everything, then Lottie announced she had some exciting news to share.

'I've met a fella; a handsome chap, we dated last night!'

'You kept that one quiet, hence the spring in your step,' Issy looked at her with beady eyes, waiting for her to fill them in with any juicy details. 'This definitely calls for a take-away tonight or a drink somewhere, what do you say?' she asked, hoping Lottie would succumb to either.

'Well, it so happens I'm home alone, the rents have escaped to the country for a few days. It's their wedding anniversary, so I'm free and dog-sitting Floss, so pop over later for a Chinese.'

'Great, say six, as it's our first week in our new jobs, we can't make it a late night,' Amy said, conscious of the time.

They carried on walking until they met loads of dogs, deciding they'd turn back, avoiding any further confrontations.

Half an hour later they were back at the bungalow, where Mum and Dad had returned from their day out.

'We took these two out for a quick walk, met up with Lottie and Floss, who invited us over for a take-away tonight. Sam and Pete are away for a few days, so she's home alone, so we thought we'd pop over to have a girly night in. We won't be late as work calls us tomorrow,' Issy explained to Mum whilst she sat down having a cuppa.

'Lovely, don't worry about us, enjoy tonight, we'll take good care of the dogs,' she added as they made their quick exit.

Chapter Thirteen

They parked up outside Lottie's house a few streets away from Mum and Dad's bungalow. It was a lovely cottage, with a good-sized front garden with assorted plant pots on either side of the house. A wrought iron garden gate with a paved path led up to the red front door. Issy rang the bell, causing Floss to scamper and bark, announcing an unexpected guest.

'It's only me, Floss,' Issy bravely peered through the letter box, hoping Floss would sniff her out, realising she wasn't an intruder! Thankfully it did the trick.

'Welcome, come on in.' Lottie opened up, holding onto Floss's collar as she started to wag her tail in acceptance.

They were led into the newly updated kitchen, with all essential mod cons which included a lovely one-touch coffee machine, as they all loved their cappuccinos and hot chocolate. A menu for a Chinese restaurant was on the table for them to peruse, ready to place their order. They all chose a chow mein with chicken and cashews, and banana fritters for after. Lottie rang through the order to the restaurant, which was on the High Street. They collected it themselves.

'So, tell us about this handsome guy you met, who is he?' Issy tentatively asked whilst she started to dish out the food in equal portions. A portion of Chinese crackers was added to the yummy meal.

'George is his name, an old name I know, but he's young at heart. I met him at the local pub a month ago. He happened to sit next to me, we got chatting, as you do, and found out we have a few things in common. He asked me out on a casual date, surprising me, our friendship blossomed from there. We've been to the cinema and a few meals out since. George is two years older than me, and also loves dogs. He lives in the nearby village of Bilbury with his parents. I've not seen or met his parents yet! See how things develop, no hurry.' She gave them the rundown.

'Sounds great, clearly you have good taste in men, Lottie, keep going!'

'Love the chow mein, just what I needed. Who's for banana fritters and a cappuccino to follow?'

'Oh yes please,' they chorused together, loving the friendship they had developed over the years.

They watched Lottie operate the new up-market coffee machine, as she made three cappuccinos. Banana fritters with a scoop of vanilla ice cream ended the evening, all feeling satisfied.

'Well, we'd best get back, work awaits us in the morning,' Amy announced as they put our coats on to brave the cold evening air.

'I've got an interview too, so wish me luck. I'll spare you the details: another time,' Lottie added.

They embraced before walking to the car. 'Good luck, sleep tight.'

Lottie had been a bookworm from a child, deciding to follow her long-time dream to work in a library. She loved working alongside people from all different walks of life. At school she enjoyed English lessons, writing chapter summaries and writing short stories. Her imagination grew from strength to strength over the years, which she developed later on in life by completing a short online writing course, submitting her essays to a famous author, the course tutor, and on completion gaining a certificate with distinction. It proved the most satisfying hobby she had ever imagined embarking on, giving her lots of satisfaction.

A week before she had seen an advertisement in the window of a library she frequently walked past.

An assistant librarian is required to help set up our new computer system. A love of books is essential as well as interacting with members of the public. Apply within to start as soon as possible.

Lottie was clearly very interested, wanting to know more,

which could lead to other opportunities further down the line. She was subsequently offered an interview on Wednesday at 11am.

The morning of the interview Lottie made an effort to look her best, taking out a red block coloured dress and wearing a black pair of tights to keep warm. A bit of natural lipstick added to her chic look. She quickly let Floss out into the garden, kissing her smooth head, before she picked up her coat and bag and keys to walk out to the car. As it was only a few minutes up the road she could then do a quick food shop on her way home, making the most of her time home alone whilst her parents were out.

'Good morning, how can I help you?' asked the lady at the library.

'I'm here for the assistant librarian position for an interview at eleven o'clock. My name is Lottie, by the way.'

'Oh yes, we're expecting you today,' glancing at a sheet on the counter. She turned her head to see if she could see the lady she was looking for. Within minutes a tall lady walked over to greet her.

'Miss Higgins. Pleased to meet you, Lottie, thank you for coming in this morning. Please follow me through to my office where we can talk more, not wishing to disturb the readers.'

She opened her office door to a chaotic scene of books littered everywhere, piled up high from the floor. Her desk wasn't much better, with a two-tier filing system rack on one corner of her messy desk, with more paperwork on the other side, leaving little room for a cup of coffee!

'Sorry about the mess, I've only just taken over this office and haven't had any time to declutter yet, which is next on my to-do list. Please take a seat. I'm so sorry it looks like a mess in here,' she repeated, embarrassed. 'I'm on the case, so it should look a bit better by Friday! So what type of books do you like reading; romance, contemporary or a thriller? The choice is endless,' she wittered on, getting straight into the interview, trying to find out a bit more about what made Lottie tick.

'Oh, I prefer contemporary romance set in the country or a good series of them.'

'Favourite author?' she asked.

'Victoria Walters springs to mind, or Lisa Jewell. I love her latest mystery books, perfect to get stuck into.' Lottie concluded by giving her a wide selection of different genres of books.

'Good, that satisfies me that you definitely love your books, with a wide range of genres. Well, we are presently expanding our library here and currently installing a new updated computer system, which will hopefully be user friendly for our members too. That's where you come in. We need you to input our books; a booking system if you like, helping others get to grips with it. Shelving books when they are returned to us. Everything to do with being a librarian, basically,' she explained, making it sound easier than it probably was. 'Does that sound like something you could offer?'

Lottie swallowed hard as she took it all in, then nodded, listening as she rambled on. 'Yes, that all sounds very interesting,' she confirmed.

'Lastly, the hours are flexible, though generally 9 to 5 with a half hour lunch break. Like I said, it's a flexible team we operate here, we all muck in together,' she concluded, moving her chair back, getting up to show me to the door, noting the interview was over.

'I'll be in touch soon, Lottie, and thank you again for coming.'

Miss 'posh' Higgins stretched her hand out to grasp Lottie's, before she walked out with her head held high, giving the impression she was super confident.

'Bye for now,' a lady behind the desk said as Lottie walked past her to head out into the street. She turned around, giving her a smile.

After a quick food shop she was back home, before Floss got up to any mischief. She unpacked, putting everything away in its rightful place, until she was told otherwise when her parents returned, not knowing where things went. Her mum sent her a message, asking if everything was OK, to which Lottie replied that it was all good, and there was nothing to worry about. *Enjoy your stay,* she added. She would spare her mum the details until she had heard back from Miss Higgins.

The week progressed without any major issues. Both Issy and Amy soon acclimatised to their new jobs, enjoying the variety of tasks during the day. Lottie heard back from Miss Higgins on Friday, offering her the position in the local library, which she was thrilled about.

All felt good in the world until she had a disturbing message from her mum, Sam, saying her stepdad had taken a tumble whilst they were away. They were on a ramble along a coastal path when he tripped over a fallen branch, losing his footing. He fell backwards, causing minor bruising. Arnica cream would sort him right, Sam thought, so fortunately no lasting damage.

Hope you're both OK and enjoying your weekend despite Dad's mishap, more water needed lol, Lottie replied.

Mum replied: *We're back in our hotel where he's taking it easy and drinking lots of water!*

Issy and Amy made the most of their time with Lottie whilst she was home alone with Floss, needing their company too. After work they'd often arrange a pub night out or go to the cinema. *Wonka* was the latest, in which Rowan Atkinson's short role as a priest was always amusing to watch with popcorn. Lottie clearly divided her time wisely now she had George on the scene. She was pacing herself, not rushing into anything: time would tell if anything serious was going to develop.

Day three at the vets proved a busy one, as more dogs of various breeds invaded the place during the course of the day. Some were more lively than others: they screeched across the floor, either desperately trying to escape their fate, or just eager to sniff the others out in the waiting room. It was a dog lover's paradise, as their humans watched on, often in fits of giggles. Naturally, many came in feeling very poorly, some needing emergency treatment due to life-threatening injuries. There were sad cases where animals had to be euthanised, causing huge upset to their owners, which was the worst part of owning a pet, saying your final goodbyes. All pet lovers experienced the heartbreak of losing their furry companion one day.

Today was one of those tough days, as suddenly the practice door was pushed open. A young, injured dog was carried in by his owner, wrapped in a big blanket, shivering with shock after an RTA. A male vet rushed out to greet him and then hurried into his surgery. The door was firmly closed as he took a thorough look at the poor dog's injuries. Fortunately, this one had a lucky escape, just a broken leg, and after a month's rest at home, the dog made a good recovery. A happy ending for the dog and his owner that afternoon.

Life at Oak Place residential care home, however, carried on much as usual with their day-to-day routines, although no two days were ever the same.

Friday afternoon was a sing-along afternoon. A lady from a local choir came along, performing popular folk songs where everyone could clap and sing along, which they all loved. Musical shakers and hand-held tambourines were handed out, to add to the lively event. Music was a great form of therapy for them, especially for those who had Alzheimer's or a different form of dementia. Afternoon tea followed, with a variety of sandwiches and cakes and tea or coffee, satisfying everyone. A lovely afternoon's entertainment.

The day drew to a close at five o'clock; another successful week, time to have a relaxing weekend.

Amy's week, however, wasn't that straightforward; with two dog operations, an RTA and sadly having to send one over the rainbow bridge. Old age creeps on faster in dogs than in humans. That summed up a typical week in life at a vets' practice.

The weekend started with a much-needed long lie-in to recharge from the week just gone. Mum and Dad did the same until the dogs disturbed them, by whimpering by the back door in the kitchen, itching to be let out into the garden. The weather was fortunately on the change, warming up slowly, enabling the dogs to enjoy their outside space more, sniffing around, enjoying the scent of spring as the daffodils started to emerge.

As it was a reasonable hour Mum put the kettle on the Aga to boil, to make her first tea of the morning, time alone with the dogs, only to be distracted by Dad walking into the kitchen, never wanting to be left out of the picture, greeted by the dogs as they circled around him, nudging him for some attention.

Jodie got the mugs out and the teapot from the cupboard, placing two tea bags in, before pouring out for a welcoming brew.

'Good morning, lovely, did you sleep well?' he asked, looking at her with puppy eyes.

'Good, thank you,' handing him his tea in his retirement mug which he cherished from his carpentry days.

Just as he sat down Jodie's phone began to ring; although not recognising the number, she still answered it.

'Is that Jodie?'

'It might be, who's this please?' she pondered, wondering who would ring at this hour on a Saturday morning.

'You clearly don't recognise my voice, it's James, your long-lost brother!' he played along with her interrogations.

'Oh yes, of course it is,' teasing him, not really recognising his voice. 'So how are you, any juicy news at your end?'

'Well, if I do then I'd have to see you in person, so what are you doing this weekend? I'm in your neck of the woods with work, so I could pop in for a cuppa if that suits you? Sorry it's short notice.'

'Err, well,' hesitating, 'why not; go on then, it's been a while. Come for coffee, whatever suits you best, we are generally very flexible here,' Jodie added with a touch of excitement in her voice, eager to hear his latest news. He had either found a girlfriend or married and was expecting their first child, something on those lines, she thought. He was twenty-odd years younger, after all.

'Well, blow me, that was James, he's popping in to visit today. Not having seen him in a while sounds fishy to me!'

'Surely he can come over for no particular reason, love, is that not allowed?' Dad remarked.

'I suppose so, he's now trying to make up for lost time and why not, water under the bridge and all that, it's the here and now that matters most,' she added, feeling more comfortable in herself.

A few minutes later she got a text confirming his time of arrival, as he'd forgotten to mention it on the phone.

About eleven o'clock, if that's OK?'

Yes, that's fine, we look forward to seeing you at our new home. The postcode is: ST5 8LR for your satnav thingy machine!

'Well, that's our weekend sorted, never a dull moment in this house!' Dad remarked, secretly looking forward to the surprise visit. 'We had better get some cake and sandwiches in, I remember he loves his cake.'

Mum added cake to the shopping list on her app; everything these days was an app for this and that, pen and paper seemed definitely a distant memory, despite having everything in one place on your iPhone making life simpler.

She took a quick walk down to the local bakery just outside the village, recently opened, with a variety of homemade cakes; she chose a boxful to offer later. The clock had just struck eleven when the doorbell rang, announcing his arrival. Rosie raced to see who it was, barking as she went.

'I'm coming,' Jodie shouted as she followed Rosie to the front door, picking up her key from the table as she passed. She unlocked it to peer behind the slightly ajar door, seeing a tall, dark-haired man standing holding what looked like a bunch of flowers in one hand.

'It's only me, Jodie, James!'

'Oh yes of course, just a tick,' she said, opening the door to let him in.

'Well, and who have we here?' he said, pointing to Rosie, eager to bend down, unsure if she would like strangers.

'James, meet Rosie,' she introduced her, 'this is my brother James!' As if Rosie understood!

'Hello Rosie, you're lovely aren't you, can I stroke you?' looking at Jodie, asking her permission before he did.

'But of course, she loves attention!' she added, before taking the beautiful bunch of flowers from him.

'Oh, these are for you, Sis, hope you like them,' he added, leaning in to kiss her on the cheek.

'Oh, they are lovely, thank you, come on in and I'll put them in water,' she said, blushing, closing the door behind him as he viewed the hall.

'You've got a lovely bungalow. I assume you haven't been in long?' he asked, as he took his jacket off, giving it to her to hang on the coat stand.

'Only a few months now, we love it in our old age.' She smiled at him, noticing his big blue eyes and a small beard forming around his chin. He followed her into the kitchen, where the girls had finally gathered, casually dressed in their joggers and jumpers.

'Girls, meet my brother James.' Mum introduced him to them as he reached out his hand to shake theirs in turn.

'Take a seat, tea or coffee?' Amy asked, to take the role of mum.

'Oh, coffee if that's OK, I'm not a tea lover myself,' he added.

'I'll switch the coffee machine on. You can have an ordinary coffee or a latte or a cappuccino, it's up to you.'

'Oh, a cappuccino please, that's a treat.' James smiled at her. She placed a red mug under the spout and pressed the cappuccino picture to start the process. James eagerly watched her, intrigued how it all worked, sending coffee aromas wafting throughout the kitchen as it spurted out the freshly ground coffee followed by the frothy milk.

'Et voila!' She handed him the ready-made coffee, which he took in his hand.

'Thank you.'

"Enjoy,' she added, smiling back at him.

'Cake?' Mum asked, placing a variety of cakes on a plate in the middle of the table, giving out white plates and small forks with yellow paper napkins.

'So what's the news you were wanting to tell me?' Jodie asked, feeling rather nosy.

'Oh yes, I was coming to that one … I've met someone, Julie, we met a few months ago through an online dating site. We had a meal one evening, and it seemed to go well, so we went on a second date and things just blossomed from there. Three months later, we're still going strong,' James added, feeling chuffed with himself.

'Perfect, I'm pleased for you, if that's what you want, she sounds like a keeper. Good for you,' Jodie said, feeling more in the know.

'More coffee or cake?' she asked, after he had finished, placing his mug next to his plate.

'One for the road, I can't stay long as I'm meeting up with Julie later. We're off to the cinema, to see what's on! Lovely to see you, let's get together soon. I'll be in touch shortly, we can go out somewhere, or you come over to mine, bye for now, Sis.' He gave Jodie a hug before opening the door, pointing the car fob to unlock his four by four.

Chapter Fourteen

Monday morning came around too soon. Mum had loved James' surprise visit, despite it being short and sweet. Next time they would hopefully meet his new girlfriend, Julie, who sounded like a keeper. Amy and Issy approved of him, knowing he was a good brother to their mum.

'Good morning girls, here's to a new week, where anything can happen, it's a fresh start,' Mum said, as she walked into the kitchen and unlocked the back door to let the dogs out. There was a slight covering of an early morning frost on the lawn; seeing the dogs had imprinted their little paw marks, you could only imagine a crunchy noise as they trotted along.

'Any plans for you two today, the dogs would love a good walk? You don't neglect them, just saying.'

'A possible fishing trip for Jack and Dad, don't think he'll take them. I might meet Elaine for lunch, see how she feels, she didn't feel very well over the weekend. Reminds me, I must ring her later.'

'Well, enjoy your day and I'll see you later. Just text me if you need me, OK?'

'Will do, and you, bye for now.' She hugged Amy before she closed the door behind her.

On arrival at the practice, they had a quick staff chat about the week ahead as a few operations were planned; they never knew if there would be any RTAs coming through the door, each day was different, which made it more interesting. No sooner had Amy made herself comfortable behind reception for the morning shift than the doors flew open as people brought in their sick pets one by one, mainly cats and dogs with various ailments.

Amongst the people in the queue was Lottie, with her Floss, who fortunately only needed a check-up.

'Good morning, Lottie, a lovely surprise seeing you both this morning. What's Floss here for today? I'll take a check,' she said, tapping into the computer. 'Oh, here we go; a check-up with Steve, one of the vets here today. He's a locum while our regular vet is on leave. Please take a seat and he'll be out shortly,' she explained, as she did to all pet owners.

'Thank you,' Lottie replied, gently pulling Floss's lead to heel.

Minutes later, a lady stormed in with her little Westie dog snuggled up in her arms. She was clearly upset.

'Please can you help me, this one isn't feeling herself this morning, I think she's eaten something she shouldn't have,' she explained, fighting back tears.

'OK, don't worry, we're here to help. Can you tell me what happened? I'll need to take some details, before a vet can see her.' Amy had quickly noticed it was a girl.

'Your dog's name?' she asked.

'Poppy,' she replied, smiling back at her.

'Oh, I love that name.' Amy tried to distract her.

'Aww thanks,' she added, feeling less panicked by the situation.

A few minutes later she was checked over by Steve, the locum vet, who gave her an injection to help. The customer had only been in there a few minutes, but had a bit of a shock on seeing the bill, once Amy gave it to her to pay. *That's vets for you*, she thought, after seeing her reaction.

'Thank you for your help earlier, sorry I panicked,' the owner added, feeling grateful for Amy's patience.

'You're very welcome, I know how upsetting these situations can be. They're our much-loved pets after all. All the best,' Amy replied as she walked towards the door.

Amy enjoyed being receptionist for the morning until she swapped hats in the afternoon, looking after recovering animals after their procedures. She received ongoing training alongside a veterinary nurse, making sure the animals had their medications, keeping a diary during the day. This part of the job was the hardest, yet the most rewarding one, watching their recovery.

The day continued running smoothly until five o'clock when her shift came to an end and the evening staff took over. A number of patients were discharged after the vet had been fully satisfied with their progress, to recover further at home in their own environment. Their owners came to collect them, sometimes accompanied by their children or grandparents. It was always good to see the whole family getting involved, often bringing a tear to her eye.

Her last task of the day was to do a handover to the evening receptionist, making her life easier. It was a satisfying feeling knowing they didn't have to muddle their way through, not knowing where the last person had left off, leaving them frustrated. It was Amy's responsibility to leave the desk clear of clutter so the next person felt ready to start her shift from a clean sheet. Amy didn't fancy any backlash the morning after: her motto was always to do a job well.

'See you in the morning, I hope your shift goes well,' was her usual reaction before she left the building.

She felt confident and held her head up high, knowing she had done her best for the animals and everyone who walked through the practice doors.

Back at the bungalow all seemed calm. Mum and Dad had been out doing their individual pursuits. Jack came over, all ready to set off on a fishing trip with Dad. Elaine popped over to take Mum out for a day trip around the National Trust Cotswold Wildlife Park and Gardens in Burford. Looking on their website they also had a variety of animals, giraffes, buffaloes and zebras, amongst others. A perfect day out for them, knowing Mum would love that and ending the day in a tearoom. They all sat around the kitchen table, reminiscing later with plenty of stories to tell.

Issy had had a full day at the care home, another craft day, making cards from discarded old ones, cutting and sticking on various coloured cards. A lovely selection of cakes and sandwiches had been the perfect ending to a long day.

'Which animals did you prefer, Mum?' she asked, eager to know how her day had gone.

'All of the animals were lovely, especially the giraffes with their beautiful markings and elongated necks. We were very lucky with the weather, too, it stayed dry, with the sun eventually appearing from behind the clouds.'

'A good day then, with best friend Elaine! What about you, Dad, another good catch?'

'Definitely, a couple of huge pikes, beautiful scales, both weighing in at 40 pounds.' He showed her the pictures to prove his catch, not that she disbelieved him!

Just then her phone buzzed on the table. She noticed it was from the estate agent. Feeling excited she accepted the call, hoping it would be good news.

'Good afternoon, it's Trudy from the estate agents. I've been asked to update you on your house in question. I'm delighted to tell you that all the surveyor's reports have been successfully completed. Everything has been signed off, which means you can now arrange a moving-in date with an assigned removal company. We highly recommend Jason from The Big Move Company. They are local to this area, on the industrial estate. I'll email their details to you, to take a look at. May I congratulate you both and wish you every success as you move into your new home. It's a very beautiful, well-kept place, Mrs Roberts has done you proud. She moves out in a week's time on a Friday, the usual exchange day these days. Please don't hesitate to ring me once you have fixed a moving in date. Jason is the guy in charge, he is a very pleasant man. Good luck.'

She ended the call on a high.

'Issy, that was the estate agent … we can move in within the next week or so. She sent me an email with a removal company's contact, we just need to phone them to confirm a moving in date,' Amy told her excitedly.

'Wow, that's the best news today ... we're getting our own place soon, Sis.' Issy joined her in the kitchen after giving the dogs some much-needed attention.

"We just need to sort out a date with Jason, the guy who runs the company, then it's all systems go. We need to take Friday off work, as we then have all weekend to move in,' Amy added, giving her the heads up.

Within minutes Amy was on the phone to the company and they agreed to move in on Friday week. All furniture was stored in Mum and Dad's garage, ready to be placed on the van. The rest they could buy in slow time. The main thing was they would have moved in. Time to pack their suitcases, leaving a few essentials at the bungalow to sleep over. The next few days were going to be busy, yet the most exciting time in their lives.

Chapter Fifteen

The date and time had been confirmed in writing from the removal firm, so now it was all hands to the pump, all systems go as the big day was ever drawing closer. A sense of overwhelming excitement was definitely in the air, very little else was talked about over the next week.

Amy and Issy started writing lists to remind themselves what they needed, not forgetting anything important. One list for clothes to pack, another for all and sundry. Essentially it wasn't rocket science, just ticking off the jobs once completed … easy really, or was it? They would soon find out.

'This is it, we're actually on the move, the day has finally come.' Issy high-fived Amy after they had compiled their to-do lists.

Mum and Dad soon realised something was going on, hearing the screams of joy echoing around the bungalow.

'So, what's the happy news, girls?' Mum asked, as she walked into the kitchen, filling the kettle up for their morning cuppa.

'Well, we've just heard the surveyor's report that our house has been successfully completed and we can move in a week on Friday. I have arranged everything with the removal company, so all systems go now, Mum … we're moving out, giving you your home back again. We might need to sleep over a few nights until we've moved in completely. We are grateful to you both for everything for letting us stay here.'

'Oh, don't be silly, you're family. We are always here to help whilst we still can!' Mum added, blowing us a kiss.

Our next evenings and weekend were now taken up with packing after packing, until we were satisfied that we had packed all the essentials to the rafters. The weather was improving all the time as the spring made its appearance; daffodil bulbs and other flowers sprouting, such a lovely change being back in the warmer months again.

Issy had a few extra shifts as staff either took their leave or fell sick. This obviously proved very handy financially as the move became imminent. Issy's patient, Freda, also preferred her regular helper as she got to know her individual needs and quirks during her time working there, suffering from dementia.

'Any news from James and Julie?' Amy asked her, hoping they could meet up with them soon.

'Nothing yet,' Mum replied, hoping he would get in touch soon.

James lived in the town of Burford in the beautiful county of West Oxfordshire, along the River Windrush. Mum had gone there with Elaine to view the gardens the other day. Mum only found out later that James lived there. He was an accountant who set himself up in business, travelling around the surrounding areas to clients. Julie, however, worked in a nearby florist's. She was a very practical person in her craft, arranging beautiful flowers for all occasions.

'Anyone fancy a walk? The dogs need exercise. As it's a sunny day we could go to the arboretum, have an ice cream from Mr Whippy, if he's there today.'

'I'll join you both, I could do with a walk myself,' Mum put her hand up, as if she was back at school!

The park was full of people ambling around, some with their dogs, others with their children playing in the designated play area with a wooden climbing frame with tyres hanging down, ready to be sat in and swung around. There was something for everyone, benches for the adults to sit and chat, generally passing the time whilst watching their kids enjoying themselves.

They spotted Mr Whippy from afar and headed towards the van with the dogs in tow, each wanting a 99 before the machine ran out. Rosie and Bessy had a small tub too, lapping up the vanilla ice cream whilst they devoured theirs.

They eventually went home, deciding to have a takeaway, pizza night to celebrate the news of the house, before a more official move-in later in the month after they had settled in. They played a quick game of Scrabble before retiring to bed.

The day of the move had finally arrived. Their phone alarms were set for 6.30am, leaving them plenty of time to get ready, have breakfast and think about anything they had missed off their checklists. There was nearly always something that been forgotten or left out. The Big Move Company was due at eight o'clock, ready to load up from the garage where they had stored the furniture from the various antique stores. It was then out of their hands how the van was packed. Each item was wrapped in bubble wrap to ensure less damage en route to the new abode. Mum and Dad had come down a bit earlier to look after the dogs, so they wouldn't become confused by the day's events.

The doorbell rang bang on eight o'clock, alerting the dogs as they scampered across towards the hall. Mum unlocked the door, seeing a tall dark, handsome man in blue overalls dressed for the job.

'Good morning, my name is Jason, from Big Move. Here to move Amy and Issy,' he explained, confusing Mum slightly.

'Oh yes, they are my daughters. They are eagerly expecting you.' Mum smiled at him, noting his brown eyes. She looked over her shoulder to see Amy coming to her rescue.

'Mum, this is Jason, he's going to move our furniture today to our new house. I need you to look after the dogs today, please.'

'Yes, I know who he is, he just told me, and we'll take good care of the dogs, so don't worry, OK? We will have lots of fun together,' Mum reassured her, clearly looking forward to her time with them. She returned to the kitchen with the dogs leading the way, leaving Amy and Issy to get on with the move.

Mum had clicked the garage door fob to open, so Jason and his two colleagues could start to move the furniture into the van.

'Thank you, I'm Jonathan, by the way.' He stretched out his hand, giving Amy a firm shake.

'Hi, I'm Amy and this is my sister, Issy. It's our first house move and we're super excited.'

'Lovely, please ask us anything today, we're here to make your move as smooth as possible,' he reassured them. 'OK, right, let's get this move started. Any chance of a cup of tea? We've just come from our depot, it's a bit further away.'

'Absolutely, I'll get that going while you make a start on the garage. So, two teas with milk and sugar?' Issy asked.

'Just milk for us, thank you.'

'Perfect, coming right up.'

Issy made the teas in old mugs, as Amy supervised the transferring of furniture into the van. All was going to plan until a loud meow was heard from the garage, alerting them that something was amiss.

'Oh, I know, it's the black and white cat from next door. She's clearly found her way in and is snuggled up on a rug at the back of the garage. She's meowing loudly, I'm thinking she's hungry and wants to be reunited with her owner. I'll try and pick her up. Good job I work at the veterinary practice, we have cats come in every week, curled up in their small crates,' Amy announced, seeing a glimpse of black fur.

Just at that moment, Issy came back with the teas, which were to their liking, with enough milk! She also brought in a plate of digestives to keep them going.

'Perhaps I could tempt her with a bit of a digestive, before you start moving the furniture. We don't want to scare her even more,' Amy suggested while handing over their teas.

'Good idea, you clearly know your stuff, give me a shout once you've safely rescued her. We'll have our tea now,' Jason smiled back at her.

She slowly approached the meowing cat, holding out a small bit of digestive in her hand to entice her. The cat uncurled herself and did a quick cat's cowl yoga pose, before moving in slowly towards her, sniffing out the biscuit, deciding it was OK to investigate further. Amy was getting ready with her arms stretched out to grasp her, holding her in her arms like a baby, supporting her under her bottom. She was now out of danger, safely snuggled up in her blanket in Amy's arms, purring to thank her. She decided to take her back to her humans across the street, in another bungalow with pretty borders in front of the small garden.

She rang the doorbell and soon heard steps to open it.

'Yes, can I help you?' An old woman with a wrinkled face appeared from behind the door, looking a bit frail.

'I found this cat in my parents' garage across the way, I believe she belongs to you, noting the number on the disc on her collar,' Amy said, feeling a bit concerned.

'Oh, my Smokey, she's been missing for a few days now, I thought she'd turn up again soon, where did you find her?' she asked, relieved to see her again.

'She was in my mum's garage hiding, must have sneaked in. She's safe now, which is all that matters.'

'Yes, thank goodness, she is, thank you again. She's my baby.' She winked at me, smiling.

'My name is Maggy, I've lived here over 30 years now, so I guess I'm part of the street! she chuckled with a slight snort. 'I haven't met your parents though, are they new around here?'

'They've only just moved in this year, so it's all new to them.' She pointed to their bungalow across the way.

'Well, I'd best go now and give the movers a hand, my sister and I are moving out today to our new house. It was lovely meeting you, Maggy, and I'm glad Smokey is back safe with you again.' Amy waved goodbye as she crossed over the road.

'Hope all goes smoothly for you both, see you soon.'

No sooner had Amy walked back, than the garage had been emptied of all the furniture, neatly stored in the van, to be delivered shortly to the new house. They were given the heads up, so Amy and Issy jumped into their red Polo to drive the short distance to the house.

'Oh, this is so exciting, Issy, belt up, here we go!' Amy turned and smiled, giving her the thumbs up.

They arrived in good time before the van parked on the street by their new home, where they waited for someone from the estate agent to hand over the keys. They sat patiently in the car, becoming increasingly anxious by the moment. It seemed like the longest ten minutes of their lives as they stared out of the window, the sun blinding them occasionally.

A horn announced the arrival of the lorry, then five minutes later a car pulled up behind theirs. They looked at each other, holding hands, knowing this could be the lady who would hand over a bunch of keys.

A slim tall lady dressed in a smart navy blue suit placed one foot out of the car, straightened herself up and locked the car before she walked towards their car. Amy depressed the notch to wind down the window as she approached.

'Good morning. I'm Tracy from the estate agent with the keys for your new house. I assume you are Miss Stevens?' she asked, whilst Amy opened the car door to step out and shake her hand.

'Oh yes, pleased to meet you and thank you for driving over this morning.'

'You're welcome. If you could just scribble on my iPad saying you received the keys from me, then that's all completed.' She handed me her iPad and Amy scribbled her signature on the screen.

'Perfect, and these are for you too,' handing her a small bunch of keys and a beautiful bouquet of flowers with a box of Roses chocolates.

'Oh, that's very kind of you, they are beautiful, the chocolates will go down well too, thank you,' she added, smiling at her as she walked up to her car.

Within a few hours, after all the furniture had been finally placed in the house, it began to feel like the cosy home they could call their own. They would add to it as the weeks went by, but for now they could just enjoy their new space. They had Mrs Roberts to ultimately thank for leaving the house well decorated, so that they could just move in. After walking into the kitchen, they found a white envelope addressed to them lying on a worktop by the sink. It read:

Dear Amy and Issy,

I hope your move went as smoothly as possible without any major hitches and you can now call this place your own home. I hope you will be happy and have many friends around over the years. It was lovely to meet you both.

Please accept this bottle of fizz to celebrate your new home.

To your health and happiness,
Best wishes,
Muriel Roberts xx

'Oh, look at this, Issy, she's left us a sweet card with roses on the front and a bottle of fizz, how touching is that?' Amy read it aloud, hoping Issy was in earshot.

'That's so special, she really didn't have to do that.' Issy came over to see for herself.

'Perhaps we can find out her address to send her a thank you card too. I'll ask the estate agent if they could forward her address to us.'

Chapter Sixteen

They spent their first night in their new home. Jason and Jonathan had kindly assembled the bed frames in their chosen bedrooms. They had chosen a floral design duvet set with a cream-coloured bottom sheet. Tomorrow they would continue sorting out the rest and moving furniture into its desired location. They then stepped back, admiring their efforts.

'We're in, we did it, Sis!' Issy high-fived Amy, feeling so proud of themselves.

'It's the best feeling isn't it, lovely! How exciting,' Amy added, taking charge of the situation, with a huge smile on her face.

'Onwards and upwards!' Issy said, feeling elated.

It was all about firsts. Their first breakfast, coffee and cake, a meal later and so it continued, until firsts became many. A routine was soon adopted, letting the dogs out before they both left the house for work. Mum offered to have one or both to start with, before a good routine was well established. Both enjoyed their company until Mum became ill one day, or needed her space, finding it too difficult to cope with them. That was life, it changed all the time, and they all needed to adjust. Work continued pretty much as normal with their busy schedules. Once home, they either did a weekly online shop or went to Morrisons up the road, until they established what worked best for them.

A few weeks passed and they decided to have a moving in party with family and friends, a low key gathering where everyone could share their new home. They started to make a list of people they wanted to invite, comparing their lists at the end. The list grew and grew, until they were forced to limit the numbers, otherwise they would feel squashed like sardines.

'I'll make us a drink and we'll sit down and chat about who to invite, we also don't want someone to be left out who should be here, Amy.'

'Absolutely, immediate family followed by our best friends. We can't please everyone after all, can we? These occasions always prove very difficult,' she added.

She placed two mugs of coffee on coasters on the kitchen table with a slice of lemon cheesecake each.

'I'll read mine out, and you can tell me what you think after,' Issy told Amy.

'Here's mine:

> Mum and Dad and the dogs
> Sam and Pete
> James and Julie
> Elaine
> Jack, Dad's fishing mate

'Now mine,' Amy continued:
> our friends
> Lottie and Grace
> George if he's still on the scene!

'Well that sounds about right, the house won't feel overcrowded, giving everyone space to mingle around.' Amy looked at both lists approvingly.

'Now we just have to sort out the date and time. We can message them instead of invites, keeping it on a budget; the food and drink being the most important one.'

'Absolutely, so let's say next weekend, hopefully that's not too short notice, if many can't make it, then the weekend after.'

'One problem, I don't know everyone's number. We'll have to ask Mum and Dad to tell James, Elaine and Jack. We can text Lottie to tell Grace. The dogs don't need messaging, lol.'

'Very funny,' Amy smiled, feeling amused.

Just at that moment, Issy's phone buzzed beside her as she picked up her coffee mug to drain the last drops. Placing it down again, she recognised the incoming number.

'Mum, I was just about to ring you, you beat me to it.'

'Great minds!' she giggled down the line. 'We wondered if you were both OK, it's so quiet without you two. You bring life into our bungalow.'

'Aww, well, it's our turn to host now. So next weekend we are holding our first party here, you're both invited. We thought we would invite James, if he's around, with Julie. Mum, can you ask Elaine please, and Dad can ask Jack. How does that sound?' Issy continued, hoping they would agree to it all.

'That sounds perfect to me, I'll see what James says. I think he would love to see where you both live now. Time has moved on, so we are all good friends now. So, let's be clear on the day, Friday or Saturday? I think Saturday would be better, as work has then finished for the week?' Mum asked again.

'Saturday it is, then, if you could let them know please, say seven o'clock.'

'Don't panic, I'm on the case straight away while it's fresh in my mind. I'll come over with Dad once we have answers,' Mum concluded before hanging up.

They decided to take it in turns to check up on the dogs in their individual lunch breaks, knowing it wasn't the best idea to leave them with their parents, they were their responsibility after all. Besides, Mum and Dad had their own independent lives to lead, as they were getting older too. What if they forgot to let the dogs out, or worse, one or both fell ill, the ultimate responsibility would be on the girls themselves. It was a risk they couldn't afford to take. They were satisfied they would soon get used to their new surroundings, claiming them as their own.

Monday morning soon came around, waking up in their new house. Pulling the blind up by the bedroom window to reveal a small, yet beautiful garden, with daffodils and snowdrops sprouting up everywhere, a delightful sight. Spring had definitely sprung. That overwhelming feeling that they could finally call this place their home was the best ever.

Issy sneaked downstairs to open the kitchen door, hoping to find two pooches curled up in their fluffy beds.

She slowly opened the door ajar, peering around it, only to find two beady eyes looking straight back at her; clearly they must have heard her tiptoeing down the stairs.

'Well, hello there my lovelies, let's get you both outside!' She opened the door wider to be greeted by two excited waggy-tailed girls. She opened the back door for them to dash out.

As per routine she filled the kettle up for a refreshing green tea, being health conscious, knowing it did wonders for the soul. She watched from the window as the dogs sniffed around the garden, as they raced around and jumped about. She always enjoyed seeing their energetic sense of adventure, like children, and all that was before their breakfast.

'Good morning Issy,' Amy sneaked in from nowhere. Issy was miles away in her own little world.

'Oh, morning Sis, you made me jump! I was just watching Rosie and Bessy enjoying their new space in the garden. I was impressed not to be greeted by any puddles, being their first morning in the house.'

'Clearly, yes, they have settled in nicely. Going to work and leaving them is the next challenge. I've got a good feeling though they'll be happy keeping one other company.'

The week continued pretty much as normal, the only difference being that they took it in turns to nip home in their lunch hour to check up on the dogs. After two days they had settled in well. They gave Mum a key so they enjoyed popping in, taking the dogs back to theirs, especially if the girls were going to be late home. They enjoyed their company on days when they had nothing planned, reassuring them they were well looked after.

Mum left sticky notes in the kitchen, updating them who was coming to the party.

James and Julie are looking forward to seeing you, one of her notes read, placed on the counter-top. Dad heard from Jack, who felt it wasn't his place to impose on a family occasion, so he bailed out this time. He lived alone after his wife died, finding socializing slightly awkward, which was totally understandable, despite their trying to convince him to come.

Sam had texted Mum, saying she and Pete would be delighted to come: after all they had been best friends since they were at primary school, an added bonus of Pete appearing on the scene much later on.

The day of the party was fast approaching, everyone was getting excited for the big day. All food bought, cakes ordered from the coffee shop down the road, to be delivered Saturday morning. A buffet was laid out in the kitchen, using any clear space available. They placed crockery with plates and paper napkins ready for a feast. Assorted sandwiches and nibbles with a dish of dips for crackers with thinly sliced carrot and celery sticks. They had a variety of different pizzas which were to be placed in the oven, once all the guests had arrived.

Time for a quick change into a smart yet casual look, before the bell announced their guests' arrival. A quick glance in the mirror adding a bit of natural glossy lippy, they were satisfied with their look.

'Ready Issy, five minutes to go before our guests arrive, setting the dogs off in a wild frenzy,' Amy shouted upstairs as Issy rushed downstairs to do any last-minute preparations.

'On my way, Sis,' she replied, greeted by two excitable hounds once downstairs, as if they knew something was about to happen.

The first to arrive were Mum and Dad. They rang the doorbell twice, knowing that was their secret code, announcing it was them.

'Good evening you two strangers, come on in, you're the first to arrive, to be followed by others shortly, we hope,' Amy added, feeling hopeful. Rosie and Bessy soon heard the commotion as they raced towards them, nearly knocking Mum off balance.

'I'll go into the kitchen and help myself to a soft drink, if that's OK.' Mum was eager to make herself scarce, as she probably didn't want to be seen by the rest as they arrived. They preferred to be in the background, not known as Amy and Izzy's mum and dad.

Another knock on the door: it was Sam and Pete, followed by Lottie and Grace.

'George couldn't make it tonight, a work social do, which had been arranged months ago, he sends his apologies.'

'Never mind, next time. We can always go for a meal together soon,' she reassured her with a smile. 'Go on through to the kitchen and help yourselves to a drink!'

Moments later, James and Julie appeared, both looking dapper in their attire. Fortunately, no one was overdressed, which was always their concern, leading to embarrassment.

'Well, I think that's everyone, so let's get this party started,' Issy suggested, feeling enthusiastic.

Everybody gradually made their way into the kitchen, after hanging their coats on the coat stand in the hall. Some brought a plastic bag with a change of shoes for comfort and to save the carpet from becoming mucky. Mum initially played host, offering a variety of soft drinks or a glass of wine, to anyone who dared to be first in line. A few brought a bottle of wine or ground coffee for after, so they were definitely well catered for. Once everyone had their desired drink in hand, Issy stood aside to clap her hands, drawing their attention, as she spoke a few words. All eyes soon focused on her.

'A few words before we start. Thank you for coming this evening, we appreciate it. We are naturally very excited to call this place our first home, hence the reason we wanted to share it with all of you; our family and friends. So, with no further ado, I pronounce this party open, enjoy,' Issy uttered, initially feeling a bit jittery, soon relaxing into her speech.

Everyone clapped, lifting their drinks up saying, 'To Amy and Issy and Rosie and Bessy, to happy times.'

The party soon started as all mingled around the buffet table, helping themselves to anything they fancied. Meanwhile Amy took the pizzas out to place in the oven, adding to the variety on offer. Once cooled, she placed them on wooden boards to cut into equal slices for people to help themselves.

Issy and Amy mingled around making conversation with everyone, catching up on the latest gossip. The dogs behaved, returning to their beds after everyone gave them attention, and getting bored.

Issy and Amy retired into the lounge, noticing Julie sitting on the sofa, looking a bit tired.

'Julie, lovely to finally meet you. How's life with you and James?' Issy asked, trying to get a conversation started.

'Oh, hi Issy, yes, we're both OK thanks. It was a bit of a trek this morning from Cambridge, the traffic wasn't on our side, still, we're here now, which is all that matters. Lovely home you have here, you must be so proud of yourselves, 'she added, fending off a tear in one eye. Issy assumed it was for happy reasons.

'Yes, we are, thank you. I'm so pleased your mum has finally connected with James, it's never too late, is it, life is too short and all that,' Julie added, smiling.

'It is indeed, and yes Mum is thrilled to find her long-lost brother, Dad feels the same.'

'Can you keep a secret?' changing the subject as she moved in a little closer, so others wouldn't pick up on anything.

'Your secret is safe with me, I won't even tell Amy or Mum,' Issy reassured her with a slight tap on her knee.

'Thanks, well I'm expecting, only a few weeks, so early days and we are delighted.'

'Oh, that's fantastic news, Julie,' trying to keep her excitement under wraps, away from prying ears.

At that moment James walked over, noticing Issy was sitting beside Julie. 'Is everything OK here, girls?' he asked tentatively.

'It is, we're just catching up,' Julie winked at him.

James continued walking over to Mum and Dad, who looked a bit fed up, probably equally tired.

'So, when is the baby due? Any preference to a boy or girl, not that you have any say in that?' Issy questioned.

'Not sure yet, my scan is next week, a girl would be lovely, they do seem easier, they say. I've already thought of a name; Heidi or Steven!' she smiled, looking so happy.

'Oh, how lovely, both great names. We wish you both all the very best, Julie, it will be lovely to have a little one in the family. Mum and Dad will be auntie and uncle!

"We want to keep it a secret until we've had our first scan, I'll be 25 weeks then,' Julie added, placing her right hand lightly on her tummy, looking to see if anyone had noticed.

'You'll be fine,' Issy added, before she moved on to others. She wandered over to Mum, who was taking a breather from everything, needing a bit of space.

'You seem lost in your own little world, Mum, not that's it's a problem. It's an evening of relaxation now, I'll go and make some coffee in a mo.' Issy sat next to her, trying to perk her up a bit.

'Oh, thank you, that will be welcome I'm sure. It's Elaine I'm worried about, she hasn't arrived yet. I hope she's OK, Issy?' finally telling me what was bothering her, as I knew something was playing on her mind.

'Of course, I entirely forgot she hadn't turned up. Do you think you should ring her, Mum? Best check and see how she is for peace of mind,' Issy reassured her.

Mum took her phone out of her pocket, scrolled down her contacts to find the number, which she clicked on without hesitation. After six rings, Elaine finally picked up.

'Elaine, it's Jodie, are you OK? I thought you were coming to the girls' housewarming party tonight?' she asked, as she sounded a bit sleepy.

'Oh, sorry, I totally forgot, I'm not feeling my best today, I think I've got a cold coming on,' she continued, sounding a bit low.

'Oh dear, never mind, rest well and we'll meet up soon,' Mum concluded before hanging up.

'I heard that, at least you're in the know now, you can relax now and enjoy yourself again.'

'Thanks, Issy, now where's that coffee you were offering?' Mum chuckled cheekily.

'Coming right up,' as Issy got up to stretch to walk towards the kitchen. Mum had brought a second cafetière from hers, so Issy spooned the already ground coffee she made at home, equally into them, before pouring water into them, to settle for a few minutes. Amy came in; seeing her making up the cafetières, gave her a helping hand. She got four mugs from the cupboard, placing them on a tray, carrying them into the lounge, Issy followed with the coffee and a milk jug. 'Here you go, coffee as you like it,' placing a mug down beside her.

'Thank you love, 'Mum added, feeling more alert after taking her first sip.

'Where's Dad gone? He's mingling, I guess, he loves a good chat. Shame Jack isn't here today, I can understand how he might feel like an outsider, but he is now a big part of Dad's life, bless him.'

'Right, I'd better ask if anyone else wants coffee, see you later Mum.'

A few moments later James spotted Mum sitting on her own, looking as if she needed company. Issy had whispered to him earlier to keep an eye on her. It was a chance to rekindle their relationship again after many years being separated.

'Jodie, how are you doing? I thought I'd best come over and chat to you before the evening passes us by.' He sat down next to her on the new plush sofa.

'Well, if I'm honest I feel a bit out of my depth here, it's me getting old, seeing these youngsters hanging out with each other. Still, I'm not complaining, our girls turned out well and they are enjoying life, which is all that matters. Oh to be young, free and single, as they say, life soon changes once you settle down and you get married and have a family. Twenty years later, you're back to being on your own again. Life turns around full circle.' James listened with interest.

'So, tell me, how's life treating you, James?' Mum asked inquisitively.

'Well, life is good at the moment, my job is going well and Julie and I are enjoying one another, too. So we're all good, thanks.' He successfully avoided mentioning she was expecting, until after their first scan.

The evening was drawing to a close, Mum and Dad being the first ones to leave, thanking them for a lovely evening, hoping they would see one another over the weekend. Their usual dog walks and a cuppa sprang to mind.

'Thanks for coming and helping us out with the move, we couldn't have done it without you both.' Amy gave them a hug before sending them on their way.

'That's what we're here for, girls,' Mum and Dad said in unison.

Both dogs got the vibe that they were about to leave, as they rushed into the hall so they could be in on the act, hoping to get stroked, which they were.

Sam and Pete soon followed behind them with Lottie and Grace in tow. James and Julie helped to clear up, taking coffee mugs into the kitchen, as Issy started to load up the dishwasher. Amy followed with empty plates, discarding food into a bin bag, generally clearing up and bringing back a bit of order into the home, rather than face it on Sunday morning, never a good idea. The rest could wait till the morning as it was getting late for James and Julie.

'You are very welcome to stay over, start your journey afresh after two cups of coffee in the morning. One can sleep on the sofa, the other on a blow-up bed I borrowed from Mum and Dad's loft. They'll never know or use it again, those days have long gone,' Issy added, trying to make it easier for them.

'Well, that's a lovely thought, it's a long trip home, if you are really OK with that.'

'Absolutely, I wouldn't have suggested it otherwise. I'll get the blow-up bed and put it in the lounge, if you could blow it up, I haven't got enough puff!' At that moment Julie appeared looking exhausted, so she welcomed the offer to sleep over.

'That's so kind of you both, really appreciate it, Issy. We'll leave after a coffee in the morning. I'll take the sofa,' as she plumped up the cushions to get comfortable. James checked the car, bringing back a blanket he had in case he ever broke down, so Julie could feel cosy on the sofa.

'The bathroom is upstairs on the left,' Issy added before wishing them goodnight.

Amy let the dogs out for a final pee, before they ran back in and snuggled up in their cosy beds. It was now nearly midnight before they made their way upstairs to bed themselves, a long but successful party had by all.

Chapter Seventeen

Sunday morning soon came around despite feeling a bit weary, still a coffee and a healthy breakfast would fix that, Amy thought, as she rolled out of bed, put her house shoes on then slipped on a pair of her flowery joggers, to prepare breakfast and to let the dogs out.

The sun was just appearing from behind the clouds from the east, which was a good sign. Issy filled the kettle to boil, making them filter coffee in the cafetière.

'Good morning, Amy, I hope you both slept well,' Julie walked into the kitchen all dressed, ready for the day ahead.

'Morning Julie, coffee and a fried egg on toast?' Issy gestured.

'Oh, yes please, that sounds perfect, thank you,' as she took a seat at the table, stroking the dogs as they made a beeline towards her, wanting some love.

Issy put the cafetière on the table, placing 4 mugs alongside, ready to be poured out. Julie played mum, soon to be one herself!

'How do you like your eggs in the morning?' Issy asked, coining the phrase.

'Oh yes, ha ha, fried for us if that's still on offer,' she chuckled.

'Absolutely is, help yourself to coffee, just press the plunger, it should be strong enough now.' Issy turned to get eggs from the fridge, before taking a frying pan out and olive oil, ready to cook.

She placed two slices of brown bread in the toaster, ready to serve the eggs on top.

'Morning, lovely,' James sneaked up from behind, giving Julie a kiss on the lips.

'Oh, you made me jump, James, Issy made coffee and a croque Madame is on its way.'

'A what? That's foreign language to me!' he replied questioningly.

'That's a fried egg on toast to you and me, love!'

'Parfait!' he chuckled, 'I do understand a bit of French.' He winked at her.

'Et voila!' Issy brought over the plates with the eggs on toast, with a slice of tomato on the side.

'Bon appetit!' she said.

Silence descended as they tucked into their croque madame, polishing it off in no time, drinking their coffee in between bites.

'So, any plans next week?' Issy asked, hoping one of them would reveal their baby news. They looked at one other, as if to say should we tell them? After a few minutes James couldn't contain it any longer.

'Well, we weren't going to say anything, but Julie is expecting and we're having the first scan on Tuesday morning. Please don't say anything to Jodie and Ralph, as we only wanted to tell them after we had the scan.'

'Oh, that's lovely, yes of course your secret is safe with us.' Amy placed a hand on top of Julie's, knowing she already knew, but James wasn't aware of it yet!

'Everything is crossed for you both, don't worry, all will be fine,' Amy reassured them.

'Thanks, and thank you for last night, we will love you and leave you now.' He pulled back his chair, then helped Julie out of hers. They made their way to the front door, grabbing their coats on their way out. Amy and Issy leant in for French kisses, before waving them off, seeing them drive off up the road.

'And breathe, our house in the middle of the street is ours again, to coin another phrase,' Amy chuckled.

'Indeed, I'll have another coffee, Sis, if you don't mind.' Issy got up to make a fresh pot of coffee. Do you think we can stretch to a decent coffee machine yet?' Issy asked, missing a cappuccino in the morning before work.

'I think we could, we just need to look online to see what's available for our set budget or wait for the right one, Amy replied, feeling hopeful.

'Something to look forward to then, I guess,' Issy smiled.

'OK, I'll feed the dogs before changing into something more suitable, we can then take them out to the park, we need a change of scenery, some down time, before another week hits us tomorrow morning. We could ask Mum if she will have them tomorrow for a while, save us coming back at lunchtime. I think I will soon have weekly meetings at the care home, to bring us all up to date with the patients' well-being. We'll just have to review the dog situation here, as and when, depending on Mum's and Dad's agendas.'

Walking around the park was pleasant, seeing everything gradually coming into full bloom. A lawn, with a blanket of bluebells, was a picture postcard in itself. They let the dogs of the lead to sniff around, enjoying the spring scents. Rosie suddenly took off, after seeing something from a distance, another furry friend recognised her as they soon collided. As Issy sped up her pace to catch up, I soon recognised it was Floss, Lottie's dog.

'Hello Floss, where's Lottie? I guess she's catching you up,' Issy bent down to stroke her.

'Issy, fancy meeting you here,' a slightly out of breath Lottie said, grabbing Floss's collar so she wouldn't run off again. 'Well, Floss and I needed a walk,' Lottie added, smiling. 'We loved it at yours last night. Mum and Pete are having a lazy Sunday. Grace and I thought we might go to the pub later, fancy joining us? I bet you can't be bothered to cook today!'

'Actually, we thought the same, a lovely treat before a new week.'

'Sorted, let's meet at The Queen's Head, just up the road, they do a good carvery on Sundays.'

They walked on together for a while before turning back, going their separate ways home to settle the dogs, before they jumped in the car to meet Lottie at the pub at two o'clock for a meal.

The pub was a lovely old traditional pub with an old water mill, dating back from 1827, where it was still being used to brew beer today. Issy loved how Stow on the Wold was steeped in history, something as a child you don't take much notice about, it's only as an adult you tend to appreciate everything around you more.

They parked up in the car park, noticing Lottie soon drive up in the pub's car park next to them.

'Perfect timing,' Amy announced as they stepped out of the car, locking it up after. They walked in together, hoping to find a table, as they hadn't prebooked. They were in luck as the lady by the door directed them to one in a corner overlooking the old mill.

They took their seats before ordering soft drinks with the waitress, opting for orange juice with ice. She placed their order on her mini tablet before telling them they could join the small queue for the carvery. Their tummies were already rumbling in anticipation. Within minutes their drinks were on the table. They all took a sip before joining the now growing queue for the carvery.

'Good day ladies, I have chicken, ham or lamb, what would you like today?' a tall dark-haired handsome man with a white chef's cap gave them the options. Issy and Amy chose the succulent-looking chicken, whilst Lottie and Grace opted for lamb, making them drool at the thought. They helped themselves to the various condiments on a nearby table before returning to their table.

'To us girls!' Lottie chinked glasses before they tucked into their meals.

'Bon appetit!' they chorused together. They tucked into their meals in silence whilst they were reasonably hot. Ten minutes elapsed before Issy broke the silence.

'So, what's your week looking like tomorrow?' she asked Lottie, wondering how her job interviews were going.

'Well, I've managed to secure a permanent job as a busy florist up the road, delivering flowers within a ten-mile radius, which I enjoy doing, meeting the community and spreading a bit of joy to those who need it most. I started last week, so it's early days yet, whether I continue for the foreseeable. I go out in a white van, with boxed up flowers in the back, similar to those French vans you see travelling around on the streets in France with the wood frame double doors on the back.'

'Sounds busy, yet lovely. I'm sure your customers will love you, especially the little old ladies who possibly don't see anyone but you in their day,' Amy added, smiling at her as she finished her orange juice.

'What about you, Grace?' Issy asked, unsure how she spent her time.

'Oh, I'm doing an apprenticeship at a local school, hoping to become a teaching assistant for special needs children. It's such a rewarding job in the difficult times we live in these days,' she added, feeling proud of herself.

'Oh absolutely, our mum did that when we were younger. She loved it, reading to a small group every day, learning as you go along. Well done you, Grace, you'll go far, I'm sure. Anyone for dessert?' changing the subject.

The waitress noticed they had finished, walking over to collect the plates, bringing over a blackboard stand with a choice of desserts.

'Sticky toffee pudding for me,' Lottie said, after a quick glance.

'And me,' Grace added, 'followed by a floater coffee.'

Amy and Issy chose the lemon cheesecake, their favourite.

Moments later the waitress was back to take their dessert and coffee orders.

'So desserts first, then coffees, agreed!' Issy added, 'Four floaters after, please.'

The waitress confirmed, 'Perfect, coming right away!' She smiled at them.

The mouthwatering desserts soon arrived followed by the floater coffees, which were a special treat to end the weekend on a high.

They split the bill between them before walking out into the now depleted car park to drive back home, a group hug first, wishing everyone a wonderful week before zooming off.

Chapter Eighteen

A busy week awaited them, so they needed help with looking after the dogs. They decided to ring Mum to see if she would look after them one day a week, Mondays, being a catch-up meeting in the care home. Amy was uncertain of theirs, soon to be decided. Fortunately for Issy and Amy, Mum agreed to pick them up, taking them for walks. One of them would pick them up later from theirs.

Issy left sticky notes in the kitchen, reminding her where they had left off concerning the dogs, avoiding any confusion.

Dearest Mum,
Thanks for having the dogs, they will love spending the day with you both. Any problems ring me OK. Have a great day! Xx

On arrival at the care home, her phone pinged, a message from the boss, announcing their weekly catch-up meeting held in a nearby office at 10am.

Issy placed her bag and jacket in her designated locker in the staff room. She put her phone in her back trouser pocket, before heading into the main lounge to help out with the mid-morning drinks and snacks with the patients. She noticed Freda wasn't there, surprising her. She dismissed that thought and carried on looking after the other patients who needed the extra help.

'Good morning, everyone, we have a birthday girl in our midst today. Let's wish our Patsy a happy 75th birthday!' Trixi, one of the head staff announced. Everyone began to clap and sing Happy Birthday, some waving their hands in the air, all joining in with the fun.

'Thank you, ladies and gents!' she shouted, to be heard by everyone.

On cue a lady from the kitchen brought out a huge cake, with candles around the top, placing it on a table with a red rose gingham tablecloth. Her helper wheeled her over to the table and she took one big breath, to blow out the candles. One of the staff came over to take a photo on her iPhone to add to their Facebook page, before the candles were blown out.

'One, two, three and blow,' Jane, her helper said as Patsy blew every candle out in one big puff. Everyone clapped and cheered at her profound effort.

The cake was then cut into equal slices to be handed out on plates with a fork and a yellow paper napkin for all to enjoy. The celebrations continued, after Issy had slipped away to her first catch-up meeting.

'Welcome to our weekly meeting. I'm delighted to introduce you to our newest member of staff, Issy. She joined us last week and has been assigned to look after Freda, who sadly suffers with dementia, thankfully still in its early stages. Please stand up for others to see you, Issy.'

'My name is Claire, I'm one of the coordinators here,' the host opened the meeting.

'I noticed Freda wasn't in the lounge this morning, is everything okay?' Issy asked, feeling a little concerned.

'You're right to ask that, Issy, she's not feeling her best this morning, our on-site doctor will be checking her over now as we speak. I'll keep you posted later on today. We have therefore assigned you to Ruth, a new patient who joined us last week. She's lovely, just a bit frail in her young age of 70, gets lonely, so loves to play board games or a card game of snap, to help with her memory,' she explained. 'Lastly, we have decided to have a monthly social at a local pub or restaurant, away from these four walls, which I am currently trying to arrange. It is very important for our sanity and wellbeing, as was suggested by an ex-colleague who sadly left us last month, due to family issues. Details about the social at the next meeting.

'On that note, thank you for all your support this last week,

173

onward and upwards. Keep up the great work, it's all much appreciated,' Claire concluded the meeting on a high note.

They resumed normal duties, seeing everyone enjoying their coffee and birthday cake, all enjoying a chat with others on their table. Today was games morning, which everyone enjoyed, especially Patsy, who loved a game of cards or a board game. Today an old card game of Lexicon was brought out. Seven letters from the pack of cards were handed out to make up as many words as possible, helping everyone with any memory problems. The person with the most words and with no more letters left, was the winner. The game brought hours of fun to the residents. Other tables had board games, such as snakes and ladders and Scrabble.

Lunch time was the busiest time for all staff. Patients needed taking to the bathroom before, some needing two helpers, depending on their ability, taking extra time.

On the menu today was the classic mac and cheese, with broccoli and fish fingers, which was loved by all, making the staff equally hungry. Tea and coffee after for those who desired it, before most patients were escorted back to their rooms for an afternoon nap. Others had physio or other treatments. That was a typical morning at the care home, all having fun together.

Issy woke up Tuesday morning with a surprise text from a somewhat excited, yet nervous Julie.

It's the morning of my scan, say a prayer for me please. I'm sure everything will be fine. Love J xx

Issy immediately sent one back, wishing her good luck.

All will be fine, love Issy. X

Amy's day, however, didn't quite go to plan during her day at Rowans. A few sick dogs arrived into the practice, one needing urgent surgery, after a nasty RTA, a hit and run, leaving a dog injured on the side of the road. These incidents hurt Amy the most, being so upsetting to hear about and to see, as they were carried in by their owners or a vet who had to dash out to their car to assist.

A few meowing cats in their cages; some giving a hiss as people gazed into their cages, clearly unwelcome or they felt a little frisky being trapped in their narrow confines.

The most challenging days became obvious, when the owner walked out after seeing the vet, without their beloved pet. They had to be sent over to the rainbow bridge; either due to old age or ongoing health conditions, neither was pleasant to witness. Some came out sobbing their eyes out or numb from shock. A box of tissues was always sitting on the reception desk. The bill would be settled later under such circumstances. Working at a vets' practice wasn't for the faint-hearted, there were good days and awful ones.

Losing a pet was as bad as losing their owner, you just learned to adjust to them on a daily basis.

After a long tiring day Amy walked out into the car park, taking in a deep breath to release stresses of the day, before driving off to collect the dogs from the bungalow. As soon as she turned the key of the front door, both dogs came scattering along to greet her, which was always lovely after a stressful day at work.

'Hello, you two, had a lovely day?' Their waggy tails said it all.

'Is that you, Amy, fancy a quick cuppa before you head to yours?' Mum asked, pleased to see her.

'Oh yes please, it's been one of those hectic days at Rowans. We had to put a dog to sleep, it's heartbreaking all round. No more suffering for the dog at least, just the owner, so hard Mum.'

'Sit down, darling, here's a lovely cuppa to help you along the road.' Mum handed her a large mug of tea and a plate of flapjacks.

'I'd best text Issy to tell her I'm here, before she wonders where I am, Amy added. 'Too late, as she just beat me to it.'

Where are you? I've just got home.

Just having a cuppa with Mum, collecting the dogs, home shortly.
Amy fired one back.

OK, I'm going out to a yoga class later, I saw it advertised outside
the pub the other day.

An impromptu decision, enjoy see you later. X

'Issy's joined a yoga class, so no hurry now, just me and the dogs,'
she explained it to Mum, feeling more relaxed.

'Fancy having tea with us, makes sense?' Mum asked, hoping
she'd stay.

'Oh, go on then, you've persuaded me, Mum!'

'I've made a veggie lasagne this afternoon, it's in the Aga.'

'Thanks Mum, my favourite.'

'You can take a portion for Issy, so she won't feel left out,'
Mum added.

An hour later Amy was back on the road to ours. Issy wasn't
back yet, so she had the house to herself for a while, some "me"
time. She hung her jacket up in the hall, along with the dogs'
leads, then went straight into the lounge to relax on the sofa. She
checked her phone for messages, one from Julie. She immediately
thought about the scan she had, so texted her back.

Hi Julie, I've only just seen this, how did your scan go this
morning?'

Within a few minutes she had read it, noting the two blue
ticks.

Thanks for asking, Amy, all went well. The baby is fine, we don't
want to know the sex, it will be a lovely surprise when it's ready to enter
this world.

Oh fab, I'm so happy for you both, so nothing to worry about then.
Love Amy X

Issy soon rocked up. hearing her turn the key in the door, looking rather worn out as she collapsed next to her on the sofa.

'I'll put the kettle on, you need it. Green or ordinary?'

'Green, I think,' feeling thankful.

Amy got up, followed by the dogs. 'Mum gave me a portion of lasagne. I'll heat it up for you.'

'Thanks Sis, you're a star, I'm starving after today,' she shouted back. Their new home rule was to consume all meals in the kitchen, so Amy called her over into the kitchen; the lasagne was eaten within a few minutes. She took her mug of tea back into the lounge and switched on the TV to catch up on *Eastenders*, their favourite soap drama, to unwind.

The evening was soon upon them as the sun began to hide behind the clouds, as darkness descended. She let the dogs out before they retired for the night.

Chapter Nineteen

Nine months later

The days and months of spring soon rolled into early summer. They had now been in their new house for nearly six months, a place they could finally call home. They continued visiting furniture stores and art galleries to add to their home, aware of not over-furnishing the rooms, decluttering along the way.

James and Julie's baby's due date was fast approaching, a mere two weeks to go, before Amy and Issy were to become cousins, possibly godparents if they were fortunate to be asked. They could only wait and see, placing no pressure on either of them. Meanwhile they were all getting very excited to have a new arrival in the family, mum being especially keen to hold her first niece or nephew.

Lottie's sister, Grace, had finally passed her exams and was now a proud teaching assistant, securing a permanent post in a primary school, working alongside a lovely five-year-old girl with slight learning difficulties in a mainstream classroom. The family had only just moved into the area, so everything was all new to them. Grace showed her empathetic side making her transition into school life as easy as possible.

Lottie was promoted as head florist in her small company, branching out into special occasion flowers, such as weddings and funerals, creating the most beautiful bouquets made with love. The original white van got a makeover with the words *Beautiful Flowers* painted on the now blue and white van. She continued driving around, brightening up her clients' days wherever possible.

Both Lottie and Grace remained single for now, as their jobs proved demanding, leaving little time for partners, let alone other activities. Amy and Issy continued their weekly coffee and pub social gatherings as much as they could.

Dad and Jack remained the best of mates, sharing their hobby of fishing, ending up at a local pub for a pint and a good natter about their day's fishing. Finally, Elaine and Jodie continued to enjoy each other's company, going for coffee and taking the dogs out, which kept them both fit. Their latest hobby was attending a bingo night, held monthly at the community hub, making new friends. Life was looking good.

The final week of the baby's due date arrived. Mum received a text from James, explaining Julie became more and more uncomfortable, ready to pop any moment. Suddenly it was all systems go as she woke up one morning all cramped up, the baby was on its merry way. Within an hour she was at the hospital in the labour suite, fully dilated, lying on the bed as her waters just burst out all over her yellow maternity book. Julie had a lovely kind-hearted midwife, who gave her the usual gas and air to fight off the birthing pains, until she gave one final push, the baby made a grand appearance into the world, a big sigh of relief all round.

She heard the words, 'Congratulations, you have a beautiful girl, well done Julie,' setting off her hormones as she became so overwhelmed and exhausted all in one, as she opened the floodgates with tears of pure joy. Her baby girl, weighing in at 7lb 5oz, wrapped in a white blanket, was handed over to Julie, a very precious moment.

James was a very proud father, wrapping his big arms around mother and baby, planting a big kiss on each of their heads. Julie just beamed, feeling elated.

'Would you like a cup of tea, either of you? You most definitely deserve it, Julie,' the midwife asked.

'Thank you, I'd love one, it's thirsty work giving birth. That said, I would do it all again in a heartbeat, well, after a year or two!' she giggled.

Right on cue, a nurse walked in with her tea and a piece of toast, as it was breakfast time.

'Have you chosen a name for her?' the midwife asked, needing to fill out her paperwork. 'You can register her birth on the ground floor in the birth and deaths registry office.'

'Her name is Alice Maria Brown,' Julie told her, with a big smile on her face.

'Oh, such a beautiful name, perfect.'

Lisa, the midwife, handed James the paperwork to register her birth later before leaving the hospital. They both went to the registration office before they drove home later that day.

Later that afternoon she was discharged, after the doctor checked them over, giving Julie the thumbs up. The real test was after they got home, being a first-time mum, everything was new to them. James had brought in a car seat for the baby to go home in. They both went out baby item shopping weeks prior to the due date, buying larger items such as a small pram. They agreed on the name: Alice Maria Brown. She had a small amount of ginger hair, which could fall out later or change colour. Once home James sent Mum a text.

Hi Jodie, I thought we should share our news. Julie gave birth to a beautiful baby girl this morning, Alice Maria. Once we are more settled, we'll come over to show her off. Love J and J Xx

Mum picked up her phone immediately to ring Amy.

'I've just become an aunt. Julie had a girl this morning, Alice, it's such a pretty name.'

'Oh, that's fabulous news, we'll send a card, enjoy your day. I'm currently at work, chat later.'

News travelled fast as Mum soon rang Sam and Elaine, who were naturally delighted for Mum and Dad.

A few weeks had passed when they started to make christening arrangements, despite not being over religious, it seemed the done thing to do. The question of godparents arose and naturally

Julie was very keen to ask Amy and Issy, as she was the only child, leaving no one else to ask. James, however, had a brother, David, a few years younger. Julie picked up her phone to ring Amy.

'Hi Amy, how are you? I was wondering if you both would like to become godparents to Alice, as we are in the middle of arranging her christening date with the local vicar.'

'Oh yes please, we would gladly love to accept the responsibility. What an honour, thank you so much Julie, I'll pass the happy news onto Issy, who I know will agree. She's currently taking the dogs out for a quick walk.'

'Perfect, so I'll put your names down as definite godparents. I'll keep you posted of the christening date and details after we meet with the vicar next week,' she added, feeling chuffed to bits.

It's all happening in our family, Amy thought after she ended the call. More lists to be written; invites to buy and to be distributed, much like a wedding, only she was glad it wasn't her responsibility this time.

The christening soon became the event of the year and talk of the town. Mum and Dad being proud aunt and uncle couldn't withhold their excitement any longer, being the main topic to any conversation when things dried up.

James and Julie met up with a lovely vicar, Ruth Murrey, who was new to her parish. She herself had a young girl who had recently started in the town's primary school. They had to attend a few christening classes by law, explaining the great importance and role of new parents and godparents. Julie was keen to re-explore her beliefs from her school days. James, however, remained slightly sceptical, sitting on the proverbial fence, waiting to be convinced. Time would tell as he really wanted to support his wife and daughter as she grew up.

On the day of the christening, both parents had to swear on oath the Holy Bible, saying they were to follow God's instructions to share with Alice as she walked through her life. A big commitment which they felt obliged to take seriously. Ruth prayed with Julie, leaving a huge impression on her; subsequently she gave her life to the Lord, bringing her much freedom and joy especially at this time of their lives. She felt she had made the biggest, yet best decision in her entire life.

The Rev Ruth gave her details of their church services, being a more relaxed style of service, more acceptable to young people these days. They were asked to attend at least three morning worship services before the christening day, which they did. They took this very seriously, being a big commitment and responsibility for their precious girl Alice.

'How's it going, James?' Jodie rang him later that week, eager to know if she could help in any way.

'All good, thanks, we're just making lists of people to invite for the big day, then we need to organise outside caterers or something. We thought we might go to a local pub and rent a room there. So much to think about and arrange, like a wedding reception, only it's a christening instead, of equal importance,' he explained at length.

'Busy times ahead then, let me know if we can help.'

"We do have a definite date we can now work around. It's Sunday May 10th at 11 o'clock. Could you let Sam and Pete and the girls know and Elaine? We will do the rest. We've kept the numbers to a minimum which in turn will keep the overall cost down.'

'Absolutely, sounds good to me. What about the church hall, they cater for such occasions, rather than going to a pub? I don't think it's quite the appropriate venue, just saying, James. It's up to you two of course,' Mum threw that idea into the mix.

'I think we prefer the pub venue, it seems more popular these days,' he begged to differ.

After much thought James did think a pub meal might not be quite appropriate after a christening. The whole spiritual experience would soon be lost, with it being a one-off occasion, so that idea was discarded, as it just didn't feel right to Julie; a mother's instincts were usually trustworthy.

Within a few days the Rev Ruth got in touch with Julie, giving her the good news that the main hall was available, and that the church's catering company would provide a lovely buffet at a reasonable price, settling the matter once and for all. All that remained now was to agree on the music. A few hymns were suggested as well as some more modern choruses. There was something for everyone. Within the week the order of service had to be submitted to a local printer to be collected in a few days.

The Sunday before was the rehearsal, which included immediate family, going over the service, where to sit and stand in church and when to come up to the altar for the christening. The vicar had to read out statements to the parents and godparents, asking them to confirm and agree to their spoken oaths in the appropriate places. It was a very serious moment in their lives, not to be taken lightly.

'Good morning, everyone and thank you all for coming today to the christening rehearsal for Alice, next Sunday morning.' The Rev Ruth Murrey opened the casual meeting.

'Please don't be nervous on the day, just enjoy this special time together as we all partake in this memorable day. There will be a blessing at the altar after for James and Julie and godparents. I will offer the bread and wine as you kneel by the rail. The rest of the congregation will be called up in turn by row. It is entirely your choice to partake in this part of the service, where I will place my hands on you for a blessing, even if you don't believe. I look forward to seeing you all next Sunday,' the Rev Ruth explained, hoping everyone was in agreement with everything.

Everyone made their way to the front of the church, shaking Rev Ruth's hand as they walked out of the church doors.

'She's a lovely vicar, I am certainly warming to her,' Issy smiled at Amy once out of earshot from everyone.

'She is indeed,' Amy nodded in agreement.

'I need a coffee after all that, fancy going up the road before heading back to ours?' Issy locked arms with Amy as they walked along the church path to the car.

'Good idea, let's go! I can smell the coffee from here; with a piece of cake, what's not to like?'

On arrival at the coffee house they placed their jackets on the chairs by their chosen table before placing their order at the counter, drooling over the cookies and cakes underneath.

'Difficult choice, isn't it? They all look very appealing,' the young girl said, as they gazed at them intently.

'It is, so two slices of carrot cake, please, with two cappuccinos,' Amy said after a few minutes.

'I'll bring them over,' she added, as Issy swiped her card to pay before returning to their table.

Arriving back home, they were greeted by some post lying on the doormat. Sifting through it, they noticed one from the local council with important information enclosed, which they were always suspicious about, knowing there were so many scam letters flying around these days.

Amy promptly opened it, thinking it probably was genuine as it had the council's logo on.

> *Dear Miss A Stevens*
>
> *I am writing to you today as we are in the area soon to update Wi-Fi on your road. I realise this may come as an inconvenience to you, but you will definitely benefit from it as you search the internet.*
>
> *Work will commence next week. You don't need to be at home. We will update you as and when. We are just laying fibre optic cables to enhance the internet speed.*
>
> *Any questions please don't hesitate to get in touch.*
> *Yours sincerely*
> *John Watts*
> *Head of Installations*

'We're getting an internet upgrade from the council, it says here, starting next week,' Amy raised her voice to Issy whilst she was attending to the dogs.

'Cool if it's free, we need to concentrate on the christening on

Sunday, glad we don't need to be in for them. Just let them do it,' she replied.

The week continued as normal without any further dramas, until Issy had a call from Jodie, who got herself in a slight panic about Sunday. What to wear? She naturally wanted to look smart and presentable, claiming she had nothing suitable in her wardrobe, which in their opinion was never the case.

'Just pick your favourite dress, that mid-green one with the flowers on it, and a cream cardigan to match. You'll look fabulous in that, Mum,' Issy told her on the phone.

'Thank you love, it's never easy when you stand in front of a crowd of people, eyeing you up and down, I get so self-conscious.' Mum added, chuckling down the line.

'No need, silly, they're not really directly looking at you.' She thought it best not to say they were more interested in the baby, when her head gets a water blessing on her forehead from the vicar.

'OK, that settled then. I just want to make my brother proud. I can't wait now to see little Alice, smiling, hopefully,' she added, feeling more confident.

'Only three days to go, and you will, Mum,' Issy reminded her. Soon to become the talk of the town no doubt months after.

James and Julie had recently relocated to Broadway, a large village 15 minutes away from Stow on the Wold, which made life more convenient for all of them. It was a pretty village, lined with picture perfect period houses in the midst of horse chestnut trees. They were very happy there after moving into a four bedroom house with beautiful gardens to the front and rear. A perfect place to bring up young Alice with plenty of amenities scattered around the area.

Mum was nearer her long-lost brother, which made them both happier, knowing they would probably now grow old together, giving Mum a new focus, Alice appearing on the scene.

Amy's phone suddenly pinged on the kitchen table where she usually left it, spending the majority of her time in the kitchen.

'Lottie, how's it going, everything OK at your end?' she asked as Lottie sounded a bit concerned.

'I had a phone call from an unknown number the other day, only to realise it was from Julie, whose daughter is going to be christened at the church on Sunday. She sounded a bit panicked as she desperately needed flowers for the church, as their usual florists had pulled out at the last moment. I immediately reassured her it wasn't a problem, as I could provide some at a good price.'

'Oh gosh, just a minor hiccup then, still at least you can step in, which I'm sure she will appreciate,' Amy said, knowing what Julie must have felt.

'She forgot I am a florist, she just rang on the off chance. I think Mum put her in touch with me, saving the day. Absolutely, it's all sorted now. Flowers can't be done in advance anyway, so no worries there,' Lottie reminded her.

'Problem solved for them, the least of their worries now. It will be difficult enough to get everyone ready on time especially with Alice, getting feeding times and nappy changes right. All adding to the fun of being a parent, I'm sure,' Amy concluded, before hanging up.

Chapter Twenty

The day of the christening finally arrived, everyone getting excited yet a bit nervous at the same time. Julie took it all in her stride, knowing nothing much could go wrong, it wasn't an exam after all. The occasion was going to be a happy one, to be remembered for a long time after and talked about over countless social gatherings, no doubt.

'Right, I've got my check list.' Julie waved the paper at James to grab his attention, which it did, after having just changed Alice's nappy that morning.

> Alice's christening dress
> Socks and shoes
> Changing bag with lots of nappies
> Favourite Teddy
> Hats and cardigan to match.

Julie read the list out, whilst James checked the list, ticking them off rather than on a device. Julie had it on her phone for double checking.

Alice wore a beautiful light pink dress with a cream cardigan suiting her baby face complexion perfectly. Soft white socks with a bow on each side with pink ballet style shoes to finish off the outfit. Julie picked up the dress from a charity shop, only being worn once, looking as good as new. Charity shops have an array of excellent clothing for all at a reasonable price, not to be easily dismissed, perfect for those on a tight budget or for those one-off occasions.

James was clock-watching all morning, leaving ample time to park at the church and for visits to the bathroom before the service began.

It was now 10.50, everyone was walking into the church. Sidesmen escorted them to their seats, ready for the opening hymn to be played by the organist who sat in the balcony above. Silence fell as the organist played the introduction to the hymn "Morning has broken", which opened the service beautifully.

'Welcome to our special morning service, where we will be witnessing the christening of Alice Maria, the first daughter to James and Julie Brown. They have recently moved to this area, so everything is still very new to them. Please will you bring Alice to the christening font, along with the godparents.' Rev Ruth opened up the service.

James and Julie sat in the front row, with the godparents and close family members.

'Let's go,' Julie whispered to the others as they all got up, turning around to form a line at the beginning of the row. James was holding Alice in his arms, making sure her dress stayed intact. He would hand her over to Julie once they were lined up around the christening font.

All six lined up at the front, looking out into the congregation, followed by a few latecomers as they shuffled along a pew by the front to get the best view.

'Welcome James and Julie and baby Alice and her godparents this morning to witness Alice's christening.' The Rev Ruth opened the service, as a little noise came from Alice's mouth, resembling a giggle, as if she knew they were talking about her. The congregation responded with oohs and aahs.

'Please open your service booklet and we will start the christening, affirming our commitment to God together,' she continued, looking down the line to gain their attention.

Prayers and relevant Bible verses were read out, then the response questions were asked to James and Julie, by confirming to teach Alice God's instruction until she was old enough to understand and make her own choice. The godparents had to agree to help Alice follow His instruction.

That moment was very special to all, a promise not to be taken lightly. Family and friends stood in unison with them feeling overwhelmed, and above all immensely proud of them. Alice was handed over to the Rev Ruth, to be blessed by wetting her forehead with a cross as a sign of love and blessing as she grew up. A few happy tears were seen on Julie's cheek as she witnessed her girl being christened, filling her with joy.

The organist played the all-time favourite hymn "All things bright and beautiful", as they all returned to their seats. Alice by which time fell asleep in Julie's arms, clearly the blessing had a profound effect.

The rest of the congregation were then ushered row by row to the front, to receive the bread and wine by the Rev Ruth. They formed their hands in a cup position, indicating that they wished to partake in the bread and wine. Those who didn't want the communion were offered a blessing, as she placed her hands on their heads.

Everyone returned to their pew in an orderly fashion.

The service drew to a close with another hymn appropriate for the occasion, "Be thou my vision" which was a perfect ending to the service, all standing and exercising their vocal cords.

'Please join us in the hall afterwards for refreshments and a light buffet to further celebrate Alice's christening,' she concluded the service on a high note.

Everyone started to make their way towards the hall, leaving Julie and her family to gather up their belongings. Alice was gently placed in her small, compact pram, to follow the others to the hall. Warm embraces were given to the happy couple and as they looked into Alice's pram noting her smiling face gaze back at them.

Tables with floral gingham tablecloths and chairs were laid out around the room. A buffet was set up on a centre table with plates and cutlery wrapped in white paper napkins at one end, for people to help themselves before they chose from the yummy buffet. A variety of sandwiches on white or brown bread with an assortment of cakes were on offer, making a splendid meal for all. Everyone mingled around, enjoying the delicious food.

'That was a beautiful service this morning, wasn't it,' Jodie remarked, seeing a tear emerge from Julie's eyes. 'You must be so proud of young Alice, who behaved impeccably as the Rev Ruth held her by the font.'

'She's my number one girl,' Julie remarked, with a big smile across her face.

'She is indeed. Dad and I will go home now to see to the dogs, hopefully they've not been up to any mischief,' Mum added. 'Pop over any time, you're always welcome at ours, Julie.'

'Thank you, Jodie.'

Three months had passed and Alice was growing up to be a beautiful redhead baby girl, always smiling, turning out to be the easiest little bundle of joy to everyone who paid them a visit. Mum bought her a play mobile frame, which was placed on the floor as Alice lay on a cosy patchwork quilt underneath. She enjoyed kicking her legs whilst raising her arms to grab the hanging objects dangling before her, enhancing her fine motor skills as she cooed with delight. It was now all about "firsts" at this stage in her life, especially when Alice spoke her first words, endlessly delighting her mum and dad.

A routine was soon established as Julie and James took turns in bottle feeding, once Julie's breast milk had dried up, giving them both a restful night's sleep they so longed for. James took paternity leave from work to make the most of these precious moments in Alice's young life. It proved hard for him to return to work, yet he valued the distraction of being a full-time parent, leaving little time for himself, let alone with Julie. Even cosy nights curled on the sofa became virtually non-existent.

Julie's hormones were still all over the place, turning on the floodgates at any awkward moment. Julie found this the most testing time, hoping it would soon pass her by. She refused to start HRT tablets, with the various side effects, preferring natural herbal remedies such as camomile or green tea.

They all met up a few weeks later at the weekend at Mum and Dad's bungalow, where they were keen to see Alice's reaction to the dogs. They sat on the sofa in the lounge, with Alice in her bouncy chair on the floor.

The dogs were allowed in, to be supervised by the adults as Rosie and Bessy raced up to Alice, sniffing her out in her bouncy chair.

'Slow down girls,' Amy shouted, seeing them so excited as they dashed in, wagging their tails, heading straight for Alice.

Alice enjoyed touching their soft fur on their ears and heads, soon bonding with one another which was the sole purpose. Alice was never left alone with the dogs in the room, for safety reasons.

'Who fancies a cuppa and a piece of cake?' Jodie asked, changing the subject after a while, feeling thirsty. Mum always had cake or flapjacks in the house should anyone unexpectedly pop over.

Mum and her girls went into the kitchen to help her make the tea. Issy got mugs from the cupboard and a large teapot, popped in a couple of tea bags to make a decent brew. A milk jug with spoons, carrying them on a tray into the lounge. A delicious Victoria sponge was bought from the café up the road a few days ago for the occasion, which Mum brought out on a plate with small forks and red rose napkins for those sticky fingers after! It was a joyous occasion seeing everyone gathered together, interacting with each other including the dogs, being part of the growing family.

'Please help yourselves to tea and a piece of cake,' Mum announced, after she placed the tray on the long coffee table in front of the sofa.

The chitter chatter continued for another hour, before James and Julie had to leave and drive home. Life was a bit different now with a baby on board with mealtimes and bedtimes to juggle, not veering much from their set routine.

'Thanks, Sis, for today, we loved it all. Come to ours next time and we can go for walks in the park near us, with Amy and the dogs as well,' giving Mum a hug and kiss on the cheek.

'Lovely, thanks James, see you soon.' He walked down the hallway, followed by Julie carrying Alice, to let themselves out. Mum gave Julie a kiss and baby Alice as they passed by.

Mum stood on the front doorstep to watch, as James strapped Alice into her car seat, before jumping into the driver's seat to zoom off down the road, sounding the horn as they drove off. Mum waved them goodbye.

'Well, that was a lovely afternoon spent with baby Alice, she's such a gorgeous girl for James and Julie. I'm sure she has her wobbly moments too, as all new parents do, it gets better in time, so they say. The biggest hurdle is getting them to sleep through the night. Some take longer than others. It can range from a month to six months!'

'Well, I suppose it's time for us to head home too, we need to think about dinner and feeding the dogs too,' Issy reminded her.

They gathered all their stuff, putting the leads on the dogs as they made their way to the car. Opening the hatchback, lifting them gently in. They soon became accustomed to car journeys, looking out the back window before curling up on their blanket on the floor.

'Thanks, Mum, and see you soon,' Issy added, giving her a kiss before jumping into the driver's seat to shoot off.

As they drew closer towards their house they noticed something peculiar happening in the road. On closer inspection Amy noticed not one, but two curled up hedgehogs, one in front of each other, as if they were wanting to cross the road to find shelter under a nearby bush. Clearly they had just come out of hibernation, after a long sleep, waking up to another world.

'Issy, pull over, these two need our help.' Amy patted Issy on the shoulder as she indicated to the left to park up by the kerb.

'How can you help them? They are prickly and we don't have gloves.'

'Well actually I do have an old towel in the back for such

occasions, originally for the dogs, but this will serve its purpose, just watch,' Amy added, smiling back at her.

Issy turned off the engine, not wanting to disturb them any further. Amy got out of the car and opened the hatchback to locate an old blue bath towel, used for dirty paws for the dogs, and found a pair of leather gloves tucked underneath. She put them on and grabbed the towel to walk towards the curled-up hedgehogs in the road, gently placing the towel over them, picking them up and taking them back to the car.

'Now what, we need to take them to your vet practice, they can then advise what happens next.' Issy suggested, taking her phone out ready to click on their contact number.

'You rest them on your lap, Issy, whilst I ring them, they know me after all.'

Rowan vets emergency, how can I help?' An out of hours staff answered.

'Oh, it's Amy Stevens, I have just picked up two curled-up hedgehogs on the road near our house. Should I bring them over, as we're not sure what to do? I think they've just come out of hibernation. They don't appear injured.'

'Hi Amy, it's Tracey. Thank you for rescuing them, please bring them in straight away and we will take it from there,' she advised before hanging up.

'Great, she told me to bring them in, so let's go Sis, we occasionally have hedgehogs brought in. They know a lady nearby who nurses them. They are lovely creatures, needing human intervention to see them through difficult times. I'll drive there, save you changing seats,' Amy insisted, which Issy was happy with.

On arrival, Tracey came to unlock the front entrance door, as Amy followed her into the back of the vets, where the night staff were expecting to check them over.

A vet came over to take a better look. She gently unwrapped the towel to reveal the curled-up light brown hedgehogs; their spikes nestled underneath in a ball. She picked them up to check

193

for any injuries, of which there were none. She grabbed a medium-sized cardboard box from the side, placed some soft straw bedding in the bottom and placed them on top. She placed a small blue ceramic bowl of water next to them with a few seeds and finely chopped apples to keep their weight up. A designated area was made for them until they were transferred to a local wildlife sanctuary, specifically for hedgehogs.

Chapter Twenty-One

Well, that proved to be a very eventful evening last night, seeing two sleepy hedgehogs on the road, then taking them to Rowans. A first for Amy at a busy vets practice. It showed how each day was different. Fortunately, the dogs were oblivious to the drama, only raising their heads, once the boot was opened.

'I'm glad I'm not a hedgehog wandering the streets at night looking for a bush to shelter under. I prefer my warm bed any day!' Issy remarked.

'I'll find out how they are doing next week,' Amy smiled at Issy.

'Now who's up for a Sunday roast at the pub? I'll text Lottie if she wants to join us. The dogs can come too.'

'Go on then, our regular meet-up place before the week takes over,' Issy said, eager to go.

Amy took her phone from her pocket to scroll her WhatsApp messages, finding Lottie, to text her.

Fancy Sunday dinner at the pub, bring Grace if she's free.

She instantly replied.

I was thinking that myself, Mum and Pete are out visiting friends. I'll book a table, meet you there in 10 minutes.

Issy sorted the dogs out, letting them out for a last pee, before putting their leads on. Amy checked the house and locked up.

They arrived at the Queen's Head and looked around, noticing Lottie sitting on a comfy seat by the window, waving them over. She was on her own, as they guessed, no doubt Grace had had a better offer, with George if he was still on the scene.

'We meet again, stranger. Grace not joining us?' Issy asked, wondering why she hadn't joined them.

'Oh, she's out with George, having a day out, I believe. She slept over last night,' Lottie added.

'Must be serious, then,' Amy looked at Lottie, slightly concerned, hoping it wasn't a one-night stand, knowing it wasn't the way forward for any of them.

'I think she knows what she's doing, I hope so anyway. She doesn't talk about it much, only that she's very fond of him, which is good enough for me,' Lottie concluded, trying to focus on her meal.

'Good afternoon, ladies, what drinks can I get you all?' the young waitress asked, waiting to take their order.

'Three orange juices with ice, please,' Issy said enthusiastically.

'Are you all having the carvery today? You can join the queue now if you are,' the waitress added before walking over to the bar to place their drinks orders.

They got up to join the queue before it expanded. Meanwhile she brought out their drinks for them to devour with their Sunday roast. All choosing chicken, with cranberry sauce from the condiments table, adding gravy over the broccoli and cauliflower, giving the meal a sweet rich flavour.

'To us, and to happy times.' They raised their glasses together.

'Did you hear about our adventure last night involving hedgehogs?' Amy opened up the conversation for a point of discussion over their meal.

'Wow, tell us more, sounds prickly to me, excuse the pun,' Lottie laughed, nearly spitting out a mouthful of her food.

'We were driving home from Mum's when, all of a sudden, we saw two dark objects in the road. As we approached with caution we noticed there were two curled-up hedgehogs in the middle of the road., by which time I told Issy to pull over to the kerb, we couldn't just leave them there; next thing they could be run over as cars came hurtling down the road, despite it being a 30 mile limit; people don't care about these creatures these days, just seeing them as an obstacle in their way.'

'They just want to get to their destination regardless, with no care for nature,' Issy added.

'So what happened next, did you put them back under a bush, hoping they'd survive?' Lottie asked inquisitively, eager to know the happy ending.

'I did one better than that, we took them to the vets where I work. I rang them before, saying we were on our way. They checked them over, then made a cosy bed for them in a cardboard box they had hanging around, an old veggie box, I think. We gathered up some food for them and a water bowl inside. The nurses will now care for them until they can be released back into the wild; under a leafy bush,' Amy re-told the story in full, all listening attentively.

'Yeah, a happy ending to two hedgies!' Lottie called them. 'Large and small, we love 'em all!' she added, feeling amused.

'I'll find out more tomorrow when I report for duty!' Amy laughed.

Desserts to follow with three cappuccinos, they settled the bill and walked back to the car, feeling stuffed, in a good way.

They drew themselves together for a bear hug, wishing one another a good week, before driving off separately into the distance.

'Can we stop off to get some milk? We're running low at ours, Issy,' Amy announced after reversing in the car park.

'Good idea, I think we need something for the morning,' Issy added.

Amy pulled up the blind by its cord the following morning, to reveal sun beaming through, showing a light covering of dust on the inside window, reminding her that spring had landed in their midst with gorgeous light-coloured yellow daffodils scattered around the garden beds. After a quick shower to freshen up for the day ahead, putting her usual work clothes on, she walked along the landing, knocking on Issy's door as she passed, saying, 'Rise and shine,' before running down the stairs to let the dogs out. Opening up the kitchen door to see Rose's nose up against

197

the back door, desperate to be let out, before a puddle emerged on the floor. Bessy still curled up in her bed, hearing the commotion, followed her out into the garden, wagging her tail with delight.

'Oh, morning, Sis, sleep well? I heard your knock, thanks.'

'Can't hibernate like our furry friends yesterday, can we, you've got Freda to care for today. Tea or coffee?' Amy asked after the kettle boiled.

"Green tea for me, I'll grab a coffee at the care home later,' she added, making it easier all round.

Amy took their favourite mugs out, placing a green tea bag in one and an ordinary one in the other, stirring it a few times before putting the tea bag in a small pot. They put some bran flakes in a breakfast bowl with a few mixed berries, adding a spoonful of low-fat yoghurt, creating a healthy snack to kick start the day.

Issy took her phone out to check for any urgent messages and emails, of which there were none. Sometimes the care home would send her one in advance, if something cropped up untoward.

With the dogs fed and watered and let out again, they grabbed their stuff to leave, before locking the front door behind them.

On arrival at the care home, Issy signed herself in the red staff book on the entrance table, before wandered into the staff room to hang her jacket up, leaving her bag in her locker, removing her phone to put in her trouser pocket.

'Good morning, Issy, another week adorns us,' a member of staff remarked, passing her by as she headed to Freda's room along the corridor.

'Good morning, here we go again,' Issy reacted as they passed each other by.

She knocked on Freda's door, announcing herself, and a nurse opened up, dressed in her blue plastic apron. Clearly she had just showered her, before Issy took over, bringing her into the lounge for breakfast. She was already sitting in her wheelchair for Issy to push her through into the lounge.

'How are you this morning, Freda?' Issy asked her. Freda turned to look at her gazing into her eyes with excitement.

'Oh, you know, same old, same old, nothing much to talk about, my dear. I'm sure your weekend was far more exciting. You can tell me all about it over breakfast if you want. I love listening to stories, it's like reading a book,' Freda giggled happily.

'Your wish is my command. Now let's see what the buffet cart has on offer today, before I take you to that table by the window,' Pointing to it.

'I'll have scrambled egg with some toast, please, not too much though, and a cup of tea. Help yourself to coffee and join me. You can tell me all about your weekend, if that's OK with you, of course,' she continued.

'Absolutely, I'll just take you over to the table, then I'll get your breakfast,' Issy added, wheeling her up to the table by the window.

Moments later Issy carried over the tray with Freda's breakfast and her own cappuccino.

'Here we go, a breakfast for the Queen,' placing the tray on the table, giving her a plate of scrambled egg on toast.

Issy took cutlery from the plastic tub on the table, placing it neatly on either side of her, ready for her to tuck in. Freda looked up at her, slightly confused, thinking something was amiss. She began to mouth, 'Could you cut it up for me, please,' feeling slightly embarrassed as she had difficulty using her hands.

'Of course I can, you only need to ask me, Freda.' Issy gave her a friendly hug.

'Now tell me about your weekend, did you meet a fancy chap? You're that age after all,' she gave me a wink.

'Oh, nothing like that, cheeky!' Issy smiled back at her. 'It involves two prickly animals who curl up in a ball usually in the winter months, can you guess the animal, Freda?'

'Oh, those porcupine creatures, yuck they're horrible looking things.'

'I agree, they're not my favourite either. You're wrong, it wasn't one of those. Last guess now and then I'll tell you!' she kept the guessing game going.

'I give up, I can't think of anything else, tell me, Issy,' she chuckled, feeling amused.

'Well, it was a sleepy hedgehog; two of them in fact, in the middle of the road!' Issy revealed as Freda looked at her, all surprised.

'Wow, so what happened next, did you rescue them or just leave them there?' Freda asked, eager to have a happy ending to the story.

'The short version was yes. I was in the car at the time and pulled over to stop. I grabbed a big towel from the boot, walked up to the scene, picked them up with my towel and returned to my car. My sister was with me, she held them whilst I drove to the vets where she works. The nurses came out and looked after them,' Issy continued to explain to her.

'Then what, does this story have a happy ending?'

'They were put in a cardboard box on a bed of straw with some food they like and a bowl of water. They will now be well looked after, before they fully wake up to be released back outside under a bush, their favourite spot. The end.'

'Wow, that was an eventful weekend, not every weekend is like that, at least they are safe now.' Freda got her happy ending.

'You ate all your scrambled eggs whilst I was chatting, you must have been hungry,' changing the subject back to food, seeing the clean plate.

'The story kept making me hungry. You should tell it to others, you're a talented girl.'

'Ah, thanks, Freda. I like to write stories too. Would you like a coffee now? Cos I fancy another one after all that storytelling.'

'I bet you do, go on then, make it two coffees, just ordinary for me, you chose your own, love,' Freda replied, feeling all excited.

I went up to the coffee machine to press the appropriate picture for their coffees and brought them back over to her.

'Can we play a game of animal snap? I'd like that,' she asked, hoping I would say yes.

'Sounds like a good idea, you are very alert today. It so happens it's game morning so I'll get a pack of cards from the games cupboard.'

Issy soon came back with a pack of animal cards to lay face down on the table, after she had cleared the breakfast tray. They took it in turns to pick up a card, trying to match it with another, picking up another card, before they shouted out the word snap!

'Oh, this is fun, you have to remember where the last card is,' she giggled.

'You do, that's the aim of the game, it tests your memory, which is good for all of us.'

Another member of staff came over to look after her, whilst Issy took her lunch break in the staff room.

'I'll see you later, Freda, it's my break now, OK?' Issy gave her a squeeze, before walking off.

She went off into the staff room for her lunch break which she so needed after all that storytelling, although she loved it.

A plate of various sandwiches was laid out on the table for all to help themselves, a kind gesture from the kitchen staff as an appreciation for their help. Issy plated up a few with some plain crisps to keep her energy levels up. She turned her phone back on to check for any messages. One from Mum, which always concerned her, hoping she was OK.

Just checking to see you're having a lovely day, Sam and I are meeting up for lunch later. I'll pop over and take the dogs out as it's a sunny afternoon, they'll need walking. Love Mum X

I sent one back thanking her for taking the dogs out, wishing her a lovely lunch with Sam.

The afternoon continued with a guest appearance. A local lady from a choir came over to sing for the residents. Hand-held instruments were given out to the patients, to shake to the beat of the music, all enjoying a delightful memorable afternoon's entertainment. Refreshments and cakes were on offer after, for all to indulge in. The celebrations continued throughout the afternoon until the evening staff took over, at six o'clock, when Issy wheeled a very tired Freda back to her room. Issy stayed with her until one of the night staff came into her room. A good afternoon was clearly had by one lady.

Chapter Twenty-two

'Hello, anyone at home?' Issy announced once she got home.

'In here, Sis,' Amy answered as Issy stepped into the kitchen, as she was preparing their dinner.

'Smells yummy, let me guess, a spag bol, another childhood favourite.'

'Indeed, sit down and I'll serve up, you must be starving after today's long shift,' Amy answered, seeing her look slightly weary.

'I am. I told my patient all about the hedgehogs, and I turned it into a guessing game, as to what creatures they were. She had a laugh about it all, being the main thing. How are they doing now, did you see them today?' she was eager to know.

'Oh, they are eating well and we're releasing them back outside in a few days, once we are confident, they can fend for themselves.'

'Super, that's what we like to hear.' They high fived each other.

'We also had a few baby kittens brought in today by a lady. They were so cute. The mum had just given birth to three, who were all fine. They are black and white, one of the kittens has a white fluffy bit on the tip of her tail, extra cute in my opinion. I would have one, had we not got the dogs, though dogs are more reliable, they don't suddenly disappear like cats do!'

'I've got a cat allergy, remember, so it's not an option for me, besides which we are dog lovers in our family, Amy. Yummy spag bol, by the way, we haven't had one in ages, have we? Where are the dogs, by the way?'

'They're outside somewhere, sniffing about. I let them out earlier.'

Just as she spoke, they stood by the back door, waiting patiently to be let back in. Amy opened the door as they dashed past her, checking their food bowls for any scraps.

'Hello, girls. You've just been fed, no more till breakfast, I'm afraid,' Amy reminded them, as they turned to look at her as if they understood every word.

'Who's for a cuppa before we binge watch something on TV. I'll put the kettle on while you load the dishwasher.' Issy desperately wanted to crash on the sofa before having an early night.

'Two green teas coming up.'

She clicked the remote for the TV, eager to catch up on the news on the Square in *Eastenders*, being their favourite soap, with all old characters making a brief return, adding excitement to the storylines.

Amy brought in two mugs of green tea with a small plate of digestives. By half nine Issy was ready for bed.

'I'm knackered, I need my bed. Can you let the dogs out before locking up please? See you in the morning, Amy,' as she gathered up the strength to walk up the stairs. Amy quickly stacked the dishwasher, wiping the surfaces clean before she shut up shop, as she was ready for her bed too.

Another day waking up to the sunrise as it gradually beamed through the window.

Amy sat on the edge of her bed, lifting both arms high, embracing a new day as she stretched herself up to an upright position. It felt good, it always did the trick.

It was a perfect day for releasing the hedgehogs back into their own environment, nestled under a green bush in the practice garden later today. She had a quick cool shower to invigorate her body, then rushed downstairs to let the dogs out before getting the mugs and bowls out for breakfast.

'Morning Sis, sleep well?' Issy asked, stifling a yawn. 'I need a coffee to wake me up,' taking out the cafetière, adding two scoops of ground coffee and water to stand before pushing the plunger down ready to pour. 'Did you know it's International Women's Day today. Amy? Well, that's what Facebook says anyway!

Something to embrace, strong women together making all the difference.' She walked over to Amy, giving her the biggest hug, feeling grateful to have her in her life; girls together!

'Love you to the moon and back. I'm taking these two to Mum's, as I envisage a long day ahead. They can take them out for walks.' Amy quickly messaged Mum, warning her she would just drop them off on her way to work.

All good, see you in a minute, we'll take care of them, Amy xx Mum texted back.

'Come on, you two, you're going to Grandma's for the day.' They raced back in so I could get them ready to leave for work.

'Ready, Issy? I'll drop you off after,' she shouted up the stairs.

Amy parked up at Jodie's, gathering up the dogs, and turned the key in the bungalow, to see Mum sitting in her dressing gown, ready to receive them.

'Thanks Mum, it means a lot.' Amy pecked her on the cheek before making a beeline to the car again. Next stop the care home.

'See you later, Sis,' Issy said, getting out of the car after Amy pulled up.

Arriving at the care home Issy was greeted by waving hands, seeing Freda in her wheelchair by a table near the window in the lounge. She was ready for the day. Her helper noticed me walking up to her and handed her over to me for the day shift.

'Good morning, Freda, how are you today?' Issy leant in to ask her.

'Well, I'm glad you're here, I'll have scrambled eggs on toast again please, with a cuppa,' she quickly told Issy before she could say anything else.

'Coming straight away and I'll have my usual cappuccino, as I left in a rush this morning. We dropped off our dogs to my parents today. They love having them for company, taking them out for walks.'

'What's happening with the hedgehogs, have you heard anything from your sister?'

'Wow Freda, you've got a good memory after I told you yesterday!' Issy applauded her as she passed over her breakfast with a cup of tea. Issy joined her, sipping her cappuccino in between helping her cut up her toast. 'Well, today's the day I think they get put back outside under a bush, where they belong in nature,' she explained.

'Oh, that's lovely, best news so far today!' Freda said, feeling happy. 'Could you ask your sister to take some pictures? I would love to see them.'

'I'll text her now to remind her to take some, and say that you were asking about them, Freda.'

Within minutes Amy messaged her back, saying it was happening today and she'd take some pictures when they released them. Issy confirmed to Freda they were being released today.

'I look forward to seeing them,' she replied, smiling up at Issy.

Back at the vets, Amy had a final peek at the young hedgehogs before they went outside to be released under a bush in undergrowth by the hedge. It was a memorable moment when a few staff gathered outside to witness the occasion. The weather was fortunately kind to them, as we decided that the best time to do the honours was at lunchtime, when those who wanted could join the small crowd outside.

Amy swiped her camera on her phone, to take a few photos, as the hedgehogs were carefully lifted from the cardboard box, placing them in the hedge undergrowth.

'I have the honour today to release these two hedgehogs brought in by Amy a few days ago, to continue to enjoy their lives in mother nature,' Tracey announced to the few members of staff gathered around at the rear of the garden.

'Amy, would you like to do the honourable deed of taking them out of the box, please. I'll take some photos on my phone to send you after,' she continued.

'Oh yes, thank you. I'd love to. OK here we go, camera to the ready … and off they go, slowly walking under the bush.' Amy gave a running commentary in the build-up to the moment.

There followed applause by the onlookers, and a few more photos were taken by others, enough to document the occasion in a scrapbook at the practice. Everyone made their way back inside, to continue their lunch break, before resuming the day's activities.

'Well, that was fun, I didn't expect to be asked to actually release them, ha ha fame at last,' Amy remarked to some of the other staff who had hung around for a few minutes.

'Well done, Amy, you were brilliant,' a colleague remarked. 'Back to work we go!'

'Who's next?' Amy asked, taking her seat at reception.

She started to book everyone in on the system, as different pets were brought in. One, in particular, stood out from the rest: a gorgeous-looking German short-haired pointer puppy, a not so common breed in this country. She had a beautiful soft brown and white speckled coat.

'Good morning, who have we here?' Amy looked over her desk to see a small puppy with a bright red collar attached to her lead.

'Oh, this is Luna, we've only just bought her from a good breeder. She's nine weeks young and full of life. She's here for a booster injection and anything else she needs.'

'Perfect, oh yes, I see she's registered with us, please take a seat and a vet will call you in soon.'

'Thank you. I'm Mrs Ramsey, by the way,' she added with a smile.

As Luna wagged herself across the floor in excitement, a little puddle emerged, nothing unusual with such young pups. A nurse came out from behind the reception armed with a mop!

Another lady shortly arrived with another unusual breed; a Hungarian Vizsla, a rust-coloured gorgeous dog with short smooth velvety ears. Both breeds were classed as working gundogs, in the world of Crufts, a programme Amy loved to watch every year, being a dog lover.

A few were heard in the waiting room as others passed them by; all creatures big and small.

The next lady brought in a crate with two rabbits needing some expert attention. A pure white one, the other being light brown. On closer inspection both had inflamed red eyes, causing problems with their tear ducts, eye drops would help clear that up for them.

'Luna please,' a male vet announced as he came out from his surgery door, seeing the patient dogs in the waiting room. Mrs Ramsey stood up, leading an excitable Luna into his surgery.

'Hi, and who have we here? She's a German pointer, isn't she? I've been watching them on Crufts this weekend, such beautiful dogs, aren't they?' he remarked, causing her owner to place a huge smile across her face.

'Thank you, this is Luna who is nine weeks young and needs a booster today,' she said, handing over her blue doggy passport.

'Perfect, I'll give her a good check over anyway,' he continued, lifting her onto the examination table. She was oblivious to his examinations as he was armed with some beefy smelling dog food in one hand, as he manhandled Luna with the other. He checked her heart with his stethoscope, giving the all clear, before inserting her booster into the fur of her neck. Another one squirted up Luna's nostril, causing her to sneeze a little as it irritated her, job done, she was placed back down on the Lino floor. She ate a handful of dog food as a reward. Mrs Ramsey then led her back out, as Luna skated along the floor, eager to make a quick exit, to pick up the bill from the reception.

'That was an expensive morning,' she chuckled to herself under her breath, swiping her card to pay.

Amy took her break for lunch in the staff room, pulling out her phone to check for any urgent messages. One was from Dad, which was unusual as he didn't usually bother with his phone, so Amy decided to give him a call. He picked up after two rings.

'Amy, thanks for ringing me. It's Mum, she's not well, she's feeling a bit dizzy, so I told her to lie down. She's been there a few hours now,' he continued. naturally sounding concerned.

'Oh Dad, she's probably a bit under the weather, nothing to worry about, but keep an eye on her. Make sure she drinks water and tea, no coffee though, OK? Keep me updated, please. Are the dogs OK? Let them out in the garden, that's good enough until I pick them up. Must go as I'm on my lunch break.'

Amy hung up before he got more flustered.

She texted Issy to let her know.

Thanks for telling me, I'll check in on them later too. Xx she sent one back a few minutes later.

The day at the practice continued pretty smoothly as Amy's day drew to a close. Mum was naturally on her mind so she made a quick exit, calling on her way home, relieving them of the dogs as soon as she could.

'I'm back now, Dad,' she shouted down the corridor after letting myself in.

'In our bedroom,' he bellowed back. She walked into their bedroom seeing her mum flat out in bed, looking out of sorts. She looked worn out and hardly spoke, which concerned her more.

'Have you rung the doctor, Dad? As she isn't responding too much.'

'I think you're right. She's deteriorated a bit and needs checking over,' he confirmed, looking more worried.

'I'll ring them now, 'scrolling down her contacts till she found the doctor's number, clicking it immediately.

'How can I help?' a lady answered the phone.

Amy explained the situation, classifying it as a medical emergency, so they sent out a doctor as soon as possible.

Ten minutes elapsed and a knock at the door, alerting the sleeping dogs as they raced to the front door.

'Miss Stevens? I'm Dr Russell, to see your mother, Jodie.'

'Oh yes, thank you for coming, I'll take you through to see her.' Amy led the way to her bedroom.

'Thank you, I'll check her out, it may be an infection. They can cause havoc with dizzy spells, soon to be sorted with a short course of antibiotics. Please don't worry, your mum will be fine, I promise,' she added, seeing Amy's concern. She bent over to give her mum a kiss, before leaving the doctor alone with her.

She left the room with Dad and made them a cup of tea.

'She's in good hands now, Dad.' Amy placed a hand on him to soothe his worries.

'She is, thanks to you. You're such a lovely daughter, Amy.' He reached out, placing an arm around her shoulder to comfort her.

Moments later, the doctor wandered into the kitchen.

'Well, as I expected, she's got a water infection, so I've given her a three-day course of antibiotics, which should definitely clear it up and she'll be able to get back to living again. I'll leave you with the tablets, twice daily please, drink plenty of water throughout. I know it's not easy, I'll be the first to admit that and I'm a doctor, shows we're all the same,' she added, laughing. 'I'll see myself out, thank you. Let me know if things change.'

'I will.' Amy shut the door behind her.

Half an hour later Issy walked in.

'And before you ask, I walked here, I needed the exercise. How is Mum now? I've been so worried, given her age,' she asked, feeling concerned.

'The doctor came out and she's got an infection, so she's been given a course of antibiotics. She should be fine after a few days,' Amy reassured her.

Chapter Twenty-three

They got home much later that evening, both feeling worn out from the unexpected development with their mum. They didn't have any energy to cook dinner, so scrambled eggs on toast seemed the best option. They needed to wind down before they turned in for the night, so they watched an episode of *Countryfile* on TV. Amy thought she'd best check if everything was OK at the bungalow before lights out, so she rang Dad, who answered immediately.

'How's Mum now?' she sounded overly concerned.

'Oh, I've just given her a second tablet for the night, she should start to feel better in the morning. Now you stop worrying and go to bed, you've helped us out enough today,' he insisted.

'OK Dad. Good night, sleep tight.' He hung up before she could say anything else.

The following morning Amy checked her phone again as she dressed for work.

Mum had a bad night, probably due to the tablets. She's hardly slept, don't worry, she's taking it easy today.

Not the best news to start my day, she thought.

Don't worry Dad, it's probably the antibiotics as they start to take effect. Let her sleep and drink plenty of water today. I'll pop in later. Just update me please. Amy shot one back quickly to reassure him. He sent her a thumbs up emoji.

She updated Issy before they both hit the road for work. They left the dogs curled up in their beds in the kitchen after feeding them. As much as Mum loved the dogs, she couldn't cope with them today. Dad was by her side mostly, playing nurse.

Issy chose to walk to work, needing the exercise, leaving Amy to drive straight to her practice.

'Good morning, Amy, how's your mum feeling today?' Tracy asked, as she walked past the reception to turn all the lights on and check everything was looking tidy before an onslaught of pets arrived through the doors.

'Thanks for asking, Tracy, she's not great, had a bad night so I'll pop in after work. My dad is caring for her, doing his best.'

'If you need to finish early, that's fine, just come and find me. Your mum takes priority, don't worry, lovely.' She placed a comforting arm on Amy's shoulder, which she needed.

'I will, thank you, Tracey.'

The day continued as the doors were unlocked. A few people walked in with their pets. Two cockapoos needing a check-up. It was booster day for many this morning.

The next lady to walk through the doors with a crate, with two tortoises. Amy glanced through their cage holes, noting their large green and black speckled shells. On closer inspection she saw a head peer out from in between his body, with two black eyes staring at her.

'They are lovely, what are their names?' she asked the lady, who placed the cage on the desk.

'Oh, this is Fred and his mate Bob. They are tortoiseshells with their beautiful markings. They are two years old, we think. I rescued them last year, after they were brought into a shelter,' she explained.

'That's good of you, so what can we do today for them?'

'Well, their eyes seem to be a bit bloodshot, I need them looking at, please.'

'Not a problem.' Amy started to type on her computer, to send through to the next available vet. A queuing system was quickly building up.

'Take a seat in the waiting area, a vet will be out shortly.' She indicated the patient area.

'Thank you.' She grabbed the cage from Amy's desk to take a seat in the waiting room.

Tracy brought Amy a much-welcomed cup of coffee, leaving it by the side of her desk, away from the computer!

'I thought you needed this, Amy,' placing the red mug on a coaster nearby.

'Thank you.' She took a sip before the next customer came over.

The morning carried on as normal till lunch time, when Tracey took over her shift. She was glad to take her break, hoping to catch up with Dad about Mum's recovery. She made herself a cuppa in the staff room, sitting on the sofa. She took out the sandwiches she'd bought from the supermarket. Tuna mayonnaise being her all-time favourite, with a few plain crisps on the side. What's not to like, she chuckled.

She took her phone out to ring Dad, hoping all was well.

'Dad it's me, all OK with Mum?' She had been redirected to voicemail, which wasn't good. Perhaps he was in the bathroom or taking a nap. She'd try Issy instead, knowing she might have been in touch, she thought.

Her phone suddenly burst into life.

'Amy it's me, I've spoken to Dad, ten minutes ago. Mum's resting but finding it hard to fight off the infection. Dad's taking a nap on the sofa now. Don't worry, she'll get through this, she's a fighter, Amy,' Issy reassured her aching nerves. 'Can you pick me up on your way back? I'll walk home to check on the dogs soon. Bye for now, Sis.' She hung up, blowing a kiss down the phone.

Amy was somewhat satisfied with her response yet not entirely convinced until she saw Mum later. Five o'clock couldn't come quickly enough, so Amy started to tidy up before closing time in an hour. Tracy wandered over, encouraging her to pack up and see her mum, which she was very grateful for.

'Off you go, family comes first, you've been excellent today,' Tracey wouldn't take no for an answer.

'Thank you, I appreciate it.' Amy stood up, pushing her swivel chair back to stretch her legs. She retrieved her things from her locker and headed straight to her car.

She sent a quick text to Issy to say she was on her way to the bungalow, before she zoomed off into the distance.

On the way there she thought she'd pick up a fish pie from Tesco, one from their Finest range. Dad wasn't a natural cook, and Mum definitely wasn't fit enough to cook. So a hearty fish pie it was, being a fisherman he would thank her for that. She parked up on their drive, to see James's car outside. She wasn't sure this was the best idea for them to just turn up, knowing Mum was unwell, she wouldn't exactly be in the mood for visitors.

'Hello, is anyone home?' Amy shouted out as she walked into the bungalow.

We are,' came a familiar voice from afar.

Julie appeared from nowhere, making her jump back a step.

'I hope you don't mind, Amy, your mum wanted to see me. I drove the car. James is on an overnight work course.'

'Oh, lovely to see you, Julie, I assume you brought Alice?' Amy wondered where she was.

'Absolutely, she's fast asleep in her pram in the lounge, you can have a quick peek.'

'Ooh, yes please.' Amy walked into the lounge to see her nearly stirring to wake up, dressed in a pink flowery baby jumpsuit.

'Hello Alice, it's your cousin Amy who's checking up on your aunty, she's been feeling poorly lately,' she spoke over the pram softly. At that point Alice started to wriggle her legs, slowly waking up from her deep sleep.

Amy bent down to pick her up as she raised her arms in submission. A very special moment holding her cousin in her arms. Amy gave her a big kiss on her forehead.

'There we go, shall we go and find your mum? You're probably hungry and I am too,' she giggled, looking into Alice's eyes as she gazed back into hers.

At that moment Julie came in seeing me holding Alice. 'You've definitely got the knack, Amy,' she remarked, seeing Amy and Alice snuggled up together.

'Well, she's gorgeous. I'll babysit any time when you both need a night out,' she added, beaming with joy.

'Careful, I might just take you up on that!' Julie chuckled.

The next day Mum was back to her normal self, the antibiotics had obviously worked their magic. Julie and Alice slept over in Issy's old bedroom down the corridor, as was suggested by Mum before her impromptu visit yesterday. Work for Amy and Issy carried on as usual till Friday eventually arrived, the weekend just around the corner.

'Good morning, Julie, how did you sleep last night? I hope Alice behaved!' Mum asked, as she switched the kettle on to make that all important first cup of tea of the day.

'Good thanks, Alice slept through till five o'clock, which is very good for one so young,' she announced, feeling relieved to have had a decent night's sleep in a while.

'Oh, that's brilliant, let that continue, though she may go through peaks and troughs as they all do,' Jodie smiled at Julie.

Julie's mobile rattled on the kitchen table, alerting her it was James.

'Good morning, how's your course going? I stopped off at Jodie's last night. Alice slept till five this morning, a six-hour sleep which is great.'

'All good here but boring, that's excellent news with Alice. Can't wait to see you both. Must go, love you loads.' He hung up in a hurry.

Mum took out two mugs with a tea bag to dunk in each!

'Fancy an egg on toast?' she asked, after handing over the mugs of tea.

'Yes please, I need to keep my milk flowing!' Julie added, giggling.

'It's tough work breastfeeding at all hours of the day, but we know breast is best, we all know it's so true, you just have to persevere,' Jodie explained, speaking from her own experience.

'Our two were both breast fed, then topped up with a bottle later on. That's the way to do it, Julie. OK, lecture over!' Mum said, not wanting to upset or bombard her with too much information.

'Would you like to go for a walk with the dogs and Alice, before you go home, unless you desperately need to get back. We could have lunch later as well?' Mum asked, hoping Julie would stay a bit longer.

'Actually, that would be lovely, as James won't be back till much later, with the traffic being probably heavy too.'

'Perfect, you can relax now. Put your coat on and I'll get the dogs ready to go to the park.'

They set off, with Alice tucked up in her pram and Jodie leading the way to the park. As the sun was out they enjoyed a tranquil stroll around, seeing all things brightly coloured, the daffodils and a blanket of bluebells shimmering over the grass. Birds tweeting, talking to each other, giving a sense of peace and quiet as they strolled along. They passed many dog walkers; cockapoos, Jack Russells and labradors sniffing each other out, as they stopped.

'This is very pleasant, a lovely peaceful walk to shake off any stress,' Julie remarked, feeling chilled, embracing every moment.

She spoke too soon, after hearing her phone vibrate in her pocket.

'I'd best take this, seeing it's James,' Julie announced, knowing he had little time to chat whilst at the conference.

'Hi there! How are you and Alice today? Are you still with Jodie?'

'We are out for a walk, taking the dogs too whilst Amy and Issy do a food shop this morning. I'll leave after we have lunch,' she said, before hanging up. The signal wasn't very good, so Julie only got the gist of what he was saying. She would make her own mind up when she'd leave, they would see each other anyway once at home.

Half an hour later they decided to head up to the café for lunch; a baked potato with whatever topping was on offer. They all loved tuna mayonnaise with some lettuce and tomatoes with a few plain crisps on the side if you wanted. All homemade on site, which always tasted better.

'Good afternoon, ladies, what can I get you today?' a friendly lady asked them, once they had chosen their table.

'Two baked potatoes with tuna mayonnaise, please,' Jodie smiled at her, feeling hungry.

'Of course. Any drinks?' she asked.

'Two cappuccinos, please.' She tapped in their order on her tablet.

Moments later she brought over their cappuccinos. Alice was fast asleep, so they took advantage of the time to chat about anything and everything. They became closer, enjoying each other's company on every visit, something Jodie valued so much, making up for lost time after reuniting with her long-lost brother and his now wife. Seeing them so happy with Alice meant the world.

They ate their baked potatoes, relishing every mouthful, until Alice finally started to wake up.

Julie picked her up to lie down nestled in her arms, lifting her jumper discreetly to breast feed her. She felt proud to do so in public, as it felt the most natural thing to do. Once she had found her comfortable position, Julie continued drinking her cappuccino, chatting to Jodie.

Jodie gazed up at Julie in awe as she admired her, taking everything in her stride, feeling so proud.

They arrived home feeling accomplished and relaxed. Mum let the dogs out in the garden, making the most of the sunshine and Alice, whilst Julie packed her bags to go home. Goodbyes always felt like forever, yet they only lived fifteen minutes away.

'I'll help you load the car whilst you fasten Alice in her seat,' Mum suggested.

'Thank you, I'd best get a move on or James will start worrying. Thanks for today and see you soon.'

Julie checked she had everything before jumping into the driver's seat to head off. She waved at Jodie as she watched her indicate to turn left out of her drive.

Jodie walked back into the bungalow, feeling a little sad to see them go, yet glad to have the place to herself again. Life felt good.

Chapter Twenty-four

'Is that you, love?' Dad echoed as Jodie stepped back into the bungalow.

'It is indeed, I've just waved Julie off on her way back home to James. We had a lovely time in the park, then had lunch after at the café up the road,' she recalled.

'I'm so pleased for them, they seem great parents to young Alice, who is such a cutie,' Jodie continued.

'Jack and I went fishing up the lake, caught a tench this time, our first, which was exciting. They are beautifully scaled fish with delicate fins,' Dad explained, as Jodie popped the kettle on for a much-needed green tea, taking out two mugs from the cupboard.

'Thought we might do a week's fishing trip one day in the summer, whilst we still can. Would you mind?'

'Good idea, make hay whilst the sun shines, I could spend time with Julie and Alice, though I mustn't interfere too much; she might tire of me. I don't think I could go away with Elaine, she's a bit full-on in my opinion. She prefers a quiet life, mixing with others isn't really her idea of fun. Besides, I don't like being too far from home; the girls and the dogs are my world,' Jodie chatted on, regardless.

'Time will tell,' Dad said, before going to change out of his fishing attire.

Moments afterwards, Amy and Issy appeared in the kitchen, looking rather pleased with themselves, the dogs raced up to greet them, circling around their feet as they bent down to stroke them to calm them.

'Hello, you two, you look happy-go-lucky, what's the news in Balamory? Remember that lovely children's programme on TV, set in Scotland with all the colourful houses?' Mum remarked, singing the song out loud.

'Oh yes, I think the pink house stood out the most, amongst the vibrant yellow, red and purple houses. We loved that programme, Mum.'

'Well, I just heard that Lottie is dating a handsome chap, which comes as a complete surprise to us,' Amy announced.

'Wow, that's lovely yet unexpected, don't worry, we won't say anything, we promise,' Mum added as Dad walked in, hearing the commotion.

'Well, it's definitely all happening in our circle of friends; one wedding and a christening, now a new fella on the horizon,' Dad remarked, giggling. Good news all round then, life gets better by the minute,' he added, smiling.

'So, do we know anything about this new chap, his name, where they met and his job?' Mum continued speculating.

'I know nothing, Mum, as Manuel would say in *Fawlty Towers*. I'm meeting up with Lottie later so I'll fill you in on the details then ... patience is the key, Mum,' Amy explained, wanting to close the conversation.

Monday evening was the night she was due to meet up with Lottie at the pub up the road, a full interrogation would take place about her latest chap.

'Good evening, Lottie,' Amy announced as she noticed her getting a drink from the bar.

'Oh, hi there, Amy, I didn't see you sneak up.'

'What can I get you?'

'I'll have a mocktail, an elderflower cordial on the rocks, I think it's called, anyway, it's scrummy,' Lottie confirmed.

'Perfect, coming right up, my treat.' Amy smiled at her, placing her hand on Lottie's shoulder. They walked over to a table in the corner of the room, putting their drinks on two beer coasters.

'A little dicky bird tells me you have become two; a handsome chap has sprung on the horizon, truth or is it a lie?' (Noting the program *Would I lie to you!*)

'Well . . . it is . . . the truth!'

'OK, his name, his place of work, details please, or forever hold your peace!'

'Oh, this is scary, I'd best not mess up then, Amy, or you'll never speak to your old friend again!' Lottie added, giggling, knowing Amy couldn't live without her.

They took a large sip of their drinks before replacing them on the mats so Lottie could start her side of the romantic story. Lottie started to unravel the story in small chunks as Amy listened attentively.

'So, I met George a few months ago, after several casual dates at a quiz night held at another pub where he lives. He was part of our team one night, and I was rather smitten by his good looks. We seemed to hit it off, he was always chatty and interested in my floristry job, as I travelled around in my van with bouquets of flowers in the back.'

'Go on, describe this handsome bloke to me. Is he tall, dark and clean shaven, which I could well imagine he is? That would suit you, Lottie,' Amy enquired, picturing this image in her mind.

'Correct, he is of average height, light brown hair with blue eyes, to be precise. I hope that satisfies your investigations, Miss Marple!'

'Sounds handsome to me. Tell me more, what's his job? I assume he's employed?'

'Correct again, he's a landscape gardener, self-employed, taking on numerous interesting jobs. He designed gardens of all shapes and sizes, big or small, he loves them all!'

'Very funny, he sounds a practical keeper, if you want my opinion, Lottie. You chose well there my friend. Cheers, here's to your new handsome landscaper, for want of a posher title. Seriously, that fits in nicely with your floristry work. Just one other question, before I raid the bar for two packets of nuts or whatever you fancy. Where does he live?'

'Oh yes, he's a local guy from Broadway, the next town from here, and lives in a thatched cottage near the High Street. I've not seen it yet, I'm waiting to be invited over, we'll see,' Lottie concluded, feeling in need of a packet of nuts and another drink.

'Another drink, Amy, my turn, with a packet of nuts?' Lottie announced.

'Ha ha, yes please, an orange juice this time with ice and those nuts!'

Lottie walked up to the bar to place the order.

Whilst she was walking back with the drinks, Amy's phone buzzed. She didn't recognise the number, so she hit the red button to end the call.

A few minutes later it rang again, only this time she decided to answer it, despite feeling a bit cautious.

'Amy Stevens?' a muffled voice asked.

'Who's this please?' not wanting to divulge anything.

'It's Trixi from Rowans, I'm so sorry to disturb you. It's just we had an emergency RTA this evening and we are short of staff, so I wondered on the off chance, if you would be willing to come in tomorrow morning for a few hours. You would be paid double time; however, we do understand if you can't cover,' she continued, sounding desperate.

'Trixi, I'm sorry I didn't recognise your number, hence I didn't pick up. Of course I'll come in tomorrow, I'll see you at 8am,' Amy said, hopefully making her feel at ease. She hung up before she whittled on.

'Well, that's my Saturday morning sorted then. We certainly could do with the extra money, though it's not all about that, it's animal lives at stake here.' She updated Lottie.

'We'd better make this our last drink since I've got to be up early tomorrow. So when can we meet this handsome George? Unless it's too early in the relationship to go public.'

'No, it's not a problem, I'll see him tomorrow, so I'll chat it over with him, see what he thinks.'

'Great, I look forward to meeting him, bring him to ours if you like.'

On that note they finished their drinks and walked into the car park to drive off in separate directions.

Saturday morning came as soon as Amy's alarm struck 6.30, no time to hit snooze, she had furry friends to look after at the practice. She could honestly say she loved her new vocation in life, helping others was always magical. She knocked on Issy's door, peered around the door to ask her to feed the dogs later, being such an early hour. Amy needed to head off early and would have breakfast once there. Issy raised one hand in the air from underneath her duvet, confirming her duty.

'Good morning, Amy, thanks for coming in at short notice, it's much appreciated,' Trixi said as Amy walked past her, brushing her arm against Trixi's in a friendly gesture.

'So who have we got in today?' she asked as she walked through into the recovery area, hearing a few meows and moans as she passed the kennels one by one.

'Five recovering dogs and two cats, one cat sadly being an RTA brought in last night. She's got a broken back leg. Steve, the locum, had to operate on her last night . . . a successful repair. She has a pink bandage to keep it all tightly together encouraging quicker healing.'

Amy looked at the clipboard chart to see further information and hourly observations. Clearly a nurse would assist her with the necessary injections and supervision of meds.

'Fancy a coffee before we start, with an egg muffin I picked up on the way here from a McDonalds drive through?' Trixi asked, brightening up Amy's eyes.

She handed Amy a white plate from the cupboard, placing the muffin on it. We had filter coffee; the girls having bought a cafetière with the drinks float a few weeks before.

Checking each kennel carefully, they noticed a few red inflamed eyes in some dogs who needed eye drops at regular intervals, something Amy was shown how to administer with the nurse's supervision. It was a very delicate procedure, involving two of them, one keeping the dog calm, muzzling them temporarily to avoid being bitten, whilst Amy gently dropped the drops under the eyelid, gently massaging the fluid into the eye. Once she had done a few animals, she soon perfected her technique.

Time soon passed when Amy handed over her morning shift to a colleague for the afternoon. She texted Issy to see if she wanted to meet up at the café as she was in need of a pick me up wrap and cappuccino.

Was thinking the same myself, I'm on my way back from dog walking. Meet you in five.

Amy sent a thumbs up emoji.

'Afternoon ladies, what can I offer you today?' Amy walked up to the counter, seeing an array of scrumptious wraps and toasties.

'I'll have a cheese and tomato toastie and my sister will have a mozzarella and tomato melt with two cappuccinos, please.'

'Take a seat and I'll bring them over.' The lady started to prepare their drinks and toasties. 'Enjoy,' she said as she brought them over, placing them on the table.

Amy started to chat about her morning shift whilst enjoying her delights, trying to stifle a yawn in between bites. It had been a long day so far, the coffee stop helped to perk her up.

'Sounds like you had fun, now time to relax,' Issy remarked. 'Changing the subject ... I've spoken to George, and he is coming over tomorrow to have a roast at the Toby Carvery, you're welcome to join us, he'd love to meet us both.'

'Perfect. I'll book a table for four at one o'clock tomorrow. Great, looking forward to meeting George too,' Amy added before making a move.

Saturday was a day for catching up on chores before a new week. Sunday was a day to relax, having Sunday roast at the Toby Carvery; meeting George for the first time would be very special. Amy naturally was keen to see her best friend happy. Could this be the one? Time would tell.

Amy drove home, to make a shopping list for the week, taking

Issy for good measure. The afternoon was spent walking the dogs in the park which they enjoyed as the sun shone, making everything seem more pleasant.

Chapter Twenty-five

Sunday morning was a day of rest and relaxation and today they were finally meeting George, Lottie's new chap. Would he be the one, or was it the loving boyfriend she had secretly desired over these past years. Time was ticking so perhaps she wanted to settle down, get married and have babies of her own. Life had a habit of changing without any prior warning. You never know what's around the corner, surprising you when you least expect them.

'We're going to the Toby Carvery today, Issy,' Amy shouted up the stairs, lest she forgot.

'I'm just putting a bit of lippy on. I just want to look presentable seeing George for the first time,' Issy replied.

'I'll let the dogs out as we're leaving them here today, although I'm sure George is a dog lover, seeing Floss,' Amy added.

They parked up in the car park feeling slightly nervous, knowing They were about to meet Mr Right for their best friend, Lottie. They needed to check him out to see if he was a suitable match. They were about to find out.

'Good afternoon, we have a table booked under my name, Amy,' she told the lady waiting to seat everyone waiting by the entrance.

'Oh yes, follow me.' She grabbed four menus from the pile, leading the way to their table.

'Your waitress will be over shortly to take your drinks order. Are you all having a carvery today?' she asked, tapping away on her tablet.

They made themselves comfortable as if they were waiting for royalty, till Issy spotted Lottie looking around the room, trying to find where they were sitting. She waved her over, noting she was holding hands with George. Their hearts suddenly felt more at ease, an overwhelming feeling he was in love with her, dismissing all feelings of angst.

'Hi, this is George,' Lottie introduced him as they stood up to shake his hand. 'George, these are my besties I've been telling you about, Amy and her sister Issy. We've known each other since primary school and never looked back.'

'Oh, please sit down, I'm not royalty, I'm just plain vibrant George, well I hope I am!'

'Sorry George, just wanted to show our politeness, it's lovely to meet you at last. Lottie has told us lots about you, all good! Without further ado let's order some drinks before we go up to the carvery, it comes highly recommended,' Amy added enthusiastically.

Their waitress walked over armed with her tablet, ready to take the order. They ordered a bottle of Liebfraumilch for the occasion. They then made their way to the buffet counter, all having turkey with various vegetables with components from the side table.

'This looks lovely, thank you for inviting us. It's lovely to be out without the dogs, as much as we love them, we need our time too,' Issy commented, feeling slightly guilty.

They raised their glasses, wishing everyone good health and happiness.

The mains over, they moved on to dessert. They chose the warm chocolate brownie with a scoop of vanilla ice cream being an all-time favourite. Four cappuccinos after, they finished the meal off on a high.

'Back to ours to meet our hounds, you could pick up Floss and bring her over. We can all go out for a long walk in the arboretum, it's so lovely in the spring seeing the daffodils popping out everywhere,' Amy suggested.

'Perfect weather for it too, we'll meet you there in the car park by the entrance in half an hour, just text me when you leave yours, Amy,' Lottie added, feeling enthusiastic.

They paid up to head back to collect the dogs before meeting Lottie and George at the arboretum. On opening the house, greeted by two waggy tails, they let the dogs out into the back garden, before putting their leads on ready to drive to the park.

'We made it on time,' Amy said, as she gathered up the dogs from the boot.

A few minutes sniffing each other like reunited friends, George bent over to stroke Rosie and Bessy, meeting them for the first time. They then continued towards the park. Lottie took Floss's lead as he and Lottie walked hand in hand together, smiling at each other, looking loved up. A romantic relationship in the making, making Amy and Issy so happy to see them loved up. They instantly knew this wasn't just a fling, Mr handsome Right was in their midst.

'Fancy an ice cream from Mr Whippy over there?' Issy pointed out, seeing the blue van parked up from a distance.

'Oh, I love a 99 with a flake, my perfect indulgence for the week if the weather permits,' George added, winking at Lottie as they walked towards the small queue that was forming in front of the van.

He had only just parked up, seeing he was sliding the window to open up. A few girls were ready and waiting as they lined up behind them, patiently waiting their turn.

'Good day, ladies and gents, what can I entice you with today?' the man in the van asked, as they stepped in front.

'We will all have a 99 with a flake, so four, please.'

'Right you are!' he gestured, starting to pull the lever to release the ice cream.

'Would the dogs like a little one in a tub to lick?'

'Oh yes please, they'd love that, thank you.'

He handed over the small tubs for the dogs, placing them on the ground, which they soon lapped up. They took theirs from the ice cream holder by the van's window.

They continued walking and chatting, enjoying the scenery

and seeing everyone out and about, taking in the fresh air, placing happy smiles on faces.

'So, I hear you're a landscape gardener; Lottie told us the other day, a perfect combination with her as a florist delivering bouquets around the vicinity in a French-style van,' Issy opened up the conversation, eager to get to know George more.

'Well, it wasn't always my vocation, I changed careers last year from a boring 9 to 5 office job. I was an accountant, I studied in college, seemed like a good career at the time, until I realised after many years maths was not really my friend. Day in and day out in a stuffy office proved tedious, pretty much the same old every day.

'One day I had a light bulb moment, following my sister's illness; she was diagnosed with multiple sclerosis, initially affecting her mobility. It's a slow progressive muscle weakening illness sadly afflicting millions today, particularly in women. Currently no known cure, yet plenty of self-care options such as exercise and lifestyle changes, exercise being the top priority for maintaining mobility, as indeed we all need to be aware of in later life. Fortunately for her, it's a very slow burner. She currently attends a neurological centre, on a weekly basis, offering oxygen therapy in a hyperbaric oxygen chamber, the next best thing to a cure in her opinion. At last neurologists have accepted its benefits. It is now offered in every neurological centre around the country. Every year they have an MS Awareness Week, asking people from all walks of life to sponsor the charity, by participating in fun challenges to raise much-needed monies for every neurological centre in the UK. I decided to contribute, doing a sponsored run for the centre which she attends. Sadly, there is no government funding for these centres, they are all charity based, offering life-long support to help people enjoy everyday life to the best of their abilities,' he explained at great length, leaving us all awe-inspired.

'Oh wow, I'm so sorry to hear about your sister, thumbs up to your fundraising challenge. That's pretty impressive, she must be *so* proud of you. You're giving back your time in society.'

'Susi, my sister, is one strong courageous woman, she just gets on with life, defying the odds. She benefits greatly from the therapy, keeps her going for longer, enjoying life to the full.'

"We are a family who love to help others in life, doing our bit which is so important and uplifting these days,' Lottie supported George's comment.

'Absolutely, onwards and upwards, I say,' Amy announced, feeling encouraged.

They got so caught up in the conversation as time just raced by. They started their walk back to the car. Issy unlocked the boot of the car, lifting the dogs in, who soon lay down on their blanket.

George opened his car so Lottie could put Floss in the boot to peer out of the window once the boot was shut.

We formed a friendship circle locking us into a tight hug, before we drove off in separate directions. A good day was had by all.

Monday morning soon came around and today was an extra special week in the Oak House Care home. As Easter was fast approaching, several events were organised for all patients. Today was dog therapy day, a very popular event loved by all. Helpers were encouraged to bring their dog into the home, giving all patients the opportunity to use their three senses of touch, feel and stroke a dog to help lift their mood and enjoy the experience. The dogs were perfect for offering a calm atmosphere in any given situation.

Freda had often asked to see one of Issy's dogs, so today was the day. She decided to bring in Rosie, being the older of the two.

'It's therapy dog day at the care home, so I'm taking Rosie in to meet Freda, the lady I look after,' Issy told Amy as she was having a quick breakfast.

'Wow, that's different, I hope she behaves, Rosie that is. I think it's a great idea,' Amy remarked.

Issy pecked Amy on the cheek before they went their ways to work.

On arrival at the care home Issy was greeted by Trudy as she walked towards her, seeing Rosie.

'Hello and who do we have here?' she asked, leaning over to pat Rosie lifting her head in submission.

'This is Rosie, she's a five-year-old cockapoo I rescued a few years ago. I thought I'd bring her in today to show Freda as she's been asking me about her, hoping that I could bring her in. So here she is!' Issy explained, feeling enthusiastic.

'Perfect, let's go and introduce her to Freda.'

Trudy led the way into the main lounge, spotting Freda sitting in one of the burgundy armchairs by the window. She seemed a little low in mood this morning, so who better to cheer her than Rosie. Issy led her on a tight lead as she sniffed the ground on occasions pointing her nose to the air. Freda suddenly perked up as they walked towards her, seeing Rosie's tail flicking from side to side, eager to get closer to her.

'Oh who is this Issy? Have you brought your dog in to show me today?' she questioned, peering down at her.

'Indeed I have. This is Rosie, she's a cockapoo and is five years old.' Issy told her, hoping she would understand.

'Oh, she's adorable, Issy, can I stroke her, or will she bite me?'

'She won't bite you, she's a very friendly dog who loves any attention she can get. Just place your hand on her back and stroke her gently, she will love that, Freda,' Issy encouraged her.

'Her fur is so soft, it's lovely and smooth,' Freda remarked, smiling up at her.

'Would she like a biscuit or a drink you think?' she asked, sounding helpful.

'I've got a bowl in the car, I just don't want her to have any accidents, Freda, so I'll take her back home soon and I'll come back to cover the lunch shift,' Issy explained.

'Oh yes, you're right, we don't want any puddles, do we?'

'I'll see you later, I'll take her home now, she'll be fine there with her sister Bessy.'

'Bye for now, love, come back and have a coffee with me. I would love that,' she leant in, whispering in Issy's ear.

Issy walked over towards the exit as Trudy noticed her leaving, thanking her for bringing Rosie in. Issy told her she would be back in an hour for lunch time.

At home, Issy was greeted by Bessy as she opened the kitchen door, her nose firmly pressed against it. Issy quickly unlocked the back door to let them run free around the garden to sniff around, whilst she made herself a sandwich and made a cup of tea. She checked her phone for any urgent messages; only one from Amy, saying her day was going well, just another normal day at the practice.

Tuesday was craft day, and all were invited to make Easter bonnets which they could wear whilst sitting around the table for various meals. A craft table was laid out for helpers to pick out paper and stickers to glue on their bonnets, adding to the day's enjoyment.

Wednesday was dedicated to making Easter cards for family and friends, using colour pencils as they coloured in their Easter bunnies which were drawn out on coloured card paper, increasing their fine motor skills and concentration levels. Refreshments were served after with cake.

Their working week ended on a high, as the weekend staff took over covering regular staff, whilst they spent time with their individual families and friends over the Easter holiday to resume work again on Tuesday. Close family and friends were invited to see their loved ones in the home, to ensure they wouldn't feel isolated and alone. Easter Sunday was the perfect time for everyone to take time out and reflect on life, a meaningful day in the Christian calendar.

A short worship service was held in the chapel for all who enjoyed this special quiet time of reflection which was so meaningful to so many.

Chapter Twenty-six

All was looking well in the Stevens family. Amy and Issy were settling down nicely in their new house and enjoying their latest vocations in life. Lottie had finally found love with her new partner, George, after starting his new career as a landscape gardener, ending his boring 9-5 accountancy job. Working in nature seemed much more appealing and satisfying. Fresh air is always the best therapy for happiness. You're surrounded by trees and all things budding, depending on the time of year. Spring was particularly very colourful with various shades of yellow daffodils sprouting all around the garden. A blanket of bluebells on the lawns added to a picturesque scenery.

Jodie and Ralph were enjoying their new life in their bungalow. Ralph continued going on his fishing trips with his mate Jack, catching beautiful specimens of trout and pike, to name a few, then releasing them back into the waters.

Jodie made a new friend, Elaine, recently widowed, who brought back a small rescue dog, giving her much-needed companionship. They regularly went to the local café enjoying coffee and cake having a good weekly catch up.

The biggest news however was Jodie and Ralph becoming aunt and uncle to baby Alice. Jodie's brother and his wife Julie were delighted at having their daughter christened a few weeks ago, led by the Rev Ruth Murrey, where family and friends gathered on this happy occasion. Julie soon adjusted into her new role as mum as she enjoyed spending time making forever memories with young Alice, now 18 months young. Julie made new friends in the local church mums and tots group with its regular weekly meetings in one of the cosy lounge areas, serving coffees and light refreshments to all new mums as they sat and chatted, whilst their little ones were playing on the carpet with a variety of toys, donated by other members of the congregation and the wider community.

One year passed by when the announcement was made, Lottie decided to get engaged to the handsome George. They had been engaged for two years before setting a wedding date in September to be held in her home town of Stow. A simple yet poignant occasion in the church led by the Rev Ruth Murrey, who soon became a lifelong friend to the family. The wedding day was a beautiful autumnal day, depicting its various shades of brown and yellows with a scattering of leaves around the church lawns.

A reception was held afterwards in a beautiful wood beam barn in the Victorian style Hyde house in its picturesque grounds of Stow on the Wold, an ideal venue for weddings and parties.

Lottie chose a cream colour dress with silver sequins aligned around the long dress with a simple, yet perfect headdress to match. Working as a florist had its advantages as Lottie created her own apricot and yellow carnations for her hand-held bouquet of flowers and the same for all the bridesmaids, a perfect colour to match her outfit on an autumnal day.

Grace joined Amy and Issy as bridesmaids in hot pink midi dresses with white mid heel ballet type shoes. A photographer was hired for the day taking numerous photos of the groom and bride, as they patiently stood under an arch in the garden overhung with greenery and white lily flowers.

Group photos followed with family and close relatives and friends with the bride and groom standing in front posing for the camera.

An informal reception was held afterwards in a barn with ten decorated tables with cream linen tablecloths draped over every large round table. Silver cutlery was neatly placed by the sides of individual place mats along with white Royal Doulton plates on different countryside place mats. Wine glasses and glasses for water along with a water jug on each table making all ten tables look stunning. A scattering of rose petals was sprinkled around the centre of the table with red love hearts in between, depicting a scene of love and romance as they started their marriage as husband and wife.

The day went off with a bang, all enjoying the delicious food served to them washed down with a glass of bubbly to mark the memorable occasion. Lottie and George decided on a fortnight's honeymoon in Tuscany, in a small town called Lucca, amidst vineyards and goats wandering freely around the countryside. Flying into Florence they hired a small Fiat Uno at the airport, taking them to their rustic house for the duration in the town of Lucca. The thatched roof house was offroad down an uneven side track in the middle of nowhere, before they finally parked up outside their house for the week.

The owner of the property, who lived in a separate part of the house, provided everything to ensure they had the best honeymoon they could have ever imagined. She would leave them a buffet style breakfast at 6am each morning, consisting of freshly baked bread with a selection of white and brown seeded rolls. A selection of cereals as well as fruit and yoghurt and nuts added to the variety.

Outside were olive tree vineyards producing olive oil in abundance. They were bottled up locally before they reached the supermarkets around the area. Olive oil was poured into saucers for dipping pieces of bread to soak up, savouring in your mouth promoting numerous health benefits.

Stepping outside of the kitchen back door, was a veranda with a round garden metal table with two chairs either side overlooking the extensive rough woodland below, with goats milling around as the cow bells on their collars rang out whilst they jumped around. The bells alerted farmers to their whereabouts, making life easier to retrieve them and move them on into new pastures. Lottie and George often sat meditating and drinking coffee or ice-cold drinks, admiring the picturesque views, before they started their day in earnest. It was pure escapism from stresses of daily life where they could claim back peace and tranquillity through nature, listening to bird songs and the endless sounds of crickets during the heat of the day.

After clearing the breakfast dishes away, they gathered up their day's belongings and packed everything in their backpacks as they drove off to explore the surrounding area. Public transport was non-existent in the countryside, so a car was absolutely vital, parking up in various places, walking around the streets in the heat of the day with plenty of stops for water and ice creams to hydrate as the outdoor temperatures soared during the day, slapping on factor 25 sunscreen lotion or higher, to protect from the sun's rays.

Lottie and George had programmed a week's itinerary in advance, their first trip being to the famous town of Florence, one of the busiest and most popular cities in Italy. A mere one hour fifteen minutes by train, adorned with lush scenery as the train passed through the countryside, before pulling up into Florence station. Passengers disembarked in their droves, eager to exit onto the main road which was surrounded by pedestrianized squares.

First stop was a café with mouthwatering pastries and cakes to drool over. When in Italy all diets were thrown out of the window whilst on holiday, as you only visited once or twice in your lifetime, so enjoying every moment was absolutely essential. They were on their honeymoon after all.

A handsome waiter surveyed the outside seating area with sun umbrellas over each table shielding everyone from the harmful sun's rays, then walked over to their table.

'Buongiorno, what can I bring you today?' speaking above the noise of the crowd so he could be understood.

'Two large cappuccinos with two lemon cheese gateaux, please,' George replied, before Lottie had time to think.

'I'll bring them to you in a moment.' He smiled sweetly at Lottie, striding back into the restaurant.

'He was friendly,' Lottie added with a chuckle.

'That's Italian men for you, always flirty!' winking at Lottie, showing off his romantic side.

He soon returned with their order on a tray balanced on his upturned right hand, placing it down gently on their table.

'Grazie.' George turned to look at the handsome waiter.

They enjoyed their cappuccinos and cake before settling the bill and moving on to wander the streets of Florence.

The side streets were full of small boutiques selling anything and everything from leather handbags to flowery sundresses and olive oil remedies in the form of massage oils and creams. A tourist's paradise. They meandered through the crowds avoiding bumping into other tourists. Fortunately, everyone was shielded from the day's heat as shop awnings were lowered over rooftops shielding from the heat of the day.

Moving on slowly through the hustle and bustle of the crowds, Lottie noted many postcard stands with every kind of greeting card you could possibly imagine, from animal to funny grimaces to the usual variety of picturesque postcards of nearby towns such as Siena. As was tradition on holiday Lottie bought a selection with stamps to send to her folks back home, hoping they would arrive before they returned, not that it mattered much, it was the thought that counted. They would write them once back at their base camp, sitting on the veranda with a few biros they picked up along their shopping trip with iced drinks. Lottie made a jug of orange and mango mocktail with plenty of ice cubes to keep them cool as the outside temperature lingered into the early evening, ensuring they were well hydrated. The courtyard also had a lovely swing seat with a comfortable padded floral cushion under a willow tree with evergreen tree branches towering over giving some shade.

Lunchtimes consisted of Italian style sweet or savoury crepes from the many kiosks around the side streets. Freshly made pizza baked in an open-air oven became a popular choice or a bowl of fresh salad with a variety of yoghurt dressings.

Lottie and George were blissfully happy as they walked hand

in hand up and down the streets admiring the ever-expanding views. Finally they meandered along the promenade surrounded by many posh boats in its harbour. An evening stroll was particularly magical as everything was illuminated with light bulbs hanging down from overhead street poles, as couples strolled along the promenade hand in hand with their lovers. Italy has always remained the country of fine dining and romance with so many beautiful cities to choose from and visit. They left Florence at around 5pm to catch a direct train back to Lucca, bringing their day of fun and adventure to a close.

Once home Lottie and George pulled out the mocktail jug from the large fridge, to take outside onto the veranda, to start writing their postcards ready to post in the morning. Lottie started to write hers to her side of the family and George on his side. All stamped up, they placed them in a visible place by the coffee machine so they wouldn't forget to post them wherever they went the next day.

'Let's sit on the swing and reflect on today,' before we go to bed,' George announced, taking Lottie by the hand, walking her over to the comfy garden swing, still holding hands as they sat close to each other.

'Sounds very romantic,' as she lifted her head to kiss him on the lips, drawing him into a long embrace.

'I'm glad we tied the knot, you're such a sweet caring young lady with a caring nature for all humans and animals alike,' he continued, letting his arms drop back onto his sides.

'You're making me blush saying those things, you're so sweet, darling George. I do love you so much, thank you for choosing me.' She kissed him again, drawing him into a final embrace before they walked back into the house, locking it up for the night. By the time they climbed into bed they were ready to go to sleep, a quick cuddle they rolled over till the alarm woke them in the morning.

The song "Morning has broken" was on her mind when the alarm went off at 7.15, ready for another day's adventure.

'Good morning, George, time to rise and shine, a new day is calling us.' She gently nudged him before he turned towards her, giving her her first cuddle of the day.

'Bonjourno! as they say in Italy, what's on the agenda today, Mrs Bright?'

'Funny, I could be a bright spark, lol,' she giggled, feeling loved up. 'Well, I thought we could find a local beach, have a swim, sunbathe on the sun loungers with a few mocktails to cool us off from the heat of the day, fancy that Mr B?'

'Sounds perfect, get to know the area and chill out. Tomorrow we can hit the road again and explore Siena, another must-see town.

A quick shower before breakfast they packed their swimming gear, not forgetting their sunglasses and factor 25 oil and water, before walking over to their car. Lottie had picked up a few sightseeing leaflets from the table for guests, giving them plenty of ideas for places to visit, making the most of their stay in this beautiful place of the world.

Once they pressed the button to start her up, they added the postcode of Lucca Beach to their trusty built in sat nav ready to drive off. George took the wheel, giving Lottie a well-deserved break from driving the van back home.

They arrived shortly after 8.30 to secure two sun loungers on the beach before the crowds bombarded them. The restaurant/ bar was just opening, lowering their awnings over the outside decking. White tables and chairs were evenly spread throughout the veranda with waterproof seat cushions for extra comfort to absorb wet bums after swimming.

As it was a private beach they had to pay a small fee, worth every euro as they were allocated lovely sun loungers with an umbrella and a small table for drinks and snacks as they lay back and relaxed reading their favourite book. Showers with changing huts and toilets were located by the bar, to be used before and after going into the sea to wash off salt water, before dining in the restaurant.

'This is cool, excuse the pun!' as she spread out the large bath towels across each sun bed. She made herself comfy whilst George went to change, returning with orange swim shorts with an orange chequered T-shirt. His torso was slim built with a few hairs on his chest, sending shivers all over Lottie as he walked past.

'You're looking trim in those shorts my love!' I commented as he walked towards the sun beds.

'Thank you, now it's your turn to impress, Mrs B!'

'Wait 'n see!' she chuckled as she took her bag to change at the beach hut. Within minutes she strutted her yellow flowery swimsuit as she walked towards him, wagging her bum from side to side, causing him to giggle.

'Right, race you to the water, think of that ice cream we can have at the bar after, that will take your mind off the chill as your feet hit the waters.'

'It probably will, I'm a wimp with regards to cold water still, once in the water it's a wonderful feeling. Does wonders for mental health and general wellbeing!' Lottie raised her voice as George gathered up his pace dashing into the sea. After taking the plunge he swam as fast as he could, waving his arms in the air like a numpty, no doubt cursing and swearing as he hit the freezing water.

She soon caught up with George, seeing his raised arms as he took deeper strides into the clear blue seas swept along by the occasional tidal wave. She bobbed up and down out of the sea, gasping for breath whilst keeping her mouth firmly shut each time her head emerged from the gushing water, to avoid swallowing mouthfuls of salt water. She finally stood up as she lifted her legs high, not wanting to hit her feet on any hard rocks underneath or get caught up in any slimy green seaweed or pebbles on the shallow sea bottom. George soon spotted her, as he quickly swam towards her, scooping her up into his arms in a tight embrace, causing her to shiver even more as her body left the chilly waters.

'Fancy meeting you here,' she held onto him with dear life, as her teeth began to chatter endlessly. 'This is bliss, now can we get that ice cream you promised?' she managed to say as she struggled to form her words from the chilly waters.

'We have to swim to that floating buoy over there first, before we can have our treat!' George pointed out, encouraging her, knowing she would do anything to have an ice cream with a chocolate flake sticking out of its middle. She just had to focus on that in her mind's eye until they reached the shore. He let go of her saying, 'Race you to there ... on your marks, go!' He looked at her, egging her on regardless how she felt. Lottie was now desperate to have that ice cream as her reward which she so deserved after all her efforts. She'd pay him back somehow!

The only problem was, they had to swim back again, by which time they had warmed up, eager to get to the finishing line ... "the beach", to coin the phrase Mr Bean used in the Cannes movie.

'Yeah! Beat you there, Mr B!' She raised her arms in triumph to show him she was quite capable of the challenge he set earlier. She loved a challenge really, life would be so boring without any goals to meet after all.

She quickly skipped up the sandy beach, soon realising how hot it became, as the soles of her feet started to burn, hence she lifted her feet as high as possible, taking big strides to avoid further burning.

She plonked herself down on the blue beach towel laid on the sun bed, letting her feet dangle over the edge to dry off, before putting on her shorts and T-shirt and placing her feet into her pink Croc sandals. George was two steps behind her, dusting his feet off, before he put his brown velcro sandals on, then grabbed her hand as they headed towards the bar to get their ice cream cones; their reward with a chocolate flake sticking out from the middle. The handsome guy added it to their tab at the bar, before they took their leave later.

'Oh, this was worth every minute of the dip in those icy cold waters. I'm now in heaven on earth, that is, not wishing my life away. I've only just found the man of my dreams after all,' she added, licking the sides of the cone, before it trickled down the sides, seeing endless drops as it leaked onto her new pink shorts, causing that horrible sticky feeling. A girl never felt good with sticky fingers, now in desperate need for some wet wipes, another purchase the next time we saw a supermarket.

They walked back arm in arm to their cozy spot, to kick back and relax, people-watching, before they ordered their next cool mocktail from a passing waiter perusing the beach, making sure everyone was kept happy and safe.

'Excuse me,' Lottie raised her hand to grab his attention.

'Can I order two orange and mango cocktails please?' she smiled, noticing his slightly red face.

'Of course, madam, I'll bring them to you,' he added, smiling back at her.

'You're getting bolder asking these dishy blokes!' George winked at her, feeling slightly jealous.

'When in Italy . . .' she giggled as she stared into his blue eyes.

Five minutes later he walked back towards them with two wide-neck mocktail glasses, with a purple umbrella held up by a cocktail stick, with a mint leaf floating on top.

They sipped their drinks slowly whilst they surveyed the beach. A few young children braved the heat of the day as they dashed in and out of the water, bringing buckets of water back to make sandcastles filling the surrounding moats with water. They soon gathered a crowd with older children giving a helping hand. All was happy at Lucca beach.

'I could get used to this, George, let's come back here tomorrow, we don't have a fixed itinerary, we're on honeymoon after all, away from our busy hectic lives back home. A slower pace of life is what we're looking for, we'll only regret it once we're on the flight home,' she reminded him.

'Can't say much about the traffic around here as they drive like mad men everywhere. That's Italy for you,' George added, smirking. 'Let's see how we feel in the morning,' thinking it was time to pack up for the day.

They showered off before paying their tab to leave the beach. Despite not being dressed up, they walked along the promenade in search of an Italian restaurant, soon locating one overlooking palm trees from the other side of the road. George scanned the menu outside attached to an easel by the entrance.

'This looks good, let's eat here, Lottie,' he gestured, giving my hand a gentle squeeze to confirm.

A waitress asked them if we wanted to eat there. They nodded their response then showed us to a table on the terrace. A green table cloth was secured by clips on all four corners, with wine glasses either side. A tub for cutlery, individually wrapped in red paper napkins was at one end of the table. She brought over two large menus for them to peruse, bringing over a jug of water with a slice of lemon floating inside, adding to that slightly tangy taste.

'Pasta or pizza, what do you fancy?' George asked, peering over the top of his menu.

'Pasta for me … a creamy carbonara with mushrooms and parma ham, yummy!' Lottie said, licking her lips, smiling sweetly back at him.

'Well, you certainly know your palate, it sounds very tasty to me. OK I'll have a spaghetti bolognese Italian style with parmesan cheese from the mill they bring round after.'

'And two glasses of Pinot Grigio to wash it down with,' Lottie chuckled.

Their handsome waiter took their order tapping madly on his mini tablet, before he walked over to the bar for the girls to prep their drinks.

They raised their glasses toasting to a perfect honeymoon, before he brought over their meals.

'These look delicious, tuck in and enjoy my love,' she smiled up at George.

'Cheers to us, may we have many exciting years together.'

Dessert had to be tiramisu with a powdering of chocolate sprinkled over the top adding to its rich flavour.

'Two tiramisus with two cappuccinos please,' she smiled up at their table waiter as he collected the plates then took their order.

George smiled at him.

'Prego!' he replied smiling.

George showed his romantic side as he leant over to meet her lips embracing the moment.

'Steady on Mr B, you'll have everyone glaring at you with puppy eyes. You're so sweet George!'

'Ha ha, they can stare as much as they want, we're in Italy where romance is very ripe!' he chuckled.

They took their time over their desserts, relishing every bite as the flavours tickled their taste buds around their mouths.

An hour and a half later they strolled up and down the promenade as the sun set in the distance. The high temperature of the day was finally beginning to drop, yet still warm enough in a T-shirt. It still felt so warm and romantic as they walked holding hands, giving each other a gentle squeeze feeling totally in love. Eventually stopping to look at the sea as the tide washed in and out, unlocking hands to turn to one another, arms around each other's shoulders, as they drew in for a long romantic kiss enjoying every second. A memory forever etched in their minds for years to come. A match made in heaven. The clock struck midnight as they walked back towards the car park in case the barrier locked them in for the night. They thought it might be best to spend tomorrow by the beach instead, taking a trip to Siena the day after.

Back at the house they were so exhausted, they grabbed a glass of water each before walking upstairs into their bedroom. They slept in their underwear as it was so hot, pecked one another on the cheek, before falling into a deep sleep.

The cowbells around the goats were their early morning wake up call, as George opened the white window shutters, revealing another warm sunny day to the rear of the garden, lined with a few terracotta plant pots with pretty flowers suitable for the climate. George made her a refreshing mint tea from the herbal assortment of teas, placing it on her bedside table, whilst she slowly opened her eyes. He made himself an Earl Grey tea taking sips, as he sat up beside her.

'Buongiorno!' He leant over to kiss her cheek, by which time she was more awake.

'A mint tea is beside you, Mrs B!'

'Am I forever going to be known as Mrs B, sweet as it is?' she prodded him in the ribs as she giggled.

'That depends on the circumstances, it's your nickname for us only,' he quickly added.

'Just don't use it in front of our friends, or else I'll be turning red in embarrassment!' she added feeling all serious.

'Sorry, now drink up before . . .' he winked at me. She knew full well what he had in mind. 'That's it, I'm going to have a quick shower before this conversation gets out of control!' he prodded her back.

Five minutes later he stood before her with a blue towel wrapped around his torso, as she headed into the bathroom for her shower. Choosing shorts and a light T-shirt they went into the kitchen to make a healthy breakfast, consisting of low-fat yoghurt mixed with a few broken nuts and a scattering of chia seeds on top with an orange and mango juice, satisfying their cravings until they got to the beach. Sitting out on the veranda soon became their favourite morning spot, as they gazed out into the woodlands below hearing the noisy crickets in the distance.

After they cleared everything away, they packed up their rucksacks to drive into Lucca, parking up on the side of the road by the promenade.

'Buongiorno!' The same man from yesterday greeted them as they walked over towards the bar. 'How are you today? I'll take you to your sun loungers with an umbrella I put up earlier, it's going to be a hot one I think, so plenty of water and sun lotion for your well-being. Come over later to the bar for our special ice creams on offer today,' he explained whilst setting them up on the beach placing two large blue towels on both loungers.

'Have a great day,' he smiled whilst walking back to the bar.

'Grazie,' George smiled back at him.

'This is camp for today then, Lottie, kick back and enjoy the rest of the day.' He winked at her as he flicked the blue towel open to cover the full length of the sun bed.

'Hurray, I love it here. I want to stay here forever, though I'd miss Floss and Grace and the old folk!'

We walked individually back to the changing huts, before taking our first dip of the day into the sea. As freezing as it was, it felt so refreshing as we ran back to our camp, before walking over to choose our ice creams, with the usual flake in the middle. Brits loved a 99 no matter where they were in the world, it was pure tradition. They took seats on the terrace bar, whilst enjoying their ice creams, before they started to melt from the already rising heat of the morning. Whilst they were at the bar they ordered two cappuccinos to take back to their camp, it was never too hot for a cappuccino in their opinion, giving them that much-needed caffeine kick setting us up for the day ahead.

As they hadn't checked their phones recently, they thought it best to see all was well back home. Fortunately, no immediate emergencies, putting their minds at rest, they could now fully enjoy their honeymoon knowing the folk back home were well.

They continued to spend the day reading and sunbathing, dipping in and out of the sea to keep cool until midday. Walking back to the bar, showering off before they had a club sandwich with an orange and mango juice on ice. A delicious sandwich filled with egg, ham, and mozzarella shavings, with salad and a mayonnaise dressing, on a long white seeded roll. A few more swims before they packed up for the day. Tomorrow they decided on a trip to Siena, another beautiful place steeped in history with plenty of kiosks displaying their best tubs of ice cream of various flavours.

Sienna was a beautiful old town housing old medieval

buildings such as the famous squares of Piazza del Campo amongst other famous buildings, being a must see when in Italy. Despite museums and old buildings not being their top favourite places to go, it was definitely worth a visit which they could tick off on their itinerary list. Armed with water bottles they spent the day sightseeing, with frequent ice cream stops to keep them hydrated.

The day after they thought it best to explore Lucca with many different things to do. One which really appealed to them was river kayaking in single or double canoes. It seemed such a fun and challenging experience especially as the weather was sunny and warm.

Dress code was T-shirts and shorts and a comfortable pair of trainers.

They hired a twin canoe for an hour, deciding it would be more fun and relaxing. Another handsome Italian man showed them the basics to tandem rowing, which proved more difficult than they first thought, much like synchronised swimming except they had oars to push them along, using arm muscles which hadn't been exercised for years, if at all. George sat at the front on a comfortable long cushion, whilst Lottie took the rear seat. They were given yellow life jackets that were essential in case the canoe capsized or one or both of them accidentally fell into the river. Fortunately, they were confident swimmers.

'This looks like lots of fun, yet probably hard work,' Lottie reported back to George, whilst he got comfy on his seat, taking the oars in either hand with the paddles in the water, to row in and out as they paddled upstream. George soon got the hang of dipping the paddles in and out of the water, propelling them forward. Lottie sat and watched George, trying to mirror his actions, soon gaining a good rhythm making great strides along the river. They waved to others as they passed by as they tried to coordinate their kayaks and canoes steering them upstream, a comical sight causing lots of laughter.

'This is what I call living the dream, being outside in nature and having fun in the water with the one you love, George.' She raised her voice above the sound of the sloshing water as they glided along.

'Just perfect, Mrs B,' he teased, knowing she didn't like him calling her that in public, not that anyone cared.

'Just sit back and relax a while as I paddle through, we can take it in turns, Lottie, making it more enjoyable,' he suggested, smiling sweetly at her.

She lifted my head to the sky, closing her eyes, taking in the peace and tranquility of the waters, living in the present moment. This was the mindset which both she and George practiced on a daily basis, proving a very powerful tool as they all negotiated trials throughout their lives.

Half an hour passed when Lottie took the lead with the oars to navigate them back to the harbour side, whilst George kicked back and relaxed, keeping an eye on her lest she got into trouble, which she did after a while. This rowing business wasn't all plain sailing yet heaps of fun.

The handsome guy was ready waiting as we approached the decking for him to tie the rope around the black buoy so they could disembark safely.

'Grazie Mille,' she thanked him as he took her hand to disembark from the kayak, glad to be on terra firma again in one piece.

'Prego, see you again soon,' he said, knowing they were Brits.

'Coffee and cake for my girl?' George took her hand, leading her to the promenade seeing some tables and chairs a few yards away. They took their seats glad to be on dry land again. A young woman walked over taking their orders of two cappuccinos with a mouthwatering apple tart each.

'This is pleasant sitting in the sun, people-watching, casting all cares into the seas,' she placed one hand on his knee under the table.

She brought over their orders on a tray, placing them in front of them. Lottie took out her phone to capture the moment for ever more. The lady turned round and took a few photos of them as they pulled up their chairs closer, as they drew one another into a tight embrace. They swiped their card to pay, then they were free to leave to continue their promenade walk after their snack stop.

Chapter Twenty-seven

The week flew by leaving them only two days left before they boarded their flight back to London Heathrow. Their last days were spent on the beach, sipping mocktails and enjoying ice creams, with a flake of course! Back at the house they walked down to see the goats for a final time as they jumped around, putting a spectacular show on for them as they bid them farewell, hoping to revisit one sunny day.

The morning of their departure struck a sad yet hopeful chord. They would return soon to this idyllic spot in Tuscany where they had the most beautiful honeymoon they could have ever wished for. They gathered up their belongings, leaving the keys for the lady on the kitchen table, before closing the doors to pack up their car to drive to the airport. They parked up the trusty Fiat Uno in the desired bay before catching the bus to the airport. They checked in, seeing their suitcase disappear down the chute to be loaded up onto the luggage trailer waiting on the runway, to be transferred to their plane. The had an hour to spare, so they wandered around the lounge area in search of any desired items from the parade of shops, before finding a cosy place to have a final Italian cappuccino and a piece of lemon zesty cheesecake. Glancing up occasionally at the departure times, their final boarding time flashed up on the screen, as they picked up their hand luggage to walk over to the designated gate waiting with a queue of passengers to walk out onto the aircraft.

Once home they were greeted by everyone giving them a warm welcome home wanting to know all the stories. The dogs circled around them for days until they finally settled down knowing they were back home.

Everyone felt happy and fulfilled as they continued their busy lives together in the beautiful surrounding Cotswolds countryside. Jodie and Ralph had settled in nicely in their new bungalow and enjoyed family time together, often joined by their girls and their two dogs. Jodie and Elaine became best friends, spending time together enjoying coffee morning trips in the new café on the high street in Stow. Jack and Ralph became best fishing buddies, admiring their numerous catches on local rivers, armed with picnics and hot drinks to amuse themselves.

Sam and Pete continue to meet up regularly with Jodie and Ralph at various pubs especially on Sundays for a traditional carvery. Amy and Issy joined them as and when, as well as spending precious time meeting up with newlyweds Lottie and George.

Amy and Issy moved into their new house, a place they could finally call home, after moving out of their parents' bungalow, where they made many happy memories to be cherished forever. Both loved their new jobs, Issy helping the elderly in the new care home and Amy caring for all creatures great and small at the vet practice.

Grace, being the younger sister, took her time to find her forever love, preferring to remain single for now, enjoying her career and making the most of single life. She was in no hurry to change that.

James and Julie welcomed their second child, Oliver; a handsome blue-eyed boy, a brother for Alice, completing their family.

Julie continued to enjoy church life, joining a fortnightly women's choir, performing in a variety of concerts throughout the year.

Life in the country was indeed the best everyone could have ever dreamed of, surrounded by woodland and beautiful scenery, birds singing all year around. All three dogs, Rosie, Bessy and

Floss became best of friends together enjoying their play time, growing old together.

What more could the ever-expanding Stevens family wish for.

The End

As I bring this book to a close I would like to thank the team from The Choir Press for their continued support. Most importantly, I would like to thank everyone who has taken the time to read my book. I hope you enjoyed it, as much as I have loved writing it.

Life is a journey to be cherished with its peaks and troughs along the way, so embrace it all and give it your best shot!

Best wishes
Giselle x
Facebook Giselle Rozzell author

Milton Keynes UK
Ingram Content Group UK Ltd.
UKHW032148250924
448833UK00004B/81